The Empress of Tears

Part II of the
Autobiography of Empress Alexandra

by

Kathleen McKenna Hewtson

ISBN-10:   1523829753

ISBN-13:   978-1523829750

'The Empress of Tears: *Part II of The Autobiography of Empress Alexandra*' is published by Taylor Street Books.

Dedication

To Tim, who has made, and continues to make, my own story the happiest on earth.

To my family in the United Kingdom, my private Arts Council, thank you for your love and support, because saying I could not have done this without you is not an overstatement, merely the truth. I love you all. And the same to my family in the United States.

And to the great expertise and beyond-the-call caring natures of Drs. Rosenberg and Kornguth in San Francisco who saved my husband, Tim's, life this last year.

PART II

1895 - 1904

Chapter 1

In that I have chosen to write this, I have sometimes had to resort to consulting the contents of my old diaries, for without them it is impossible for one to state precisely how one felt about a given time and situation. Hindsight alone serves only to provide a view which is necessarily colored by how one feels today about those long-distant and partially forgotten times.

So it is completely possible that at my wedding I did feel something beyond the unrelenting depression and horror that I now recall, but all I can remember, without access to my contemporary impressions – because I made no record of them – are the enormous cold halls of the Winter Palace, filled with richly-dressed, icy-eyed nobles who watched my slow progress to the altar with uncharitable judgment and barely-suppressed dislike.

Was my new mother-in-law's face white and stricken because she had just lost her own husband, or was her tragic appearance also tinged by her feelings about me? Who can know?

Yet it seemed that the entire Russian court somehow did know, and had already passed this knowledge on to their servants, who in their turn had passed it on to the people who stood outside in the freezing air. One thing is clear: by the time I had reached the altar, it was obvious to everyone in my future world that somehow I was wrong.

The nobles said it was because I was ... Oh, too tall ... or was it clumsy? ... Or no, no, that is not it exactly ... I was ... well ... blotchy ... Yes, that was it! I would meet their flat, empty stares and, unforgiving, unsightly blotches would form all over my body like beacons.

Expounding upon their theme, the immediate onlookers reportedly commented that I had a small, pursed mouth and a cold, unpleasant expression. Well, they could easily have come to the same conclusions about themselves by simply gazing into the first available mirror to hand, as far as I was concerned.

All my new Russian- and French- speaking maids-of-honor, each of whom had *helpfully* been assigned to me by my mother-in-law, Dowager-Empress Minnie, no doubt agreed with them, and then contributed their own sniping assessments in addition.

It seemed that I was suffering from a confusing combination of haughtiness and stupidity. I refused to speak French and I couldn't speak Russian, facts they wantonly relayed to their servants, who, being from the peasant classes, passed this information on to their families, so that it seemed to me that, by the time I knelt alongside Nicky on my aching legs at the altar for the blessing, all of Russia had laid its collective curse upon me.

There is a word in German for my sort: *'pechvogel'*. It means a bird of ill omen, an unlucky sort of person, one who attracts and brings bad luck, and yet wasn't I now the Empress of all the Russias and therefore one of the most important people in existence? I was, and I was also Nicky's wife, but that night, the night following the endless day of my wedding, I was neither *pechvogel* nor mighty empress: I was only a terrified, cold, exhausted girl. And as our carriage pulled up to the doors of the Anichkov Palace, where Dowager-Empress Minnie had decreed that we should live, I could barely speak for fear of what lay ahead of me.

Minnie met us at the great doors of her palace.

There is an old Russian custom, passed upward from the peasants and embraced by the nobles, to greet a newly-wedded couple at the threshold of their home with bread and salt. It must be a lovely moment for most brides. I can see them now in my mind's eye: The happy, red-cheeked peasant bride comes shyly to her new little house with her strong handsome husband; the dear old mother greets them at the door and then disappears back to her own warm little house; and the young couple steps inside and sits by the fire with the bread she has left, and probably some homemade wine. Such a scene would be so cozy and happy, such a promising beginning to their lives.

Yet these simple pleasures, the very things that make up a life, are denied to us in the ruling class, or at least I have found it unerringly to be so.

I had to enter a vast fortress-like palace and had no idea what to do with the gold platter of bread and salt that the frail, tear-stained Minnie held out to us with shaking hands. As it happened, both Nicky and I reached for it simultaneously and ended up knocking it to the ground.

The palace was so grim and silent that the dish made a great clatter on the marble floor as we three stared stupidly down at the scattered salt and the upturned bread, while behind Minnie I saw the servants crossing themselves as it came to me that this was how it would always be from now on: My every action, no matter how small or inconsequential, would be imbued with cosmic significance.

The silence was broken only by Minnie's small, exaggerated exclamation of horror.

I immediately realized that this awful, awkward beginning was only going to be ended by me; for, if I had left it up to Nicky and the widowed Empress, we would, I think, have all stood there discussing the great tragedy of the spilt salt until the end of days.

So I stepped away from both of them and addressed Nicky. "I am exhausted and I have a terrible headache."

To Minnie, who was staring at me in shock at my – my what? – my *lèse majesté*, my ludicrously human needs and careless expression of them, I said, "Forgive me, Mother dear, but I really must find our rooms and rest. It has been a longer day than anyone could imagine and you must be exhausted as well."

She gazed at me.

I could tell there was so much she wanted to say to me, but she was a very clever woman and decided, on this occasion, to bide her time, merely inclining her head as she said, "Yes, of course … Your wedding day. Of course you must be quite … In fact, I can see you are. You are as white as snow. Here, I'll have Svetlana show you to your chambers. Oh, never mind," she turned to Nicky, "you can certainly take your bride to her rooms, Nicky. After all, they are your rooms as well. I'll dine alone tonight. What does it matter that I shall be dining alone every night from now on until I am permitted by God to join your father? Have a good evening, my dears."

Nicky looked at her, and then at me, and then back at her, so clearly torn. What should he do? Who needed him most? Where should his loyalties lie? Whom should he accompany?

Both his mother and I saw his struggle, but it was Minnie who smiled.

"Go! Go, Nicky, my darling boy, and be with your little bride. I'll see you at breakfast, shall I?" Her forehead wrinkled and her eyes filled with tears. It was quite a performance. "Oh no, I should not have said that, should I?" Before either of us could answer – and I wanted to – she went on, "No, it is too, too selfish of me to imagine that you should be up so early and want to take breakfast with your old mama on your first day as newlyweds. How could I have asked this of you? Forgive me, my children."

At that, exactly as she had intended he should, Nicky rushed over to her and clasped her in his arms, tenderly assuring her that he would be with her at every breakfast, and at every lunch, and at every dinner, after tonight, and that she would never eat alone again. Only tonight would be different because, "Poor Alix is feeling so unwell and I really should –"

Having achieved her gain, Minnie was gracious and interjected, "Yes, of course, darling, go with your bride tonight. It is her day after all, and tomorrow you can tell Mama all your new thoughts and feelings."

I was appalled. *What could she possibly mean by that?*

But then Nicky was beside me again and guiding me down long, wide, and then narrow, corridors to our new rooms, his old boyhood ones, small dark and cramped,

13

but that night I did not care. We were alone at last and there I became truly his bride and left the last of my girlhood behind me forever.

The next morning, when I arose, I felt filled with peace and hope for the first time since returning to Russia: The Old Emperor lay in Peter and Paul with his ancestors, his shining soul safely ascended to heaven to be with God and his forebears; Nicky's mother was now the Dowager-Empress; and I, as the reigning Empress, positioned alongside my precious husband, would always see to it that she was treated with the kindness and respect that was her due.

Filled with these charitable thoughts, which I'll freely admit were brought about by my new-found feelings of sanctioned love, I was, or so I thought, ready to rise that first morning and tackle what I believed were a few momentary inconveniences, the first being the rooms in which I found myself.

I did not blame poor Minnie: 'Poor Minnie' is how I had decided to think of her from now on. After all, how could the newly widowed, newly dowagered, former reigning Empress have been expected to consider where Nicky and I were going to live when in Petersburg? Her husband had died, chaos had reigned, and here my Nicky and I were not only married a year early but already 'Their Majesties.' Under such circumstances, both she and my darling brand-new husband could be forgiven, so I decided to view our temporary accommodation in the humorous light it called for.

Our suite comprised three tiny rooms, rooms that my Nicky and his younger brother, poor Georgie, used to share. Georgie, Nicky's own brother and the dearest companion of his youth, had contracted the dreaded tuberculosis, so now he lived far away in his palace at Abbas Tuman, high on some mountain or other, where the air was easier to breathe. The rooms still maintained the endearing, worn aspect of their boyhoods, complete with old schoolbooks and funny little drawings they had made of each other pinned to the walls. In fact, Nicky and Georgie's little army cots were still in one of the rooms. Another room, Nicky and my bridal chamber, suggested that no one had really ever expected us to lodge here, as there was merely a worn divan pressed up against a wall to make space for the double bed where we had become one the night before.

The last room had, I think, been a schoolroom, for there was a small old desk and a chalkboard where some thoughtful servant of poor Minnie had probably, at the last minute, moved in an old couch and a small table to make it into a makeshift sitting room for us, although at this moment one could barely navigate it as Grandmamma had sent over ten trunks containing my new trousseau, and some unthinking servant had hauled them in there before our arrival.

Laying still abed and drinking the tea that poor Tuttles had brought for me, I inhaled deeply, for there were so many details awaiting my attention on this my first day as Empress. But the Empress did not feel like an empress. I felt like what I was in truth – Nicky's wife, a new bride, and one who was living in the most disorganized situation imaginable, knowing that the moment I pulled my bell I would be faced with a dozen small, domestic crises that would demand my immediate attention.

My second task, as I saw it, was to establish order amongst my staff. I had brought my own two maids and my dear *lectrice*, Catherine, with me, but my dear familiar maids had been replaced by a ludicrous crew of incompetents whom poor Minnie had decided would be best for me despite the fact that they spoke neither English nor German. This had already resulted in a terribly tense morning for me upon my wedding day as they had not understood a word I had said and, worse, had openly stared at me with impudent curiosity. Until this morning I had not even known if my own poor Tuttles and Nancy had remained in Russia. They had, but until then they might as well have been exiled to Siberia for all that I saw of them.

Still, my loyal Tuttles assured me that she had not only found her way down to the kitchens and then to me, "battling savages who cannot speak a word of English all the way, pardon me for saying so, Ma'am ... I mean Your Imperial Highness. But I did it all the same and made them make you your tea. 'My poor mistress,' I said to them, 'she'd as like to starve and die of thirst, too, if left to you lot.' "

I sighed inwardly. I loved my little maids but knew that I would be held accountable for any perceived rudeness on their part, so while I understood Tuttles's frustration with the circumstances in which she found herself, I had to speak sternly to her.

"Tuttles, I do not think that you should be so dismissive of the other servants. After all, we are the foreigners here, as they see it, and it will be for us to accustom ourselves to their ways, not the other way around."

She goggled at me. "But Your Imperial Highness is Empress now and that trumps everyone here, except the Emperor, it does."

I pursed my lips to keep from laughing and shook my head at her.

"Tuttles, my dear, I am indeed the Empress, but it is still all so new to all of us, and suddenly so, you see. No one has had a moment to get used to the idea – not the members of the court, nor the servants, nor really the Russian people themselves. Change is quite difficult to accept for people and we must be understanding of that and give them more time to accustom themselves to the new order. Do you understand?"

She regarded me mutinously and I felt that I might have to reprimand her more sternly, but then I noticed that her lower lip was trembling badly and that her eyes were filling with tears.

I sat up, alarmed. "Tuttles, what is it, my dear?"

She began to sob wildly and I was forced to rise from my bed, put on my dressing gown unaided, and guide her to the seating area where I gave her the remainder of my morning's tea before she could speak coherently.

Sniffling wildly, she said, "It's Nancy, Ma'am... Your Imperial Highness –"

"Tuttles, please simply address me as 'Ma'am,' in the English way, when we are alone, and as 'Your Majesty' when we are not. I'm not the Pope and I think –"

"Nancy is gone, Ma'am," she interrupted me, an impertinence I decided to overlook on this occasion,

17

given her emotional state and despite her rather sullen mien. Still, I was even more horrified by her words.

"Tuttles, what can you possibly mean? Are you saying that Nancy has died?"

She shook her head. "No, Ma'am, but she's as good as dead, all the same."

"Tuttles, please explain yourself this instant!"

She looked at me half-angrily, half-frightened.

"She left this morning. One of them Rusky footmen saw her to the train. She said to tell you as she's sorry, but she can't stay in this terrible place, and I don't blame her because I'd like to go home too now, Ma'am, begging your pardon."

I was flabbergasted.

"Tuttles, I ... I ... Well, I really don't understand. You and Nancy have been with me for as long as I can remember. We all came here together. You have both been on visits here and –"

Tuttles stood, patted down her apron, and looked at me sorrowfully.

"I know that, Ma'am, and I'm as devoted to you as I ever could be – so is poor Nancy – but we cannot speak this heathen language and the room they put us in was ever so far up in the attics, and it has ghosts, and it is too cold for a body ... and, well, I want to go home. You'll be fine and all, being Empress and having that nice young man of yours who loves you so much ..."

She had begun to cry again as she spoke but her tone remained firm.

Now it was my turn to cry.

"You cannot leave me, Tuttles. You cannot leave me alone here. I will not let you go. And if you do go, I will

18

tell Ernie, and he will never give you another position back home. I will write him today to make sure he does not let Nancy back. Oh, such ingratitude!"

I finished on a wail, while peeping at her through my tears to gauge her level of guilt, which I hoped would be considerable, although it appeared I was mistaken.

If anything, she looked angry.

"I'm sorry you feel that way, Ma'am. I don't think we've been ungrateful. Me and Nancy, we thought we was just coming here with you for a few weeks, up until his Majesty the late Emperor was buried, and then we'd all go back to Hesse and maybe come back in a year or so when you got married, or maybe not, I don't know. I guess we didn't think too much about what living here would be like. Last time we was all here, it was in the winter and we were at that other palace, and there were lots of servants from Hesse on account of your papa and Duke Ernie being with us, and we was warm besides. Now we ... I mean I ... isn't and I'm all alone. I'll ask Miss Ella for my train fare. She's always been good to me and I know she'll see her way to helping me out. May I be excused now, Ma'am?"

I thought for a moment of doing just that, excusing her forever. Let her go to Ella, to Hesse, to Hades for all that it mattered. I was the Empress of Russia. I was a bell ring away from being able to summon a hundred servants ... or a thousand, if I felt like it. I could ... I could ... I could call for all my new maids-in-waiting that Minnie had given me. They could come and stare at me, and bustle around me, and make me feel more isolated than I had ever been. I could call for Nicky, who was somewhere in this vast fortress of a palace, and he could come and translate for me ...

Except that, if I let Tuttles go to Ella, she would tell everyone of my cruelty, and also Tuttles, my last link with home, would be gone. And if I summoned Nicky to act as a translator for my maids, the story would be all over the palace by luncheon, and all over Russia by dinnertime. *The new empress can't even manage to get dressed without the Tsar's help. She summoned him as though he were a servant. She called him from an important meeting. She's cruel, she's selfish, and she can't cope. Poor Tsar, poor Tuttles, poor Ella, poor Russia ...*

I collected myself and smiled at Tuttles.

"Tuttles, my dear, you know that you are far more than a maid to me. I consider you a member of the family. I would like it if you stayed, and I understand about your rooms and feeling lonely too. I'll tell you what: You can have these rooms and all for your own. Nicky ... I mean the Emperor ... and I will be moving right away to a different suite and these can be yours. At least stay for a bit and see if you cannot learn to like it and to help me, if you will."

Tuttles looked at me for a long moment before nodding.

"All right, Ma'am, I'll try it. But I can't make no promises. Thank you for the rooms. They is warm. When should I –?"

I smiled, relieved that at least this storm in a teacup had been dealt with.

"I imagine that you can plan on moving in the morning, after you've brought me my tea. I'll speak to

Nicky at luncheon and ask which rooms he thinks we should move to. I do not know the palace at all. Thank you, Tuttles. You may go and you can send in the Russian hordes to clean and to draw my bath."

She left without another word and soon my rooms were crowded with all my new maids-of-honor, stumbling all over each other as they tried to find my clothes, draw my bath, stare at me, and initiate conversations with me.

I ignored them. It is a gift I have, being able to shut out moments and people that I do not wish to acknowledge, thus remaining undisturbed. I was, however, perturbed by Tuttles's final words to the effect that she could not make me any promises. For my part, I would never be in a position say that to anyone ever again. I had made a promise, a sacred promise, to Nicky, and I could never leave, not that I wanted to, not that first new day, but I did feel that I should in some way be compensated for my sacrifices.

Or no, 'compensated' is not the right word. I had married him, I loved him – and both those things would always be true – but other things were true too, and I was determined to address them at luncheon that very day.

Chapter 2

I watched my own dearest one sleeping beside me and felt more resentment than tenderness. How could he sleep? Was not sleep the very gift that our Lord above accorded us as a reward – the sleep of the just? Did Nicky feel that he had been just to me; that his mother had been just to me?

I seethed. I knew I would not rest that night, oh no ... and at that moment I did not foresee how I ever could again, for I had been both betrayed and cruelly treated, and having to endure this night in the same ghastly rooms in which I had awoken at the start of this endless day did not help.

I had meant to spend a lovely luncheon with my Nicky on that our first day of newly-wedded life. I had instructed Tuttles to request the Russian maids to have a small table brought into our ugly little rooms and then to go to the kitchens and somehow make clear to the cooks that I wanted a light omelet luncheon with some caviar on the side for Nicky, and to find a nice bottle of wine to accompany all of it. Then I had bathed and dressed with particular care, putting on a rose lace gown for him. It did not constitute suitable mourning dress, I knew, but since we would be alone in our apartment I hardly felt it mattered.

As I had expected him to, Nicky appeared a few minutes before one in the afternoon, and so intent was he on coming to kiss me that at first he did not even notice my charming little table setting.

"My darling, my Sunny, my angel, I could hardly stand it all morning. I could barely bring myself to listen to a word that annoying old man Witte said to me. Not that," he smiled naughtily at me, "he had a thing to say worth attending to. I do think he just likes to hear himself speak. I truly do not know why Papa set such store by him, but Mama admires him too. 'Oh Witte, he is a brilliant man, you must listen to him, Nicky,' she keeps telling me. On that point she is most insistent."

He leaned down and kissed my neck as he spoke, sending strange and delightful shivers through me. It was all so different now, for we knew what love – physical love, married love – meant.

I wanted, of course, to listen to what Nicky had to say about the business of ruling, but I needed to tell him things as well. However, I didn't interrupt, for I knew instinctively, as often a woman does, that my very appearance would draw his attention to me more than any words could.

I was right too, for he trailed off as he gazed fully at me, and his voice was much huskier when he said, "I adore you in pink. You look like the most perfect rose imaginable. Oh, I wish we could just stay in and be alone, just the two of us. You don't know, my darling, what agony it is to be separated from you, even if only for a few hours."

I smiled, delighted. He was so deeply enamored of me that he hadn't even noticed luncheon. I kissed him again and then pulled back, waving my hand at the table and the wine.

"Precious Hubby, darling, of course we are staying in. Who would dare to come by and disturb us this early in our marriage?"

He stared at me and I could tell he was suddenly not the happy, adoring man of a moment ago.

"Sunny darling, we ... I mean ... we can't ... and even though you look so beautiful, you'll need to hurry and change or we'll be late and keep poor Mama waiting."

I understood perfectly that he expected us to luncheon with his mother and he wished for me to wear black while doing so, but I decided in an instant to pretend otherwise, so I smiled at him with apparent puzzlement and asked in a bewildered tone, "Nicky, late for what ...? And why should I change? I thought you loved me in pink. I wore this dress especially for you. I..."

My voice broke mid-sentence – that was honest, at least – although the tears I felt were of anger, not of hurt, as I was content to let him believe.

He was deeply abashed and I felt such a savage gladness at this realization that it shocked me and made me burst into deep sobs as the whole day caved in on me.

He knelt and tried to pull me into his arms.

I pushed him roughly away.

"No, no, don't embrace me. You don't like me. You hate my dress. You don't want to have lunch with me. You want to be with your mama. So go on, go be with her. I'll stay here in my ugly dress in these awful rooms and maybe, if you ever find the time, you can stop by and visit me and watch me rot here!"

He was aghast, jumping up and staring at me in horror.

"Alicky, what are you saying? You cannot mean this. You cannot think –"

"Oh, can't I, Nicky? Why can't I say so? Why can't I think so? Do you ever, even once, think of me, of what is best for me, what I might want? What do you think all this is like for me?"

He looked so sad that I almost relented, but I couldn't, so I met his heartbroken gaze with my angry tearstained face and would not look away.

He held out his hands imploringly but I only shook my head.

He straightened and sighed.

"What do you want of me, Alix? Do you want me to leave my widowed mother completely alone? Do you want me not to meet with Witte or any of my ministers? Do you want me to stay in here with you? Or no, you don't want to stay in here, do you? You think these rooms are horrible, my own boyhood rooms where Georgie and I ..."

His voice broke. He nauseated me as I got to my feet and smoothed down my gown. Moving over to the mirror above the mantelpiece, I glanced at my reflection. My eyes were slightly reddened but I looked fine – better than fine, really.

Cutting Nicky, I crossed to the door to the hallway and opened it, adding coldly over my shoulder, "Coming, dear? We do not want to keep Mother Dear waiting all alone, do we?"

He came up behind me and laid a tentative hand on my shoulder. "Thank you, Alicky, but don't you think you had better change, because if Mama sees –"

I stiffened under his hand, and still refusing to turn to look at him – rather facing resolutely ahead at the dim, carpeted corridor of our wing – I said in a flat tone, almost as though speaking to myself, which maybe I was, "Which is worse, one wonders, the terrible loneliness of sitting and waiting or the shock of a pink gown? Ah well, let us find out, shall we?"

With that I proceeded to walk, tear-blinded, down the corridor ... and then was obliged to stop because I had no idea which way to turn.

Wordlessly, Nicky reached for my hand and began to lead me through the maze that was the Anichkov Palace.

After what seemed a half-hour or so, we reached the doors to the dining room. They were flanked by two enormous, very black men in strange uniforms of an antique design, topped off with feathered turbans upon their heads.

Seeing my surprise, and so obviously, so pathetically, hopeful of speaking to me on any subject other than that which mattered, Nicky leaned to me and whispered, "They're Abyssinians, darling. They have been here since the time of Catherine the Great. Well, not these two, obviously ..."

He giggled. I didn't.

His face fell and the silent men opened the doors, ceremoniously bowing to us as they did so.

Immediately inside the doors stood two gold-braided, gray-bearded Russians who bowed to us as well and stentoriously announced, "Their Majesties, Tsar Nicholas and Tsarina Alexandra Feordorovna."

I was guided by Nicky to my chair halfway down the table and then he rushed over to his mother at the head of the table to kiss her cheek before sitting down in the chair awaiting him right beside her.

In my angry and nervous state, it was only then that I allowed myself to take in my surroundings. The dining room at Anichkov was as large as a ballroom, indeed larger by far than any ballroom I had ever seen other than that of the Winter Palace. It was a glorious room, too, resembling a giant Wedgewood plate decked out in pale green.

The table that day held some eighty people, none of whom I knew except for Nicky's youngest brother, little Michael – or "Misha," as they called him – and his younger sister, Olga. The remaining male attendees were the usual blur of old men in red jackets covered by medals and ribbons, possibly bestowed upon them by a succession of grateful emperors for their determination and fortitude in accepting many thousands of invitations to luncheon and dine with them. Next, I surveyed the women as surreptitiously as I could under my eyelashes, although I need not have bothered trying to do so unobtrusively as every single one of them, with the sole exception of Nicky's little sister, was staring right back at me.

Observing so many eyes fixed on me, I felt my face reddening – and no doubt blotching – and my hands swelling. 'There,' I thought savagely, 'that should supply them with a week's conversation,' but, then again, why were they here at all, or, more importantly, why were Nicky and I here at all? The poor, grieving, all-alone Dowager-Empress had nearly a hundred guests, and two of her own children, to console her, so why had I been subjected to this trial by endurance?

It was probably so she could lay aside her sadness while criticizing me, for it wasn't ten minutes in – as soon as the first course had been served – that she began to do just that, raising her lorgnette, which she wore despite the excellence of her vision, and declaring in a shocked tone, "Alix, my dear, is your dress *pink?*"

I pretended not to hear her and continued trying to choke down my disgusting cold beet soup in order to avoid all those eyes still scrutinizing me.

She repeated herself.

I sighed and put down my spoon. "I believe it is indeed."

Her eyebrows rose in horror and there was an audible gasp from everyone at the table. The Dowager-Empress appeared to be on the verge of fainting and in such distress that many of the guests turned towards her in profound sympathy and commiseration.

I poked at what appeared to be a ball of red slime in my bowl.

In the ghastly silence I could hear, but refused to watch, the Dowager-Empress rustling in consternation as Nicky murmured to her, "Oh Mama dearest, don't be upset, please, Mama. You see, Alix thought we would be dining alone in our rooms this afternoon, and so she –"

The Dowager-Empress interrupted him in a choked voice while all the guests cocked their heads the better not to miss a word of this developing family drama. "Oh forgive me, Nicky dearest, you see I thought we were all

29

heart-stricken at my Sasha's passing and still in mourning, but if you and Alix want to eat away from me, well whoever can blame you? I am terrible company, am I not? Barely half alive."

Before any of the dozens of guests could dutifully contradict her to assure her that she was the best of company, or Nicky could debase and humiliate us further – and indeed before I was tempted to vomit up publicly the few bites of so-called food I had been able to force down – I summoned up a huge effort of will to conquer my native shyness and proceeded to scrutinize each diner in turn in a direct challenge to their impending insolence. I was now, after all, their Empress and I would speak and be heard accordingly, and it was indeed gratifying to watch them all lower their eyes in submission before my gaze.

"Forgive me, do, Mother dear. Of course we all mourn dreadfully the passing of the late Emperor, but it is also the day after our marriage and I was hoping to spend it with my husband. You are surrounded here by so many who love you that it did not occur to me that we would be missed. In fact, I find myself to be quite tired and not at all hungry, so if all of you," I nodded to the assembled horror-stricken throng, "will excuse us, I propose that we retire to our rooms."

With that, I stood up and waited for Nicky to do the same. After a moment of agonized indecision he followed suit, obliging all the other guests, save his mother, to rise as well. My husband might appear inconsequential in the presence of his mother, but he was still their Emperor and I their Empress, and because we had risen, luncheon was now over. How funny I found that thought, and given how dreadful the food was, I hoped they would at least be grateful to me for not being obliged to eat any more of it. Maybe so, maybe not; at that moment I could not have cared less.

Back in our rooms I turned on Nicky, who was pale with shock.

"This must never happen again. I will not be criticized, not by you, not by your mother, and certainly not by those who are now as much my subjects as they are yours. Nor will I stay in these rooms another night. They are awful. There is not even enough room here to accommodate my clothes. I do not have a sitting room to receive in and I want English-speaking maids. You are the Emperor now, Nicky. Nothing is outside of your power. Start here. Start this minute!"

Nicky gripped the back of a chair as though my words were bullets and he needed to steady himself from them.

How ridiculous! I thought.

Then, in a trembling voice that made me want to throw something at him, he said, "Alix, you cannot mean any of these things. You have to be reasonable. As it is, I cannot imagine what I am going to say to Mama. We left early. We left her sitting there. Oh think what people are going to say. And how can we leave our rooms? Where would we go?"

I laughed derisively. "Oh, I don't know, Nicky. Where could we go? This palace has, what, a thousand rooms?"

"Only eight hundred," he corrected me vacuously.

I threw back my head and laughed bitterly. My head was aching beyond endurance by now.

"Forgive me, only eight hundred rooms, and each of them potentially worse than these, I suppose. Well, why not the attics then, with poor Tuttles? At least she and I would have each other's company since we are the only two people in this Godforsaken place who speak English. Nancy ran away this morning. She couldn't endure it here. I understand that well enough. You promised me you would build me a palace a day if I so wished, and yet now you cannot even organize new rooms for us? You said you would love me and that your whole life was mine, but you will not even stand up to your mother for me. And I ..."

I broke down completely then.

Sadly, this seemed to reassure Nicky in that it gave him something to do as he moved over and gathered me against him, holding me until I couldn't cry anymore.

He led me gently to the bedroom.

"Shh, darling, you are overtired, that's all, my poor Sunny. I am sorry about Nancy but it is probably for the best if she wasn't happy." The irony of his words was lost on him as he began undoing my buttons. He smiled mischievously. "I'll act as your maid tonight, darling. Ah, look how beautiful you are. I will even brush your hair for you. And tomorrow we will make a fresh start. I will not work as long as I did today and I will take you for a sleigh ride. You would like that, wouldn't you?"

I bowed my head and it felt good when he let my heavy hair down. Then I sat doll-like as he undressed me and brushed my hair, and stood woodenly, arms up, as he crashed around through my trunks trying to find my nightdresses. He gave up and rang for Tuttles, who took half an hour to arrive from her attic.

Unable to face either her reproachful looks or one more second of my husband's womanlike ministrations, I hid in the bathroom, and I stayed in there, shivering and naked, until Nicky had given up knocking and until I could not bear the cold another moment.

When I came out, the day had darkened into night, my nightdresses were waiting on the end of the bed, and Nicky was fast asleep. I donned my bed clothes and climbed carefully under the covers, lying as far away from him as possible, feeling I would never sleep again.

The next morning when I awoke it was Nicky, and not Tuttles, who was awaiting me with my tea.

I stared at him, my head aching too miserably for me to be either surprised or curious. He seemed to understand me as he handed me my tea and perched beside me on the bed.

Seeing me shy away, his face tightened but he managed a smile. "Drink your tea, darling, and then I'll ring for Tuttles so you can tell her what you want to pack today."

For a moment I thought, 'Oh, he's sending me away. That's good. No, that's terrible!' I felt frightened. I had gone too far.

He saw my fear but, fortunately, misunderstood my expression.

"No, darling, don't look so worried. You'll like this, and so will Tuttles." He laughed as though the feelings of Tuttles could hardly matter. "I am taking you away, to Tsarskoe Selo, to the Alexander Palace. It is my favorite place in the world. I was born there and I danced with you there for the first time. You like it too, don't you, darling?"

In my relief at not being sent away in disgrace, my resentment melted away and I smiled at him over my tea.

"I do, Nicky. I love it there. And I am so happy, my boysy."

I also felt generous enough to pretend to care about his mother, so I asked after her well-being and hoped he did not spot the edge of teasing in my voice.

His face opened up in innocent gratitude and I felt my heart turn over with his sweetness, at least until he answered me.

"Oh, it was Mama who suggested it. She said that she understood so well what a young bride must feel. She said she could remember it as though it was yesterday and that I must take you away. She said we could stay for three whole days. Oh, it will be bliss, my darling."

I managed a small smile. "Yes, thank you, darling. What a fine treat. Well then, you had better go off and do whatever it is you do all day and let me ring for Tuttles and get dressed and packed so that I can be ready for you."

His forehead wrinkled, puzzled.

"But you are pleased, aren't you, darling?"

I smiled as convincingly as possible. "Yes, of course I am, dearest one. I'm just all aflutter and want to get myself ready."

When he had left, I summoned Tuttles and the Russian maids, gave them my orders, and went to my bath. I knew then that the Dowager-Empress did not see herself as a Dowager. She was not going to relinquish an inch of ground to me, nor an inch of my husband. But I also knew something else: It was true that Nicky and I had only been truly man and wife for one sacred night. I would change that; I would indeed become Empress – the *only* one. There was a crude Old Russian joke that I had overheard Sergei make once at Illinskoe. "What matters the old wife of the day? It is the wife of the night who reigns supreme."

Poor Ella, it was clearly a lesson she had never learned, but I would. And in my case I would reign indeed, for I was Empress in very truth, and if I had to become the night-empress to claim the throne and the husband that were already mine by God-given right, so be it.

We left that day for Tsarskoe on the imperial train. It was a half-hour's ride and a whole world away, and it was there in the enchanted park, the special magic land built by two empresses simply to provide them with pleasure and beauty, that I felt for the first time truly queen of all I surveyed. And it was in the upper chamber at the Alexander palace, in a pretty old room – the one where Nicky had been born – that I became the wife who would always come first for him.

And it was there during those perfect days that we conceived our first child.

Chapter 3

My first pregnancy was terribly difficult for me physically. I was sick nearly all day and constantly overcome with headaches. In addition, I am quite certain that my baby was growing against my back, for within days of the confirmation of my pregnancy from silly old Dr. Ott, the Dowager-Empress's beloved physician, I had begun to have terrible leg pains at all hours of the day and night, making me an utter wreck from the point of view of my health.

Both Nicky and Dr. Ott recommended complete rest, and so, even though this left me unable to address the hundreds of matters requiring my attention, I was forced, for the good of the precious little one inside me, to do as they said. This, in turn, caused me to have to rely upon Ella for help once again; I had no other real choice if I wanted to escape from Anichkov and my mother-in-law before the arrival of our first baby.

Following our perfect days at Tsarskoe Selo, Nicky and I had made some decisions. We had determined that the small and perfect Alexander Palace, a little house of only a hundred rooms, would be our summer home. If I had been given my way over a single decision in our lives, it would have been our only home, but Nicky said it couldn't be as the Tsar had to live in Petersburg during the season, and if I didn't want to live at Anichkov with "Mama," it had to be the Winter Palace for us.

I simply hated the idea but not as much as I hated remaining at Anichkov. The Winter Palace was too vast, a place of limitless grandeur and unconquerable spaces.

It did not strike me as a house where one could live. Indeed, it could never be a house at all, only a stage setting to show off the brilliance, the power and the apparently limitless wealth of my new family.

I wanted a cozy home and everything seemed against me, even Nicky. Still, I had to escape from my present grotesque little rooms. I didn't even have a sitting room in which to entertain friends – if I were ever to have any of those, that is – or just people in general. Nicky had proposed that we simply pick a suite of rooms in the Winter Palace and have them done up to our taste. "Easier said than done," said I, suffering the utter miseries of pregnancy. "Not so," said Nicky, for he had already ordered construction of a new bathroom high up in the East Wing in some old rooms that hadn't been lived in since the time of Alexander I and the war with Napoleon. Indeed, no one at all in the family had lived in any part of the Winter Palace since the murder of Nicky's poor grandfather, Alexander II, when Nicky was twelve. It was supposed to be terribly haunted, but as nearly as I could tell, all of Russia was one great ice-cold haunted house, so I didn't let that worry me much.

This dream bathroom of Nicky's was one that he was basing on the design of a room in an old imperial hunting palace, named Spala, in Poland, where he had arranged for the bath to be filled with fresh heated saltwater, the saltwater being sent daily all the way from the Baltic Sea by train when he was in residence. It was quite an ambitious project as it would mean framing a sunken bath the size of a small pond several floors up in the East Wing, although this time the seawater would be piped into the palace, not delivered by train.

So this was where he clearly intended our winter home to be established. I was in no condition to travel back and forth by carriage from Anichkov to the Winter Palace to oversee the construction, let alone the decoration, of our new rooms, so I asked Ella to undertake this task on my behalf. Coincidentally, and unbeknownst to me, Nicky had already extended her the same invitation as he vastly admired Ella's taste and thought both her palaces were epitomes of interior comfort and elegance. I thought they were old-fashioned and fussy, but again, what had any of it to do with me?

Naturally, Ella was thrilled to take up a place right in the center of our lives and I imagine she was equally thrilled to have something ... well, anything ... to occupy her time. For, while I was, as the French say, *encouchée* after a bare two months of marriage, she remained as barren as Russia's vast Steppes ten years after her own wedding.

Predictably, she made my headaches much worse with her constant dropping in to show us color samples and furniture patterns. What did I care what it looked like as long as it removed me from here? And Ella always found the time in her busy work schedule to visit the Dowager-Empress, "poor little Minnie," for tea. There I'm certain they shook their heads like startled doves in sympathy with 'Poor Alicky. My, she is taking this pregnancy hard, isn't she? Oh, and poor Nicky. It is such a heavy burden he bears with her.'

In reality, at that time Nicky and I had returned to our usual seamless amity, but to call him "poor Nicky" would not have been misplaced ... just not for the reasons that society pitied him. Our marriage was one divinely blessed by God as we daily grew ever closer to sharing one heart and one mind, but this felicitous state of affairs was not mirrored in the burdensome duties of ruling that had been imposed upon Nicky. His mother had stuck him with that old blowhard Witte, who, according to Nicky, was filled with a ceaseless stream of advice, admonitions and arguments, and who responded to any reproach, or even questioning, from Nicky by running off to the Dowager-Empress and complaining about his misbehavior and his unfitness to be Tsar.

She, in turn, would summon Nicky and admonish him as though he were still a little childy and remind him that Witte had steered the ship of state faultlessly for Nicky's papa when he was Tsar and that he must not consider changing a thing. For, after all, what did Nicky know about the business of ruling?

Indeed, what did he know, for hadn't his imperial parents kept him completely shielded from such matters well into his young manhood? I felt it was my job, as his wife, to remind him daily that he was now the Tsar, which meant that, as the Tsar, he was divinely guided by God who had chosen him to be the Tsar, so it could only be right for Nicky to find his own way and to listen to his own inner counsel. This, I told him, would be what was best both for Russia and for us as well.

I even helped him to write his first public speech to a funny little group of people who called themselves *zemstvos*, and he was so beautifully grateful for my loving guidance, having been very dear and nervous about doing it. Zemstvos were simply a mixture of Russian peasants, lowly townspeople, and their social superiors, who had banded together to try and organize matters in each of their individual small villages or towns in accordance with the misguided social reforms of Nicky's grandfather, Tsar Alexander II, reforms that led to him getting himself blown up. I don't suppose there was any harm in them, and Nicky and I both loved the dear peasants and knew that they loved us in return, so we had no wish to hurt their feelings in any way; we only wished to remind them that Nicky was their Tsar, their 'Little Father,' and that he did, and always would, know what was best for them.

The zemstvos from a few dozen villages had over time, in some cases, learned rudimentary reading and writing skills, which was probably why they had taken it into their heads in the first place to try and run things in their villages. This kind of thing is only harmful if it creates a feeling of autonomy in one, and that is obviously what had occurred at this time. Instead of staying home and praying for the wellbeing of their new Tsar, or simply coming to Petersburg to bring him their rough little gifts as in times past at the ascension of a new Tsar, they had actually taken it upon themselves to write a collective petition, of all things.

Despite being crudely spelled and written on a dirty torn piece of paper – all of which could have been seen as endearing – it turned out to be a far from harmless document in which the zemstvos demanded that their voices in 'local guvermant' be heard, which was, in effect, to impinge on Nicky's autocratic powers. For if he acceded to the demands of these, the simplest of our subjects – half-savages, in fact – to have a voice in the government of the country, then what would he have to put up with from his uncles and the nobles in general whose voices were far too loud already.

He was being tested, and as he explained to me, "It starts at the bottom, darling. If I cannot control the lowest amongst us, then how can I ever hope to control anyone, including my own madly ambitious family?"

He was wise to see this and I vowed that he never should – that neither of us ever should – submit to the demands of others, not on this, not on anything. We would pass on a perfect, undiminished autocratic legacy to the son I knew I was carrying.

Therefore, when Nicky met the silly little zemstvos, he told them in no uncertain terms, "Forget these senseless dreams. I will maintain the autocracy as firmly as did my late, unforgettable father," and he made such an impression of strength and power in his speech that the reverberations were heard across the land.

He was my darling and my Tsar, and to reward him for his toils, and to amuse myself on my lumpy couch at Anichkov, I wrote to Ernie. "Come," I told him, "come now, and in secret." For though I was temporarily incommoded while I was growing Russia's future Emperor, my mind was running busily all the time, and after the success of Nicky's speech I realized that if things needed to be taken in hand, then I was the one to do it.

So, to this end, I sent for my dearest brother, wishing to give him *carte blanche* in recreating his triumphant Art Nouveau designs at Hesse-Darmstadt right here in Russia, specifically at the Alexander Palace at Tsarskoe Selo.

I had decided to do this without consulting with Nicky, which would have been a silly thing to do since he had to run the entire country, and I had certainly decided to do it without the input and the objections that I knew would be inevitable from Mother Dear. In her world, every change, no matter how small, was a cause for discussion, worry and tears, and an opportunity to pit Nicky and me against each other. However at the Alexander Palace there would be no Ella, and since Ernie and I had always been of one mind, I knew that he would seek my opinion on every matter large and small to do with the rooms that I planned to make into our family's primary nest. The only things for which I had asked Nicky approval were my plans for a nursery at the Alexander Palace so that we could have a place for our baby boy when we visited there in the summer. Even his mother could not object to such a small wish from the girl who had finally done one thing right by falling *enceinte* with the heir to the throne. Indeed, I had also ordered construction of a bathing room to match exactly the one Nicky was having built at the Winter Palace

This time, I can now see, was one of the most glorious periods of my life. My body was filled with that very first splendid expectation, Nicky was never more adoring, and my mother-in-law was never less grudging, not because she had come to like me, but out of the knowledge that the future of Russia lay in my womb. If gossip about me continued to circulate – and, of course, it did – I didn't hear it. I was busy from the time I woke up and moved to my couch until I fell asleep.

Ernie had accepted my invitation and was now in Russia, staying out at Tsarskoe Selo the better to supervise proceedings, although he made nearly daily trips to visit me to show me catalogs and drawings. This put Ella's nose delightfully out of joint because she considered herself to be the expert on all things decorative for the Imperial Family, which served only to add to the fun as far as I was concerned.

Nicky, however, thought I was the very devil and told me so.

"Darling, aren't you terrible to torment poor Ella so? She is only trying to be kind to us and she is working very hard over at the Winter Palace to make it nice for us and our little one."

I smiled at him, unperturbed. Little could perturb me during those months.

"No, Nicky, I am not terrible to Ella. It is Ella who is careless of my feelings. She is always here and gives off an air of such lofty self-importance at all times. Besides, she is just doing up our rooms at the Winter Palace to be around you and your mother, and to show everyone how wonderful and indispensable she is. It seems to me that she would be better served being with her husband, acting out her role as the Queen of Moscow. For that reason alone, I am happy that you have decided to keep Sergei on as Governor-General of Moscow. Darling Nicky, my own, listen to me: Ella is not what she seems. Nobody is that sweet and helpful and modest all of the time, and the Ella you see is not the sister I know. So please listen to me on this, if you never listen to anything else I might say to you, and send her back to Moscow and her husband."

Nicky lit another of his interminable sequence of cigarettes. He had always smoked, but since his father's death he seemed never to be without one.

He inhaled gratefully and looked at me oddly. "Darling Sunny, of course I'll send Ella away if you truly want me to, but there will be talk. Besides, family discord is not good at any time and Mama definitely will not like it. Speaking of Mama –"

"And don't we always? All roads lead there, don't they, Nicky?"

He acted as if I hadn't spoken at all.

"… When I saw her this morning, she asked me how long Ernie was planning to stay here and wondered if he should be away from his wife for so long."

I was completely taken aback.

"Nicky, what are you talking about? Why, Ducky is at home with their little daughter and Ernie is here at my request. Oh, isn't this just like your mother to try and spoil any pleasure I have? Fine, let Ella stay and finish what she is doing. I doubt I will like the results, but anything, anything to be out from under your darling mama's endless advice and scrutiny. Pah!"

Nicky leaned over and kissed me, simultaneously blowing smoke all over me. I made a choking noise and motioned for him to open the windows. He did so with a good-natured smile and within seconds we were both frozen solid. I knew his mother would find out about this too and lecture me about it. I really couldn't win in this family and I said as much to Nicky in a petulant tone.

He sat down next to me and cuddled my swelling body to his.

"You do not need to win, darling. You are my Tsarina and the queen of my heart. What does anything or anyone else matter? And, Sunny my angel, I do hate so to belabor a point, but well, you see, dearest, there has been some talk about Ernie and I think perhaps –"

"Talk about Ernie?" I twisted in his embrace and stared at him aghast. "What could anybody possibly have to say against my dearest brother, a man who has come here at my request to help me do up just one house, the only one of our little homes that I am interested in, and who is second only to you, Nicky, in being the most important person in the world to me. Who would dare say anything against him and what are they saying? Oh, never mind," I put my hands up over my ears, "I don't want to know. I don't, I don't. It is only because they hate me. Everybody here hates me and you don't do anything to stop them, to stop your mother and her damned endless gossiping."

I began to cry. Nicky looked as stunned as he always did whenever I shared my thoughts openly with him.

"Darling Sunny, please don't. You must not upset yourself. Think of the baby –"

I cried louder. I tended to be somewhat emotionally wrought during my pregnancy and Nicky had upset me badly.

He patted me and tutted repeatedly in a feeble attempt to soothe me.

"Please calm yourself, Alicky darling, my angel. Forget I said anything. It was quite stupid of me. Of course Ernie may stay as long as both of you wish. Now hush and tell me about this great secret you two are working on. I'll burst with curiosity if you don't."

I wondered fleetingly whether he was merely humoring me, but he did look genuinely interested, so for the sake of family happiness I responded.

"I'll never tell, naughty one. It is a surprise and it's all for you ... well, you and our coming little one. You must wait and be a patient boy. But you do not need to wait for everything. You may kiss me right this instant and then call for tea cakes, for I cannot wait a minute longer for either of those things."

In such ways did I, as the most loving of women, maintain the peace of my marriage. I never feared, nor faltered, nor doubted, even for an instant, that God had truly intended our union and it was because of the great love that I bore my husband that I was able not only to maintain my equilibrium when all was in flux around me, but I fancy I even managed to thrive a little too.

I was, for example, learning Russian. Catherine, my *lectrice*, and Nicky both read to me in Russian, mostly the novels of Tolstoy and Pushkin. It was a much more interesting way to grasp a new language than the stupid copy book monotony imposed on me by that senile old teacher Nicky had sent me. In fact, my grasp of Russian had reached the point where I felt comfortable practicing conversations in private not just with Nicky but with one of my maids of honor, Maria. As I learned Russian, so she learned English, and we were beginning to communicate rather well together.

This was beneficial as I now owned over a thousand new dresses in my trousseau and from the trunks and trunks of clothes sent to me by Worth in Paris, and each of the dresses – and the matching hats and shoes and other trimmings – had to be accounted for and cared for.

In this vein I was creating a catalog of my possessions for my own peace of mind and also so that Maria could better inform the other maids of my wishes. Tuttles resented my new closeness with one of those "horrid Ruskies," as she called them, but after all I was the Russian Empress and perforce needed to forge alliances in my new country.

I certainly wasn't finding many amongst my new family. The Dowager-Empress had seemingly come out of mourning to do nothing but try to diminish me.

First there were the prayers. At the end of each Orthodox service, all over the Russian land, the priests would intone prayers for the Tsar and the Tsarina by name, and Minnie, Mother Dear, had requested that the priests say the following:

"Pray, my brothers and sisters, for our Tsar Nicholas, his mother the Dowager-Empress, her Imperial Highness Marie Feodorovna, and her Imperial Highness Empress Alexandra Feodorovna." And then they named each member of the imperial family. It took ages, there being so many of them. I can only imagine that the poor peasants often thought, as did I, that simply saying one prayer for the entire Romanov family would have been much better, but heaven forfend that one single grand duke or grand duchess be forgotten. In the case of naming the Dowager-Empress before the reigning Empress, not only had this never been done before, but it struck me as ridiculous and, moreover, how dare she couple her name with that of my husband?

In point of fact, I had come to hate this woman. Only I would ever *know* that, but at times I think she suspected it. The prayers were one of those times, and I insisted that my own confessor, sweet old Father Yanishev, address the matter with the Holy Synod. The poor old man was reluctant to do so, but in the end he did as I bid and, lo and behold, they agreed with me.

Minnie took her defeat with good grace, stating, "So then, I see I am erased. In that case I will have no prayers said for me at all."

Nicky begged her to reconsider her decision as he feared gossip, but she, who adored gossip, refused and gave her orders to the Synod.

The brouhaha was immediate and painful ... for me. First, the grand dukes and grand duchesses all rushed Nicky at once and demanded to know why he had allowed his new wife to remove his mother's name from the prayers. *What would his father have said?* Nicky stonewalled by stating airily that this was a private matter he had no wish ever to discuss. Naturally, this unelaborated response only served to confirm their suspicions that it was I who had done this. Fine then, they said, remove our names as well.

While I was enraged at Nicky for not standing up forcefully for me, I did feel that the choice to remove their names was a good one. Although Nicky's younger siblings knew the truth and chose not to fight with their adored mama about it, they did at least leave their names up for the prayers, and Xenia had the good grace to say to me during a visit that she and Sandro both found her mama impossible, but simply judged it easier to give in to her than to endure her recriminations when she did not get her way. This was not my nature and I told Xenia as much. I would gladly have told everyone the truth if they had asked me, but no one came, no one asked – everyone just assumed.

I won't go so far as to say that Minnie had lied directly about my role in this, but I do know she did not trouble herself to clarify the sequence of events, and that is tantamount to a lie to my mind. The entire family stopped attending daily services at Anichkov. I didn't care. I liked the peace. I know Nicky did mind, but he never spoke of it to me.

And then, finally, we were the ones who were able to pass over those services, and over every other event at Anichkov, Nicky's mother's house, for both suites of our new rooms – at the Winter Palace and at the Alexander Palace – became ready simultaneously.

Ella announced the completion of her project at the Winter Palace with a simpering touch of false modesty, professing her fervent hope that we would "like it a little," and a little was indeed as much as I liked it, so her stated ambition could be said to have been satisfied. As near as I could tell, all that Ella had done was to order new fabrics and wallpapers that seemed to me only slightly more acceptable than the ugly red and gold ones that had dominated the previous décor. She had consulted with me at length as to my color preferences and then apparently proceeded to ignore my wishes entirely.

When Nicky and I went to inspect our Winter Palace apartments, she foolishly insisted on accompanying us. I say 'foolishly,' as it seems to me that if she had wanted me to lavish compliments on her, it would have been better for her to have waited until I had been given the time to order my thoughts, and especially my facial expression of those thoughts, as my initial impression of the results of her toils was far from favorable.

Naturally, being Ella, all had to be spoken of, and because Nicky was there, she poured on the theatrics.

With a creased forehead and hands held out in submission, she said in a broken voice. "Oh, you don't like it. Oh no! And I so wanted everything to be perfect for you … and with the heir coming. Oh, I feel so dreadful!"

She then sunk gracefully down on a taupe-and-gray-striped chaise and buried her face in her hands.

I said nothing. I was in my wheeling chair because of my leg pains, and felt sick and angry.

Nicky jumped in, of course.

"Ella, darling Auntie-Sister, of course we like it. We adore it, it's wonderful. You have the most exquisite taste. I cannot wait to bring Mama here to see what you have done."

A small smile crept across her face.

"Truly, Nicky? And 'Auntie-Sister,' aren't you the very one? What a name!"

He grinned back, delighted by his success in cheering her up, and probably thinking to himself how easy-natured she was compared to his wife. I'm certain that's exactly what he was thinking.

What he said was, "Well, isn't that just who you are, beautiful Ella, my aunt by one marriage and my sister by another? And now I will add that you are a genius of a decorator to the list as well. I cannot imagine a nicer set of rooms, can you, darling?"

He said this to me, looking down at me in my chair, his lips smiling, his eyes pleading, but that sort of thing is no good with me; I am constitutionally incapable of the dishonesty required for empty flattery.

Ella knew this well enough, and before I could answer Nicky, she gave a false little laugh and interjected, "Never mind, Nicky, I know Alix isn't pleased, but," she shrugged prettily, "I simply could not bring myself to destroy these wonderful rooms by lowering all the ceilings and making everything pink and purple. It seemed wrong. I think in the end you will both enjoy my silly, old-fashioned, quiet décors longer. These new fads, one finds, grow tiresome rather quickly, don't you think?"

Nicky nodded eagerly. "Oh, I do, you're quite right. And besides, Ella Auntie-Sister, I would look rather funny amidst such freakish fancies and I hardly think Sunny would like them. She has perfect taste. Why, just look at her!"

He looked at me, hoping that his sweetly turned compliment would turn my own obvious tide of rising annoyance, but considering that I was at that moment clad in a pale pink gown adorned with deeper pink roses and overlaid with a mauve velvet cape, it fell flat. He knew it too and shifted uncomfortably.

I smiled thinly at both of them.

"Well, Ella knows best, I suppose, and of course, Nicky darling, we would not want you to have to live with, as you say, 'freakish fancies.' Or was that you, Ella? It is hard to remember, what with you two being in such perfect accord."

Nicky looked away but Ella gazed at me placidly.

"I'm sorry, Alix, but then maybe I was only trying to be fair, to Nicky, to Minnie, to you too, because, after all, you do have your own perfect nest, don't you, just the way you wanted it. Maybe this can be Nicky's special place and the one Ernie has created, as a *surprise for Nicky*, can be yours." She turned, shrugging, to a puzzled-looking Nicky. "As you can see from my sister's face, not all surprises are welcomed."

I was beyond angry. I wanted to hit her. I wanted to scream at them both, but mostly at Ella, but I didn't. I was much cleverer than Ella and I merely clutched at my mid-section, which was churning, and gave a little moan.

My visit was over, so was Nicky's, and Ella's triumph was in ashes.

Funnily, she and Minnie both chose to accompany Nicky and me two days later when we went to meet Ernie at the Alexander Palace to unveil my real home. Both Nicky and Ella were quiet during the tour. I think Nicky was simply overcome. He smiled when he saw his special bathing room, but as for the rest he was so moved he had to sit down and gape, at least that is how I chose to see it. Ernie had created a perfect cozy nest for us and our coming baby.

All the main rooms were perfect Art Nouveau designs, with cozy corners and low charming ceilings, and hung with rose trellised paper and matching curtains and carpets, so that one felt one were in a nosegay. Our bedroom was all in pink and green to match the other rooms, but here Ernie had even ordered bedding to match. I had a stunningly beautiful boudoir all in mauve – mauve rose wallpaper and carpet, white and mauve

53

furniture, a mauve chaise to rest on and admire it all, and a suite of rooms in bright chintz for our coming little one.

Nicky's study and bath and billiards rooms had not been done in an Art Nouveau way. Ernie and I had decided to honor him with our vision of a Russian-German Gothic re-creation of old castles or hunting lodges so that visitors, upon entering the rooms, could imagine that they were in a time of ancient tsars or German kings.

The Dowager-Empress was the first to speak.

"This furniture … good God, what is it?"

I inclined my head proudly.

"It's new, all brand new, like Nicky's reign, and our marriage, and like our baby will be. Ernie found it. It's from a wonderful company in London called Maples. Not everyone, Mother Dear, wishes to surround themselves with remnants of past glories. I prefer to create future ones."

She laughed. She could always find humor at my expense, the light-minded creature.

"Well, I can only applaud you, Alix. You've taken an Italian masterpiece of a palace and turned it into a bourgeois nightmare. One can only hope that not too much money was wasted upon it."

To my surprise, it was Ella who answered her. "Oh I don't know, Minnie. It reminds me of Balmoral and Grandmamma."

I looked at her with the old love that I sometimes forgot was still there. "Ella, dearest, then you do see. Yes, it is just like Osbourne and Balmoral."

54

She nodded. "I do, and now I'll pray that, like Grandmamma, you have a dozen happy children to fill your rooms. It is all that really matters, isn't it?" She turned to Minnie and Nicky and Ernie.

There were nods all round, champagne was called for, and later that night, when Nicky and I were alone for the first time in our new bedroom, he held me tenderly and said, "I do love what you've made here, my darling."

I gazed back at him adoringly, until he laid his hand on my stomach and I realized he was referring not to Ernie and my décor but to our child who was growing inside of me.

No matter, I said to myself, no matter. We are here, he will come to love it, he will come to see that I know best. After his heir is born, everyone will come to see that.

Chapter 4

Our daughter was born in November. She was several weeks late and by the time I had delivered her, following an excruciating twenty-three hours of hellish labor, the court and the country in general had already pronounced the following 'facts' about me: that I had never been pregnant at all; that I had, in fact, been pregnant with a boy, but that I had lost him early on in the pregnancy and that I had asked that a peasant baby boy be smuggled in his stead; and that I had asked that a peasant baby boy be smuggled in but a girl had been brought to me by accident (as they were to add later, upon the actual announcement of the birth).

As I lay exhausted but still glad, oh so very glad, to have my baby, I listened to the distant firing of guns – one hundred and one times for the birth of my little girl, our little girl. I knew that was the traditional salute.

Nicky's face was as radiant as I had ever seen it, and what did it matter? We had our beautiful baby, safely – if painfully – delivered, and boys would follow, so many boys, and in the meantime here we were, a real little family of our own at last.

Nicky suggested naming her 'Olga' after the oldest daughter in 'Eugene Onegin,' a book by one of Russia's greatest poets, Alexander Pushkin, made into an opera by one of Russia's greatest composers, Pyotr Ilyich Tchaikovsky … although we both much preferred the exquisite works of Marie Corelli.

Once again,
Oh once again,
Once again,
Oh nightingale.

He smiled down at us and said, "Then, darling, if we have another girl, we can call her Tatiana."

I smiled weakly back at him, and he must have seen something in my exhausted countenance that worried him for he stroked my face and said earnestly, "Alicky, my Sunny, my darling, please don't look worried. I do not care if we never have another child. Watching you suffer was the worst experience of my life. I only even mentioned the name Tatiana because of the book and –"

I grasped his hand. "But of course we shall have another child, Nicky... lots of them ... boys. You know we will. I know you want a son. You must have a son and I will give him to you. It is –"

"It is what God wills, my darling. Oh Sunny, don't you know that even we, a Tsar and his Tsaritsa, are at the mercy of God? And darling, you are wrong about a son. If God sends us one, then, yes, I'll be glad, but I won't love him more than I love you or our new little one, and I won't rail at fate if such a thing does not come to pass. I have only ever asked one thing from God and that was that he give you to me as my bride. Having received such an undeserved blessing, don't you think I would be an ungrateful fellow to ask for more?"

I loved him, I adored him, he was my one-and-all, and as long as he loved me too I knew I was safe. I looked down at the little one in my arms and then at him. I was safe, I was. I was loved and wanted and a mother, and I knew that these things would always be true here at Tsarskoe Selo, inside the walls of our little home.

I knew, too, that outside the walls lay an enormous, nearly endless, land filled with strange people whom I did not understand but so much wanted to. They, in their turn, did not seem to like me and I could not for the life of me work out why. It couldn't be as a result of the Petersburg gossip: after all, how would a peasant ever hear that across the vast expanse of Russia? I could not believe that it was simply because I had arrived in their midst after the death of Nicky's papa: the new Tsar obviously had to marry someone, so why not me, and so why dislike me for it? If it was because I was foreign – German – I could not change that. It certainly could not be personal: the people had never even seen me, except for at brief moments during our wedding procession.

No, it must have been because of my birthplace, but their opinions would change the very second I gave the country its heir. I would not be the 'German Empress' then. I would be the mother of their Tsarevich and they would all love me at last; even those at the horrible court of Nicky's mama would love me then.

I did not say any of this to Nicky. Why make myself look desperate or less than I was to the one person in the world who did not see me that way? One of two, I mentally corrected myself – my baby would love me uncritically as well. So I only thanked Nicky and covered his hand with kisses. We three were as one and I told myself that was all that should ever matter.

If only that had been true.

The next weeks passed more quickly than at any time since my arrival in Russia. I loved every moment of being a mother, I gloried in it, and here was a thing I could do well and be praised for doing well, for Nicky felt that my decision to breastfeed Olga was the only right and natural thing to do.

My mother-in-law carped at this, of course, and even wrote to dear Grandmamma to criticize my choice, but I didn't care.

Grandmamma's letter made Nicky and me laugh, in fact.

> *Dearest Little Alicky,*
>
> *I congratulate you and your dear Nicky on the birth of your first child. My dearest Albert and I too suffered the disappointment of a daughter as our first child. However, in time, this proved to be less of a grief to us than one might imagine as we then went on to have several sons, who mostly were much more disappointing than your dear Aunt Vicky and your saintly mother turned out to be.*
>
> *Yes, a daughter can be a great comfort to one, as you may find. Still, my dearest child, I have heard from dear Aunt Minnie that you have chosen to feed your daughter yourself. This was the only thing that your poor dear mama did which ever truly disappointed me. It is not what women*

born to great houses undertake. Her strange choice ruined her health, which is why I am sure she succumbed to Diphtheria in her later years. Nor is it becoming.

But let me say more on this, for I fear you have not yet understood, my dear child, what it means to be an Empress. Alix, my dear, you must show yourself to your court and to your people to be loved. Minnie tells me that you and Nicky have virtually disappeared from your capital and that no balls were arranged in honor of your daughter's birth!

My dear child, what can you be thinking of? My Albert and I constantly presented ourselves and our family to the people of England. We did this at great personal cost to ourselves and our own dear family life, a life that, as you know, would turn out to be all too brief. Yet, my dear, we did our duty, for that is a sovereign's burden and I urge you and your own dearest Nicky not to shirk from it.

I write and say these difficult things to you as you are like my very own child to me, Alicky, and, as ever, I care only for your happiness.

Oh yes, Nicky and I were able to laugh at poor old Grandmamma's silly letter, for, as I said to Nicky, was not I a wife and a mother first? He agreed wholeheartedly, and as for showing ourselves to the court and the people, well of course we would. The coronation was coming in May.

Preparations for this event were so intense and time-consuming that poor Nicky had been inundated on every side by church officials, by Sergei in his position as Governor-General of Moscow, and by the ambassadors of every country in Europe. Not only would we be showing ourselves to our people at the coronation and the series of balls and events surrounding it, why, the whole world would be reading about us and seeing the photographs, for never had a Tsar been crowned in such modern times.

Grandmamma lived in a lost world, so I did not take offense. As for Nicky's mother's interference, I simply prayed for her indulgence as she would soon see that I alone was the Empress of Russia and, along with Nicky, of course, and the children we would have, I remained the best hope for the future of the Romanovs.

May dawned that year of 1895 with an almost preternatural beauty, even in Petersburg, which, as Nicky so correctly stated, has less of a spring season than a mud season.

Oh, Tsarskoe Selo was enchanting that season! I was up and walking again, and Olga – in her perambulator – and I were taken for daily promenades through the park with Nicky. I remember the air was laden with the perfume of lilac both outside and inside my boudoir, for

I adored the scent and had almost an excessive amount of it placed throughout all our rooms. I will admit that I was not looking forward to our trip to Moscow with its predictably endless and exhausting rounds of receptions and balls and appearances, but then, too, I felt a strange anticipation for all of that, even for the silly balls and parades. It was unusual for me to feel this way about such things, but at least these would be to celebrate our coronation. The crowning of an Emperor and his Empress is the holiest of rites here on Earth, a true marriage, if you will, between those who are set by God to rule over others and those who are likewise ruled. This ceremony would surely draw together what had been lost at my unsettling funeral-wedding and allow Nicky and me to unite our own souls once again, and this time additionally with those of our people.

If there were harbingers that all would not go as I was wishing for, I tried very hard to ignore them.

The first of these was when the old dear who was in charge of court protocol, Count Fredericks, formally requested an appointment with me. Count Fredericks was a charming old man and so fond of Nicky and me that he referred to us as *"mes enfants"* or *"mes chères."* He was like a sweet old grandfather to us both, so we condoned this *lèse majesté* in his addressing of us, but for him to request a formal meeting with me was completely out of character for him. I normally left him to his own devices, which were primarily to decide who should have an audience with Nicky, and when and to whom to award those honorary ribbons so prized by the Russian nobility.

Still, as I liked him so much, I agreed to the meeting, and because I could not think that we would be discussing anything of importance, I summoned him to my boudoir rather than to my formal audience chamber, something I regretted immediately for his news was of the sort that made me wish I could pace up and down a long room angrily instead of having to lie on my chaise and simply try to take in what he was telling me.

He twisted his aged hands, he hung his head against my railing, he shuffled, he shifted, he mumbled, he apologized and none of it mattered, for, in this, ancient protocol had won. What he was here to inform me about was that the Dowager-Empress, should she so choose – and she had so chosen – was entitled to take precedence over me in any ceremony. Minnie had not forgiven the kerfuffle over the prayers and now she would have her revenge: on the ride to the Kremlin on our entry into Moscow for the coronation, her carriage would go after Nicky's and before mine.

I was angry, I was hurt, and I wanted Nicky to order a change in the order of precedence. I told Fredericks I would *make* Nicky change it or, failing that, I would ride beside him in his carriage, which made more sense anyway.

He shook his old head sadly.

"It cannot be, Your Majesty. It is an old rule of protocol from the time of a far-distant widowed Empress. She instituted it so that her son's wife, her majesty who became Empress, could not take precedence over her, and –"

64

"And Empress Elizabeth and Empress Catherine stood for this and did not change it in their own times?" I interrupted incredulously.

He smiled sadly at me.

"No, Your Majesty, they did not change the protocol, for I believe that they believed, as did your own ancestress the great Queen Elizabeth of England, that the people will always look to the rising sun over the setting one, and so for those who would come after them they left the protocol in place."

I was touched by his mention of Queen Elizabeth of England and my temper cooled. Poor Minnie, I thought, hanging on to her pathetic shreds of royalty.

It was a few days later, when Fredericks officially requested another audience with me, that my sympathy for her vanished forever. We met in the Maple Room this time and it was there that Count Fredericks informed me that, despite the fact that protocol demanded that I wear certain of the crown jewels – jewels that this time did by every right and tradition belong to the reigning Empress – Minnie had not returned them and had no intention of so doing.

I could not believe this nonsense. To begin with, I didn't even like the crown jewels. Nicky had given, and continued to give me, magnificent jewels almost on a daily basis. I had a young baby, a coronation to prepare for, daily dress fittings, a thousand telegrams and letters to answer … and now this. I considered letting it pass, but I couldn't, not this time, and I knew exactly what to do.

I ordered Fredericks to contact the Montenegrin Grand Duchesses, Anastasia and Militza. Known familiarly as 'Stana' and 'Mitsia' respectively, they were the wives of two more of Nicky's interminable uncles and considered strange even by Romanov standards. They both had (what was rumored to be dyed) black hair and a great love for any occult practices, and were thus called the 'Black Sisters.' They were also renowned gossips and Minnie hated them. Therefore, however inconvenient the timing, I decided to deepen my acquaintance with these ladies.

Naturally, they arrived on receipt of my request. Given my pregnancy and then the raising of the baby, I had been little seen in the capital and had not entertained at all. So an invitation from me was both a great honor and an opportunity to peek inside what Russian society was beginning to refer to as "the secret court." That there was nothing to see at Tsarskoe Selo besides a small, loving, united family was beside the point.

The Ladies Montenegrin were seated in my red drawing room all aflutter with excitement. Oh what might be revealed! They could entertain on this for years and I did not disappoint them. Tea was poured and obviously insincere compliments about the décor of my home were given. They duly admired my baby, they spoke in gushing terms of the upcoming festivities in Moscow, and they breathlessly asked about my wardrobe, as I knew they would.

I smiled and pounced.

"Oh yes, the coronation. What a grand occasion! I've been quite swept off my feet preparing for it and I really believed, ladies, that I was finally ready, but now ..."

I held up my hands and shrugged, smiling. They were all agog.

Anastasia leaned in breathlessly. "Oh, Your Imperial Highness, is a new baby coming?"

I looked at her aghast, for in fact I had just begun to believe that, yes indeed, Nicky and I were to be so blessed, but that topic was hardly up for discussion on this occasion.

I shook my head in pretend amusement. "Oh, I think not quite yet, Grand Duchess. Olga is still feeding and …" I noted their exchange of looks and raised eyebrows. This was not going well; I hardly needed to encourage more criticism. I continued cheerfully, "Nicky and I will have a dozen or so children, but no, I cannot give you such news today, though of course you two will be the first to hear when there is some. No, I'm afraid it is a more prosaic matter, that old bugbear protocol again, and I really cannot think what to do."

I had to smother a laugh as I saw their faces fall in disappointment. *Oh, a boring matter, then.*

Anastasia tried to rally herself, asking with false concern, "Are you disappointed with your new gowns, then, Your Highness? We heard you had ordered hundreds from Worth for the occasion? Do they not suit?"

I gritted my teeth. *Hundreds of new gowns.* Good old Minnie was at it again. I deepened my smile and gave what I hoped was a tinkling laugh.

"Oh no, Monsieur Worth's gowns are lovely, though not as numerous as has apparently been supposed. It is just that I have recently found that I must appear in the crown jewels and –"

Mitsia yawned. "I know they are quite heavy, and maybe the settings are more Russian than German, but–"

Oh these people, these awful, judging, prejudiced Russians, and these two weren't any more Russian than I was, having arrived to marry their bombastic old grand dukes from Montenegro.

I held my smile carefully in position. My face would hurt later.

"Oh, I wouldn't know about that. I am not particularly interested in jewels, though I do like the pearls Nicky has given me. No, no, it is that I am supposed to wear certain jewels and it seems they are not available, so –"

They interrupted in unison their faces avid now.

"Not available? Oh no, is it –?"

I had them: a great scandal was here, they could taste it. Had the crown jewels been stolen – and if so, by whom? Had they been sold? Was the crown bankrupt? They were breathless with anticipation. What wonders would I share?

I gave them even better than they were dreaming of. I sighed and looked down in feigned sadness as I fidgeted with my rings.

"I'm afraid it is the Dowager-Empress, you see." They were both nearly falling off their chairs, so eager were they to hear what I would say next. "She, well … I … Oh, I hardly know what to say. You see, the Dowager-Empress will not relinquish the crown jewels, even for the coronation. As I said, I do not even like them, let alone want them, but it seems that a reigning Empress must wear them on certain occasions, this being one of them, and yet …" I raised my eyes and let my shoulders droop a bit.

It was brilliant; they were horrified, shocked to their very cores.

"Why, how could such a thing occur?" asked Mitsia.

"Do you think, Your Highness, the Dowager-Empress may have become distracted in her grief?" suggested Anastasia.

I shook my head with the greatest look of sympathy that I could summon and murmured that I hoped it was not so. God bless the Dowager-Empress and keep her safe.

That night I nearly told Nicky what I had done but an inner voice cautioned me against it. Instead, I told him what I hoped for us, for the new baby.

Initially, he was literally struck dumb with delight, and when he could finally speak again he assured me that never before had a man been given a greater treasure than me.

Two days later, Count Fredericks was again requesting an audience. I was just beginning to feel the first pangs of morning illness, so I greeted him as before in my boudoir.

He was there, with evident surprise, to tell me that he had just received a phone call from Minnie's Chief of Staff to announce that the Dowager-Empress was releasing all the crown jewels in her keeping to me immediately.

I nodded at Fredericks and thanked him for the message.

That afternoon, as I lay in the soft spring light, stroking the new hope of Russia inside me, I understood that I was ready now to be crowned, to become the mother of Russia's heir, to represent the sole image of a Russian empress for our people, and that in fact I was actually looking forward to the forthcoming festivities in Moscow.

Chapter 5

It was said later that nearly a million people came to Moscow to see Nicky and me crowned. I don't know about that. I did notice the crowds and that dear Georgie and May had come from England, and awful cousin Willie from Germany, and also a whole raft of lesser royals who probably had little else to do and wished to be caught up in our reflected glory. That did not happen, but maybe they felt better about their lesser stations in life after it was all over.

The whole sequence of events can, I think, be summed up in the color red: the red of the endless carpet leading up to the throne at the Kremlin, its color contrasting with that of the diamond chain of Nicky's ancestors which broke from his shoulders and fell with a muted thump to the carpet – an ill omen they said; the red of the lifeblood of our heir that ran down my thighs and stained my legs two nights later; and the dark brownish-red of all the blood – rivers and lakes of it – that covered the field of Khodynka and the carts and the streets of Moscow as the dead and dying rolled through them.

The Kremlin itself is red, a vast series of buildings – some whimsical, some forbidding – all gathered behind an enormous wall. It could be called, I suppose, another Tsarskoe Selo as it was once a tsars' village, but that is no longer true. Tsars come there little now, usually only to be crowned. The ancient seat of Romanov power, the Kremlin and the city of Moscow itself, is but a reminder of what it once was. While, every generation or so (for

71

Russian Tsars but rarely make old bones), a new Tsar is crowned there, nevertheless since the time of Peter the Great they have reigned and been buried in Petersburg.

Given the odd and hurried way in which I had entered my new country, and then my pregnancy and the delivery of my child, the coronation was my first opportunity to see the seat of the ancient Muscovite tsars that my husband so admired, waxing lyrical about that old city in the weeks leading up to the coronation.

"It is the true heart of Russia, darling, not a falsely envisioned sort of place as Petersburg is. They call it the "city of forty times forty churches" and I believe that is true. If I had my way, we would restore it as the capital. You know my favorite ancestor was Tsar Alexei. They called him the "Mild." It is what I hope to be called too, darling. He was Peter the Great's father, the last of the real Muscovite tsars. Papa used to tell me all about them. He loved Moscow too and –"

Laughing up at him, delighted by his boyish enthusiasm, I interrupted him with, "And just why can't you restore it as the capital if you so wish, darling? Are you not the Tsar?"

He smiled adoringly at me and shook his head.

"I suppose I am, and I certainly shall be when I am crowned, but it is not that easy to undo so-called progress, Sunny, and besides, I don't think my wify would want to move to Moscow. It is a bit of trip from here to there."

I shuddered. No, I absolutely would not want to move out of Tsarskoe Selo. I never planned on us leaving our perfect little home here at the Alexander Palace if I could help it, and I knew that I could indeed help it.

I nodded at him complacently and patted my just rounding stomach.

"That is true, my huzzy, but I'll tell you this. We can name this little one after your favorite ancestor, if you wish it."

His face lit up. Really, I tended to forget how little it took to make Nicky happy.

"I do wish it, my darling, and thank you. You are an angel in very truth. Now, I have wanted to keep this a surprise as a present to you, but since you are giving me my greatest desire," he glanced hungrily at my stomach, "I think I shall tell you now."

"You will indeed, my boy, although I cannot imagine that there is anything I am lacking."

It was only the truth. My coffers had enough jewelry for a hundred empresses, and I had my husband and my baby and a new one to come, all in our sweet little home. What more could I possibly need?

"Oh, you are lacking, though, Your Highness, though certainly not in beauty, or in jewels for that matter. It is just that you are so wonderfully beautiful that I cannot help wanting to decorate you, and –"

"Decorate me?" I laughed up at him. "You make me sound like a Christmas tree."

"No, darling, more like a palace or a ..." he paused dramatically, "... or a yacht, although as this one is all yours, I suppose you will be the one to decorate it."

I tried to look interested; I was quite unfamiliar with boats and didn't know if I liked them. I smiled all the same.

"Well, thank you, dearest. That sounds awfully nice, but don't you have one already?"

73

He laughed happily.

"Oh well, I do, or rather *we* do, the Polar Star, but that is really Mama's yacht. Of course, technically it belongs to –"

"Technically?" I asked, ice in my voice.

A moment ago I hadn't cared about boats, or yachts, or whatever they were called, a bit, but this Polar Star business sounded a little too much like the wrangling over the crown jewels to me, and if Minnie was calling it hers when it was really ours, I would be forced to step in.

Somehow Nicky knew what I was thinking because he began to speak very quickly.

"No, no, Sunny, you misunderstood me. Yes, Mother is fond of the Polar Star, but I assure you that she would like The Standart much more. That is the name of the new yacht – The Standart. You see, Papa started building it, and then he ... well, you know. But it is going to be the grandest yacht that ever sailed the seas. Why, it will positively dwarf your grandmamma's ship The Britannia and –"

"Grandmamma's Britannia? Bigger than that, truly?"

He nodded enthusiastically.

"Much bigger, and it will positively dwarf Willy's silly old Hohenzollern. And because of our trip you will be able to show it off to everyone, darling. Why, they will –"

I put my hand to my stomach.

"What trip, Nicky?"

He looked confused. I had noted this before, my husband's inability to sustain more than one thought in his head at a time. I repeated myself and he shook his head as though to clear it and then smiled brilliantly.

"Oh yes, our trip ... Well, you see, darling, it is what new rulers always do. They pay visits to other heads of states, at least to those of a comparable size and importance. In our case, we will have to go to Germany, of course," he raised a finger to ward off my expression of anger, "and to England to see your dearest grandmamma, and there we won't only be showing off your yacht, but our baby as well!" Rewarded by my smile, he continued. "And France, of course. They are our only European allies, so we will have to show ourselves there. But don't worry, dearest, now that the baby is coming we will obviously wait to go until after he is here. Still, you can plan your decoration of The Standart before then, after the coronation. It will give you something interesting to do while you wait for his Imperial Highness the Tsarevich, Grand Duke Alexei Nikolaevich, to arrive."

I held out my arms to him. "Yes, it will, my huzzy, and I know just what I am going to do. I will make The Standart look exactly like our rooms here. That way we will always feel right at home."

He creased his forehead. "Well, darling, they don't have to look *exactly* the same. After all –"

"Oh I see, so it is true what Ella and your mama think, that what Ernie and I created here, in our home, our little home," my voice broke, "is ugly. Maybe it is too *parvenu* for you, Nicky, not quite up to snuff, as they say. Maybe I'm not, either?"

It took him long minutes to comfort and reassure me, and by then I was tired and wanted my bed.

So it was all of these events, and of course our great expectation, that I suppose distracted me from thinking overmuch about what awaited us in Moscow.

I had mostly read Count Fredericks's endless notes on the schedules, and consulted with Maria about my wardrobe until I was heartily sick, and read Ella's boring notes on her decoration of our rooms at the Kremlin. Yes, all of those things had been done, but I could not see ahead. I could never have imagined any of it, really.

We left Tsarskoe Selo by train a week before the coronation, although we would not enter Moscow itself until a day later. This was all based upon some arcane ritual worked out long ago. In order to be in Moscow, and yet not to be seen to be there, we were to be temporarily housed at one of Russia's more bizarre places. It was called either the Petrovsky Palace or St. Peters Arrival Palace, depending on who was telling the story, and was a striking red brick castle that had been commissioned by Catherine as a sort of royal hotel so that the Imperial Family could rest overnight there before formally entering Moscow and moving into the Kremlin. Why she conceived this idea, I cannot imagine.

So, as with any whim of hers – or of any tsar, I suppose – she had this magnificent structure built over a period of four years and, when it was completed, she stayed there only one night. Her son, Emperor Paul, never spent a single night there, and eventually Napoleon invaded Russia and burned it to the ground, only for it to be rebuilt by Tsar Nicholas I, who again failed to use it even once. After that, it lay empty and falling into disrepair for nearly fifty years until Nicky's grandfather, Alexander II, decided it had to be brought back yet again – this time on an even more magnificent scale to accommodate both of his families, that of his wife and their children and that of his mistress and their children – in case he ever wished to travel to Moscow and stay there instead of at Kremlin. They never used it, either, as Nicky's grandpapa was considered to be constantly at risk of being hunted down by anarchists – there were three attempts on his life before the one that killed him – and the Petrovsky Palace was not considered secure enough. Nor did Nicky's papa use it, for he too was concerned about the risk of assassination. So the palace lay as empty as it had since its creation, until Nicky decided, for no good reason that I could see, that he, Olga and I would stay there before our formal entrance into Moscow.

With that history, one would think one could count on it being empty with the exception of ourselves and our entourage, but Nicky woke me up that night from my uneasy sleep to inform me that he was being haunted by the ghosts of his ancestors, and he knew exactly which ones.

"I hate this place, darling. Can't you hear them, can't you see them, the ones who were murdered before they were crowned – the betrayed ones?"

I lay against his shoulder, my eyes squeezed shut. I felt Nicky tremble beside me. Of course I knew all about the ghosts, but once again I had to be brave enough for the both of us.

"It is nothing, darling. I have always been surrounded by the dead since my childhood in Hesse-Darmstadt. They are only shades. They cannot hurt us. They are what remains on this earth of lonely royal men and women who were unable to fulfill their destinies. They will do nothing to you, my darling."

As I said it, I prayed that it was so.

I don't think Nicky really heard me. Caressing me with shaking hands, he said, "No, they are here to warn me. I was born on the Day of Job and I feel that they are telling me that I will pay for the sins of my ancestors –"

"Oh don't, Nicky. The dead cannot tell us anything. Everybody has to be born on some day. I am certain that if we knew the history of every day on earth, we would discover that both good and terrible things happened on each day. You cannot think like this. You will drive yourself mad, and me too, and I have your darling mama here to do that for me already."

That at least made him chuckle, and within a few moments I heard his soft snoring resume. Sleep did not come so easily to me, for it had not been wholly true what I had said to Nicky. No, I did not believe the dead came to hurt us, but they did indeed come to warn us, and I had seen the dead tsars too, I had heard their sad cries in the corridors of this palace that should not have existed.

What were they saying to us? Can anyone ever understand messages from those who have come before us and failed at their lives, and if we could understand would it make us do things differently?

I stroked my stomach and fancied I felt a small returning flutter under my hand. We would be different, my family, my son, I knew that this was so and that this was the message from the ancestors, and that it was less a warning than a benediction.

Chapter 6

It started well, at least from the standpoint of the weather. That alone is rare enough in Russia to raise one's hopes sky high.

It had been decided by Nicky, against all advice to the contrary, that, for his official entrance into the City of Moscow, he would ride alone and on horseback. This was, of course, how the old tsars had done it – 'the Tsar and his people' – but that was long ago, and now tsars were being hunted by some of those same people, and his ministers felt it was a reckless, even mad, move.

I supported Nicky's decision: On horseback, he looked tall and commanding; on foot, or even in a carriage, he appeared a tad ... well, squat and small, if the truth has to be told.

Everyone in Petersburg knew him to be a man of small stature. All those who mattered in the court and in the ministries knew this as well, but the people of Moscow had never seen him, and since we had been informed that nearly a million of them had left their peasant villages to do exactly that, this was his chance to present himself as the legendary Tsar of their dreams.

So it was arranged that, on the day of his grand entry into Moscow, which would culminate in us following him into the city and joining him in the procession at the Chapel of Our Lady of Iver, where we would pray to the holy icon of the Blessed Virgin of Iver, Nicky would be mounted on a white horse, wearing his humble colonel's uniform. Behind him would come the Dowager-Empress in her carriage, and then I in my carriage behind her.

I had suggested, I thought quite reasonably, as a compromise that instead of being made to seem secondary to the Dowager-Empress in the eyes of the crowds, it would be better for her and I to enter the city riding in one glass carriage, not least as it would be a demonstration of family unity and avoid the inevitable confusion of the people who would otherwise be asking themselves why I was not following behind my husband.

This time I put my argument forcibly to Sergei, my brother-in-law, the Governor-General of Moscow, who was in charge of all of the ceremonies pertaining to the coronation alongside the Coronation Commission, as I felt he would be more understanding of the situation than the aged Count Fredericks, or that sorry bunch of hidebound ministers Nicky had to deal with, or even, sadly, my own husband. Sergei agreed with me completely and proceeded to liaise diligently between my court and that of the Dowager-Empress in the days leading up to our departure from Petersburg.

Naturally, Minnie absolutely refused to give an inch, even to Sergei. Family unity be damned, and giving my people a chance to see me as their rightful Empress be damned, too. Not that she put it that way. What she said, with a sad little shrug as though it was all beyond her, was, "Oh, I do wish that poor little Alicky and I could ride together, of course I do. It would be so cozy, wouldn't it? But it can't be done. My carriage will have an imperial crown on it, as I am an anointed Empress, and Alicky, who of course will be," shrug, sigh, "is not one quite yet. It would simply confuse the dear people if they saw her riding beside me, do you not think, Sergei?"

Sergei, who it must be said was no stranger to the writings of Machiavelli, knew when he had been beaten and reported to me later to that effect.

"She is brilliant, Alix, and stubborn, and prideful, and magnificent, and if we push this, she will tell everyone that you stole away all her rights and privileges on the very first day of her son's coronation celebrations. You cannot really take the censure that would come from that. Bow your beautiful head and ride behind her on the way there, while remembering who will come before her out of the doors of the cathedral after you have been crowned but a few days later."

I railed at him, since he was the only one I could rail at.

"Oh yes indeed, Sergei, I am allowed to precede her *after* I am crowned –"

"And on the way into the cathedral for the coronation itself, don't forget," he interrupted, amused.

I glared at him. "Oh, of course, how *ungrateful* of me to forget that. And then, after those sole instances – what? A lifetime of following her skirts, because, sure as sure can be, that horrible woman will probably outlive me if just for spite alone."

Sergei choked on his tea in laughter.

"Ah, I adore you, Alix. And, anyway, you are wrong. She is just milking her final days in the sun. When everyone has seen how beautiful you are and what a glory you and your children will be to the realm ... and when you have given Nicky and Russia a son ... why then," he set down his cup and spread his hands expansively, "why then, she will go the way of all old empresses."

Somewhat mollified, I still asked tartly, "And where is that Sergei, to Hades?"

He laughed aloud. "Well, almost ... It will be to the oblivion of retirement. I imagine, in Minnie's case, that she will take herself back to Denmark, or maybe on to England where she can spend the rest of her life moaning about you to her sister Alexandra, or off to Livadia ... Who knows, Alix? But she won't be around forever. She is just having her last hurrah. Let her do it and smile all the way into your glorious future, Your Majesty."

According to a sensationalist rumor that spread like wildfire throughout the world a few months later, I ended up not being completely overshadowed by the Dowager-Empress – more by yet another corpse. It was said that our Foreign Minister, Prince Lobanov-Rostovsky, had suffered a fatal heart attack two days before our formal entry into Moscow, and with the usual Russian deep respect for the dead, combined with excruciating bad taste, it must be assumed, it was decided to have him laid out on his funeral bier and to include his remains in the procession directly behind Nicky's horse and guards, and ahead of Minnie.

When I heard the rumor, my first thought was 'How dreadful! How could anyone think that?' Then I am ashamed to admit that I briefly gloated over the fantasy of a discommoded Minnie having to follow immediately behind a dead man. Then I came to what I believe is a true realization: that some people in Russia were prepared to go to almost any lengths to associate me with death, funerals, and I suppose in the end, putrefaction. From my very beginnings in Russia, I was being cast as the Empress of Death and Destruction … but by whom?

In point of fact, Minister Alexei Borisovich was very much alive during our week-long coronation ceremonies. There are photographs of him taken on the day of the coronation itself, at the end of that hectic week, and several days later he even ratified a treaty with Japan together with Nicky, as Nicky pointed out with extreme exasperation when I reported the rumor to him with a hollow laugh. "Not to mention that he died in my service three months later on his way to meet horrid Cousin Willy."

All the emotions I went through during my entanglements with the Dowager-Empress leading up to our coronation served to put bright color into my face for the first day of the celebrations, which was much needed as I woke up terribly nauseous and pale, and I would be spending the whole day in a glass carriage, the better to be viewed!

Given my placement in the procession, I could not see Nicky, only the Dowager-Empress's own glass carriage before me and the people on either side of the route. There were so many of them. I had never seen so many people in my life, some in gay dresses and best-bib-and-tucker suits, but mostly they were peasants, solemnly curious in their black ragged clothing, who stood outnumbering members of the wealthier classes a thousand fold. The peasants, the true Russian people, lined our processional route seemingly thousands deep and a mile long. Every bell in Moscow was ringing out but the cheers of the multitude nearly drowned their chimes and I knew where Nicky was ahead of me by their lusty cheers as he passed them by. I shivered with delight as I heard, too, the mighty cries of veneration, "God save the Tsar!" that rode up into the air and scattered Moscow's crows. On and on they shouted, joyful at the sight of Nicky, and in due time I saw some who had fallen to the ground to kiss the shadow he had thrown.

As the Dowager-Empress came into sight, if anything the cheering grew even more frenzied.

It was then my turn to crest to where the people lined the road and I heard them shout again ... and then the cheering stopped. It stopped when they saw me. I saw them as well. I watched them straighten from their bows and clumsy curtsies and stare mutely right into my eyes, all of them. They stood upright, still staring, and they became so silent that I fancied that even in that massive crowd, and with all the bells still ringing. I could hear the clop-clop of the horses leading my carriage.

An exertion of will alone kept my head up; will alone kept me from fainting or vomiting or, worst of all, from asking *'Why, why don't you like me? Why don't you want me? You don't even know me!'* Instead, I inclined my head and bit down on the inside of my cheek to keep my lips from trembling.

I heard later from Maria that they interpreted even this expression as one of haughtiness and coldness, not of rejection and fear.

Cold I was indeed, despite the bright sunlight of Moscow and the thickness of my velvet gown. I was shaking so hard from shock and pain that later that evening, during a private family supper at the Kremlin, the Dowager-Empress reproved me.

"Alix, when we entered the city, I am told all one could see were your diamonds heaving up and down on your chest. It was quite distracting and I feel, and I'm certain that Nicky does as well, that it detracted a great deal from the ceremony. Why are you always so nervous and afraid in public? Can you not manage to rise to the occasion as the occasion demands it?"

Oh she was vile, and in that moment of complete, devastated exhaustion, I decided to tell her so ... but Nicky knew immediately what I was planning to do. He never could bear a single criticism of his mother, or maybe he could not bear to witness an ugly scene, I don't know. In some ways I never knew what made Nicky do or say anything. This sense of uncertainty, of course, lay at the root of my unhappiness and was why our nearly perfect union could not achieve the heights I have always believed it was capable of.

He therefore spoke before I could, asking fatuously, "What are you wearing tomorrow, Mama?"

The Dowager-Empress obviously thought this as stupid a question as I did, for keeping her eyes on me, she bit off impatiently, "A gown, Nicky ... but Alix, really, what were you –?"

I assumed that merely ignoring her attack would fuel her simmering resentment further, and that really Nicky might after all know how to handle her, so I clasped my hands and said with great feigned interest, "Ah, but I think, Mother Dear, Nicky wants to know what sort of gown and what jewels you will be wearing with it. We know that you will outshine everyone, but –"

"A white gown, obviously, Alix, as is expected. You do know that much, don't you?" Then, waving her small hand in irritation, she continued, "And as for my jewels, or what is left of them since you have seen fit to appropriate *all* the crown jewels, and I mean that in the most literal sense, I suppose I shall wear some of the diamonds that Nicky's papa gave me, in remembrance of him." She paused to see the effect of her words on Nicky and wiped an invisible tear from her eye, before laying out some more poison on me. "So, one would assume you will be wearing all of the crown jewels between now and your sacred coronation, would that be correct, Alix?"

I caught Nicky's eye and saw that in his apprehension as to how I might respond he was struggling against an outburst of nervous laughter.

I managed to keep my face straight and to look contemplative as I answered her forthrightly.

"Well, that might be difficult …"

"Difficult? How so, Alix? Are your maids having trouble dealing with all those jewels? Is that it?"

I nodded.

"Yes, there is that of course, but I meant difficult in that if I were to wear so many necklaces at once, would that not be excessive? I suppose I might find a space for all of the brooches, but for the life of me I cannot puzzle out how to wear all the tiaras at one go, only having one head. Would it be overdoing it to wear two of them at the same time, do you think?"

Nicky broke into the exchange to deflect any angry rejoinder from his mother, his voice full of suppressed giggles.

"Sunny darling, I think you will find that if you wear even one of the tiaras on the day of the sacred coronation, we will have the very devil of a time finding room for your crown. It might not fit and then where would we be?"

I couldn't help it, I burst into helpless laughter, and so did Nicky, and every time we glanced down at Minnie's thunder-filled face, we got worse.

We were still howling with laughter when she left us in high dudgeon.

Later, cuddled together in our bed in the Kremlin, we took it in turns to imitate her and set each other off again. Nicky tried to say that we were too bad and must stop, and "Poor old Mama ..." but for my part I could not remember passing a better evening.

We went to sleep that night, still laughing. That is what I try to remember, too, when I think of those times.

The day of the coronation dawned as beautifully as the day we processed into Moscow and Nicky held me against him as we stared out of the window of our chamber at the red towers of the Kremlin and the lovely old city beyond them.

Nicky kissed the back of my neck and put his hand on my stomach.

"Are you ready to be crowned, Your Highnesses?"

I caressed his hand and my tummy at the same time, my heart too full to speak. He then had to leave as I began my own preparations.

I wanted only Maria to attend to me that day. While she could be stubborn, and while her English was somewhat labored, I enjoyed her calm, competent demeanor and a real friendship had formed between us. However, as a holy wedding was to take place between Russia and me this day, I found myself surrounded by a dozen maids, while my toilette was constantly interrupted by grand ladies paying their respects seemingly from across the four corners of Russia.

I had anticipated this and arranged a secret signal with Maria whereby I would raise one eyebrow in the mirror and she would know it was time to usher them all out. It worked beautifully, so it was only Maria who saw to my final preparations.

I was wearing a very plain white satin gown, and with it I had chosen only a single strand of pearls. My hairdresser had, as arranged, done my hair in a simple *chignon* with two long side curls, in the style of the ancient tsaritsas.

Maria, a woman not given to false flattery or awe, had tears in her eyes as she gazed at me.

"Your Majesty, I do not believe I have ever seen anyone as beautiful as you are. All of Russia will be filled with pride today at the sight of their new Empress."

Impulsively, I kissed her.

"Thank you, Maria, and now could you send someone to tell His Majesty that I am ready?"

Nicky and I were to walk from the Kremlin's red porch to the Dormition Cathedral under a canopy held by thirty-two generals and officers, and as we began our slow progress I fell as if into a dream state. Here there were hundreds of people lining our way, but only drawn from the ranks of the nobility and the army. The people, the real Russians, waited outside the gates. Their allotted time with us was not to be until the following day, but I felt their prayers and their love for us as I walked.

Nicky and I were met at the door of the cathedral by Russia's chief priest, the Patriarch, who offered us the holy cross to kiss. We were then sprinkled with holy water and jointly invited to kiss the selected sacred icons three times. As I did so, I felt God in me and I saw him in Nicky, who seemed to grow in stature with every step as we were escorted to our thrones upon the dais.

I looked out over the seated crowd and saw Georgie and May, and Queen Olga of Greece, seated next to Nicky's mother. I noticed, and tried not to see, Xenia winking at me from her seat beside Sandro. Sergei stood alongside us in his role of Governor-General of Moscow, with Ella positioned behind him. I could almost feel her sense of self-importance radiating over us, but it didn't matter. The priests were chanting and the incense was heavy and hypnotizing, and I drifted pleasantly into a trance again, aware of what was happening around me but as though I were watching myself as part of a tableau taking place in front of me.

Nicky began to recite the Nicene Creed and then read aloud the prayer.

> *Thy faithful servant, Nicholas, whom thou*
> *hast been pleased to establish as king over*
> *thy people, clothe him with power from on*
> *high, set on his head a crown of precious*
> *stones.*

At that moment the diamond chain of St. Andrew, the holiest of symbols, broke and fell from Nicky's shoulders, to land on the ground with a muted thump that was nevertheless loud enough to provoke staccato gasps of horror from all over the cathedral that in their turn drew me, with great reluctance, out of my trance in time to see a priest quickly scrabble the sacred cross to safety under a table skirt. *What did that mean?*

Nicky had stumbled on the prayer but managed to resume.

> *For thine is the might and thine is the kingdom and the power, now and ever, and unto the ages.*
>
> *Amen.*

The crowd intoned, "Peace be with you."

Then the Patriarch handed Nicky the imperial crown, for in Russia only God is set above the Tsar, so it follows that only the Tsar can crown himself.

> *Most God-fearing, absolute, and mighty Lord, Tsar of all the Russias, this visible and tangible adornment of thy head is an eloquent symbol that thou, as the head of the whole Russian people, art invisibly crowned by the King of kings, Christ, with a most ample blessing, seeing that He bestows upon thee entire authority over His people.*

Then I rose from my throne and knelt at Nicky's feet. Nicky removed his crown and held it upon my head briefly, and then an aide brought a smaller crown which Nicky gently placed upon my head, briefly allowing his fingers to caress the side of my face as he did so. A priest placed a purple mantle over my shoulders to signify that Nicky wished to share his dignity and responsibility for the nation's welfare with me.

It was done and I was Empress in very truth now.

And then the bells began to ring, not just in the cathedral but also outside, throughout Moscow, and Sergei whispered to me that ten thousand bells were being rung in joy at our ascension. There was gun fire, too – one hundred and one shots – to signify, I suppose, the birth of a new king to his people, which I considered odd. There had been that number of gun shots to welcome Olga's birth. Shouldn't there have been three hundred, as at the birth of an heir? The thought made me smile. I was now formally the Empress of Russia and soon the guns of Russia would fire that number of times for the birth of our son. Russia had given me her crown and I would return the love of the Russian people, and their faith in me, with an heir meant for all of them.

It is odd but I did not once feel exhausted during the whole six hours it took to wed Nicky and me to our kingdom, yet as soon as the ceremony had concluded and we exited the cathedral to a still-blinding sun, I could barely keep my footing for the wave of tiredness that overcame me. Nicky was immediately aware of my predicament and grasped my arm firmly during our return walk to the Kremlin.

I would have time to rest for a few hours before yet another banquet, and I duly did so.

Rising later to be dressed for the evening, this time in cloth of gold, I reflected that from somewhere I seemed to be being provided mysteriously with enough strength to face the crushing burden of even a week's worth of public ceremonies. I had yet to experience even one of my terrible headaches, and though my legs ached, as did my back, I found that I could go on.

As I sat regally beside Nicky that night at the coronation banquet, managing to gaze benevolently upon all our assembled guests, meeting their avid and judging looks with an expression of tranquility and serenity set lightly on my own face, it no longer mattered to me what anyone thought or said about me.

My place at my husband's side, my place in the history of Imperial Russia itself, had been set in stone by God Himself.

Chapter 7

I can freely admit that, following the coronation and the subsequent banquet, I felt ready to return immediately to our cozy nest in our dear Alexander Palace, where our small family could quietly enjoy the spring and summer months and I could be left to rest amid familiar surroundings to finish growing my son.

Naturally this wish was scorned by Nicky's family, and by his mother in particular. After a casual "family breakfast" for thirty or so people, we royal ladies were still lingering over a second cup of tea – or, in my case, coffee – when Minnie seized the occasion to attack me after I had innocently given voice to my twin pressing afflictions of exhaustion and homesickness.

"Alix, my dear, the whole world has gathered here in Moscow to see you and Nicky. Do you think it is wise to send out the unfortunate message that the new Empress cannot even cope with the minimal expectations placed upon her and instead prefers to ignore all her guests – the crowned heads of state and the members of her court, who have all gone to great expense and inconvenience to attend her coronation, and her own people – because she is tired of them? Is that how you wish to begin your reign? If you cannot think of your own majesty, perhaps you could at least manage to consider that everything you do reflects upon the majesty of my son as the Emperor and Father of the Russian people?"

A film of red filled my vision. That woman was the evil genius of the Romanov dynasty! That she had managed to insult me so many times and in so many different ways, and done it all flagrantly in front of Ella, Xenia, May, Aunt Miechen, and the silly aged Olga of Greece, was breathtaking.

I had to take several breaths before I could answer. The ladies, with the exception of Xenia, watched me with malicious curiosity as I tried to gather myself together. In Xenia's eyes there was real sympathy, but like Nicky she feared her mother, so she merely murmured a placating, "Mama, I don't think Alicky meant to say that she was going to leave, only that she was tired. I know the feeling,"

She patted her own rounding stomach. Xenia and I, it seemed, were going to be pregnant in tandem once a year into the foreseeable future.

I threw her a smile. The Dowager-Empress threw her an annoyed glance and opened her mouth to speak again.

I intercepted.

"Xenia is right, Mother Dear, I am delighted to be here with all of you. I simply find that I am a bit tired, and of course I am nesting." I patted my stomach.

May spoke then.

"Yes, Aunt Minnie, I must agree with poor Alicky. All of this looks terribly tiring. In fact, I was saying to Georgie just last night after the banquet that I was most awfully glad that in England this sort of thing happens so seldom. And, good heavens, the crush of people ... These peasants of yours are completely overwhelming. Why are they all still here? Do they not have homes and work to return to? I cannot imagine such a thing in England. I do not know, of course, I would have to ask Georgie's grandmamma, but I simply cannot imagine that so many of our own people had the leisure to hang

94

about in London after she was crowned. As for nesting," she smiled at me complacently, "last year, after our second boy came, why, I told Georgie that I hoped we would be able to have a year or so's respite before the next, and he said," she giggled girlishly – I thought I might slap her to silence her but, of course, I did not, and, of course, she went on under the now approving eyes of every woman present, save my own – "that he thought it would be so nice to have a little girl to name after his own beloved mama, your dearest sister, Auntie Minnie, but I said that I hoped our little girl would wait a bit to come as I did not want to have to have all the seams of my new dresses let out again before we came here to see Alicky and Nicky be crowned, and now of course ..."

She trailed off, blushing, and all the ladies proceeded to coo adoringly. What a wonder was May, a third baby coming in only three years and two boys already. How proud Georgie must be!

Ella, my eternally barren sister, was particularly fawning. "Oh May, aren't you the most fortunate of women, and to think that you have been bearing up so beautifully during all of this. Why, Alicky, it really makes one –"

Sadly for Ella, before she could fully sink her teeth into the shoddy showing I made in comparison with May, Minnie unexpectedly deflected her. I suppose any admiration that wasn't directed at her was too much. Still, it was a relief.

"May, my dear, I am sure we are all most proud of you, although at your age I too had given my husband two sons and a little girl to spoil as well." She smiled at

Xenia who beamed adoringly back. "But I must say," she blinked as though to keep the tears in, so brave was she, "I must say that your mentioning how infrequently your own nation has gone through a coronation was somewhat painful to me."

May looked aghast, as well she might have done, for the Dowager-Empress was only warming up.

"After my Sasha became Tsar so suddenly upon the unspeakable murder of his papa, we had hoped to reign in peace and love over our people for many long years, but it was not to be. You are so fortunate to live in a country where violent death does not stalk the throne, May."

May gulped nervously and tried to answer her, clearly not knowing that Mother Dear's every question was intended to be rhetorical.

Minnie continued in broken tones. "As for all the people still gathered here in Moscow ... our dear peasants ... you see they come to see their new Tsar, and their new Tsaristsa as well, I suppose, and maybe even to see me, whom they have always treated with such kindness and consideration."

To emphasize her point, she glibly tossed a triumphant glance towards me, whom we all knew they were not so kind about, *not yet anyway*, I thought with a little *frisson. When my boy is born ...*

Minnie wasn't through.

Addressing the group at large, she ruminated with charming modesty about the relationship between them and their *Little Empress*. "At the coronation of my dear Sasha, they said that two hundred thousand peasants came to see us to celebrate our ascension."

I snapped at her, unable to help myself. "Yes, and Count Fredericks informed me yesterday that he believes the numbers have been nearer five hundred thousand for Nicky and me."

Ella jumped in, wanting to show off the part she had played in this.

"Well naturally, the people all want to see their beloved Tsar and both wonderful Empresses, I am sure. Sergei anticipated just this sort of thing. I mean," she blushed, "he hoped for it, is what I meant to say, and he wanted to honor dearest Nicky's faith in him as Governor-General, so he came up with a rather ingenious idea for gifts."

No one said anything for an awkward moment, until kindly little Xenia asked, "Oh yes, and what are the gifts, Ella darling? I know Sergei is so clever about this sort of thing."

Ella nodded at her gratefully.

"He really is, Xenia dear. Well, you see, Sergei was of course at dearest Sasha and Minnie's coronation –" Minnie snorted rudely, which startled Ella but she gathered herself. "... and while he thought it was just lovely the way they gave little treats out to each of the peasants, he thought to himself, 'Oh how can I make this coronation eternally memorable for them?' "

Minnie interjected, "More free beer, I imagine."

There was smothered merriment, my own, I am embarrassed to recall, amongst them.

Ella, ever the sensitive one, looked as though she had been slapped. She did so wish for Minnie's good opinion and couldn't ever quite manage to achieve it. Her relationship to me counted against her there, I imagine. Still, she plowed on into the disinterested silence.

"Well yes, Minnie dearest, more beer. I mean not more beer, but *enough* beer to, you know, accommodate so many more people, but that is not the marvelous thing. You see, they will each get a cup, a special coronation cup. It is made of painted enamel too. Isn't Sergei just marvelous?"

"A cup?" said May in an incredulous voice. "Why would they want a cup?"

Ella, who I do not think cared much for May, shot back, "Well, May dear, you see, as I have already said, it is an enamel cup and it even has a picture of Nicky and Alicky on it. It is a cup they can keep forever. Oh, if you could only understand the excitement the people expressed when they heard of it."

"Because no one has ever seen a cup before?" May asked slowly.

Xenia laughingly answered before Ella could continue her boring recitation.

"No, May darling. Well, they have, I think – I mean, at least people in Petersburg and Moscow have – but I am not sure the peasants have. I believe they drink out of bark receptacles. Heaven knows, it is what they wear on their feet. So, you see, a permanent cup, that is rather a tremendous gift for them. I do have to agree with Ella that this time Sergei has been rather brilliant."

May gave a tinkling little laugh. "Well, I must say, I cannot wait to tell Georgie and his papa and mama. If that sad day ever comes when we in England must crown a new ruler, then I imagine all of them, as well as our stingy old parliament, will be more than delighted to hand out a cup rather than provide wine fountains and banquets for the people. Of course, what the English would think of such a device I can only imagine. I guess that perhaps our ancestors could have got away with it in medieval times."

I actually agreed with May but did not dare to say so. The Russians were a terribly primitive people with their bark shoes and lack of tableware. If May wanted to laugh at them with Georgie, I secretly wanted to do the same with Ernie if I could get a minute to myself.

I saw that Minnie was about to explode again, so as the reigning Empress I decided to end this somewhat fraught peroration by rising and announcing, "Ladies, I fear that despite deriving much enjoyment from your company, I must leave you now. Nicky and I are scheduled to appear at some tedious affair this afternoon where Nicky has to give a speech and so I will see you all again at dinner tonight. And tomorrow we can all gather at Sergei's invitation to judge the wonder of these cups with our own eyes."

I bowed my head briefly to all of them and left.

Was May the thirtieth of the year 1896 the beginning of the end for all of us?

I think so, but most claim that they did not know it at the time and that they could not possibly have foreseen how events would eventually unfold. Probably closer to the truth is that they wilfully refused to recognize the storm that was gathering which would inevitably be heading their way.

I will not be lumped in with this wilfully purblind crowd. I would consent to it if I felt, deep in my heart, that I should, but for me to do so would be both wrong and untruthful, for while it seems that all the hatred and rejection of the Russian people was focused on me, I alone did understand what was happening to us and its dreadful implications. I alone bled for Russia. It is the court and the people who did not see that.

Nicky invariably rises at 7am. Nothing changes that. I, on the other hand, have need of more sleep and that morning I had not risen until ten, my pregnancy and the relentless spate of banquets and balls having worn me down. I mention this only to illustrate that it is clear that the ministers of the court, and even the imperial family, had begun to see that if something important needed to be communicated or decided upon, then it was better if I were there.

No one approached Nicky until ten-thirty that morning and then it was old Count Fredericks who asked us for an urgent audience. I was still abed, having just received my chocolate from Maria, and, as always, Nicky had just bustled in happily to have a cigarette – or ten – and spend a few minutes with me. I nearly told Maria to send Count Fredericks away until later – maybe I actually did – but then something in her transparent face made me reverse my order and in he came, trembling.

"Your Majesties ... I ... there has been ... I ... oh, it is terrible ..."

Nicky, who hated any abrupt change in his schedule, as did I, spoke rather unkindly to poor old Count Fredericks.

"What is it, Fredericks? Please stop mumbling and shuffling. Her Majesty and I are just having our morning visit and I hope, for your sake, that this is important."

To me, Nicky rolled his eyes and whispered, "Flower arrangements, no doubt."

I giggled. There had recently been a whole parade of visits to discuss that night's ball. The French, our sole European allies, were throwing it for us, and they deemed it necessary to stop in and discuss every small detail, including the ten thousand roses that had been sent from France for the occasion, lest Nicky and I fail to gain a full appreciation of their myriad, nay Herculean, efforts.

So we can't be blamed for thinking what we did.

Count Frederick's eyes boggled at us alarmingly and he almost barked back at Nicky, "*Flowers,* Your Majesty? Oh good God, if only it were so. No, no. It is the dead, hundreds of them – some are saying thousands – and we don't know what to do. Should you address the crowd? Should we cancel the festivities? Should you go to the hospitals? We don't –"

"What? What?" Nicky shouted.

This made Count Fredericks begin to shake.

I looked at Maria. "Maria, please get Count Fredericks some water so that he can settle himself down and be of a disposition to tell us *intelligibly* what this is all about."

Maria nodded and fetched Count Fredericks his water. Count Fredericks gradually composed himself and began. "There has been a tragedy out at Khodynka Field, Your Majesty. The peasants broke through the barricade, and –"

101

Nicky, immediately flustered, shouted at him again, "What, the Khodynka parade grounds? What are you attempting to tell us, you idiot?"

I looked Count Fredericks directly in the eye. "Count Fredericks, His Majesty is understandably upset. Please address me. Speak calmly. No one is angry with you. Just tell us whatever it is that you are trying to tell us."

Nicky was on the verge of saying something else until I silenced him with a glare.

Count Fredericks continued.

"As I'm certain Your Majesties are aware, food booths and popular entertainment were planned for your people at Khodynka Field, the parade grounds as you correctly surmised, Your Majesty." Nicky nodded sagely at this courteous reference to his infallibility. "Somehow a rumor began last night that there would not be enough gifts or food to go around, so at dawn the people began to break through the barricades. There are holes and ditches all over the field –"

"Because it is used for all our military parades," Nicky interjected superfluously.

"Go on, Count Fredericks," I said, trying to keep my voice even.

Count Fredericks was reduced to sobbing. "Yes, Your Majesties, it is used for parades, that is right, and so there are ditches and holes, you see, and when the people from behind began pushing the people in front –"

"They fell into the holes!" Nicky exclaimed loudly. "This is terrible! Are there many hurt?"

Count Fredericks nodded gravely. "Yes, Your Majesty, many are hurt, many are dead."

Nicky sprang to his feet in agitation. "But when … when did this happen?"

"Early this morning, Your Majesty. I have heard that the barricades began to break near dawn –"

"*Near dawn?* But it is nearly eleven now. Did no one notice until just this moment? Count Fredericks, explain this to me."

Poor old Count Fredericks's skin looked like green cheese. Shakily he rose and in broken tones said, "The Governor-General, His Highness the Grand Duke Sergei, did not wish for Your Majesties to be disturbed. He felt that he had brought the matter under control, and –"

"And was it all brought under control, Count Fredericks? Is that why you are standing here looking as though the world has ended, because everything is in hand?"

I shook my head at Nicky.

"Please, darling, don't shout at Count Fredericks. He's obviously been most shaken up by this tragedy. Please, Count Fredericks, tell us, if you can, why, if everything has been dealt with, you are looking so upset."

My tone calmed him. He drew a long breath and gripped his hands to stop them shaking.

"Yes, Your Majesty, thank you. You see, his Highness the Grand Duke, I do not think he understood the full extent of the disaster. The injured and dead … there are thousands of them. He sent in the guards to try and break up the crowds, you see, but they were so densely packed that, as I understand it, the hooves of their horses simply knocked more into the ditches, mostly women and children, and then trampled on them too –"

"Oh good God, no," groaned Nicky.

I held out my hand to him and he gripped it in a most pained manner.

"Go on, Count Fredericks," I said quietly.

"Yes, thank you, Your Majesty. As I said, it seems the Grand Duke did not wish to disturb Your Majesties, so after the incident with the troops, he ordered ambulances to the Field to collect up the injured, and…"

"Count Fredericks, please!" Nicky all but screamed.

"… But there were not enough ambulances, Your Majesty. There could never have been enough. The dead are everywhere. The children … Oh God save Russia!"

And with that, poor Count Fredericks fainted dead away.

There was a silence during which Nicky stared at me, panicked.

I rose to my feet, my stomach churning and my head beginning to pound. "Nicky, go assemble your ministers and your uncles, and your mother too. Find out exactly what is going on so that we can … Oh, so that we can do something, I don't know … Go! Hurry!"

He continued to stare at me, lost, until something in my eyes rallied him.

"Yes, yes, that's right. I shall go and find out what this is about. I am sure that … Well, once we know, it will not seem so bad, will it, Sunny?

"Quite possibly … I mean, people exaggerate so, and should we not do something about poor Count Fredericks here?"

Nicky glanced down at the unconscious old man at his feet. I bit down hard on my lip, drawing blood, but held my composure.

"Don't worry. Maria and I will take care of him. Go now! Please, whatever it is, we have to know."

"Yes, of course, you are right. Thank you, darling."

He left and I turned to Maria, the self-control written in her face helping me to remain calm in my turn.

"Maria, go find Dr. Botkin and have him attend to Colonel Fredericks. Then ring for some other maids to assist me. I must dress immediately and join His Majesty and find out ..."

The look on her face stopped me.

"What, Maria?"

She shook her head. "Go there, Your Majesty," she said, gesturing towards my long windows now curtained off from the morning sun.

We gazed at each other for a long moment before I nodded at her silently.

She curtsied and went off to do my bidding, and I was left alone, save for the presence of the seemingly comatose Count Fredericks. Slowly I crossed the room, and with my own trembling hands parted the curtains and looked out.

Far down below me, and just over the walls of the Kremlin, I saw that the usually busy streets of Moscow were silent and empty, save for a long row of peasants' carts that stretched as far as the eye could see. Some of them were covered with blood-soaked tarps, yet hands and legs were to be seen everywhere. There was a long, bloody trail forming behind them, and as I stood there, sickened and shocked, I observed a small body − a tiny child, of maybe three or four – fall off one of the heaped carts and roll into the gutter.

The silent people pulling the carts did not even stop or notice what had happened.

I could not bear it. I began to pound on the glass and shout, "The little one, the baby, it has fallen. Help it! Help it. Somebody … Oh God, please help it!" No one heard me, or if they did, they failed to turn from their dogged forward motion, which prompted me to scream much louder, "God, please, please … God, come and help the baby."

The glass cracked under my fists but no one heard me, God least of all. I was alone. All of us in Russia were alone.

Of course, that was a silly thing to think. We were far from alone, Nicky and me. We were absolutely surrounded by advice. Sandro and Xenia and Nicky's mama blamed poor Sergei and said we had to call off the French ball and go to visit the hospitals. Nicky said he did not blame Sergei and that he himself preferred to retire for prayer to a monastery. Ella cried terribly, and when Xenia asked outright if it was for shame, Ella stared at her nonplussed and said, "Shame? No. Why? I am upset for the poor victims but at the same time I thank God that Sergei had nothing to do with this."

Sergei, somewhat prickly, opined that if we were going to go on and on about it, he would tender his resignation as Governor-General of Moscow on the spot. Nicky's uncles, Vladimir and Paul, threatened that they would leave Russia immediately and forever if Sergei were to be blamed. Nicky shook his head, and since no one could interpret that, they all of them turned on him simultaneously, demanding that he state his views.

I could have explained to them the futility of such an expectation, but no one was consulting me on anything. I think it was because they could not quite figure out a way to blame me for the tragedy that had taken place on Khodynka Field.

I took advantage of this temporary reprieve by sitting quietly and observing the proceedings. This annoyed the Dowager-Empress who broke off from the quarreling uncles to snap at me, "Alix, are you planning on attending the French Ball tonight?"

I shook my aching head.

"I will, of course, attend the ball if that is what Nicky wishes, but for my own part I feel that it would look very bad to the people."

Though she had voiced that very sentiment not ten minutes beforehand, she now rolled her eyes as though disgusted by my answer.

Somehow in the *mêlée* of shouting and contention, Nicky overheard me and rushed to my side, nodding eagerly. "I think Alix is right. We should cancel the ball. We will go to the hospitals and see the poor people, and –"

Uncle Vladimir's howl of outrage cut him off.

"... And offend our sole European allies, Nicky? Is that what you want to do, demolish your late and revered father's entire foreign policy at one blow? I assure you that the French will take enormous offense should you do so after all the effort they have put into preparing for it."

Grand Duke Paul joined in with his own forcefully expressed observations. "If you give in to your wife's wishes on this, Nicky, you will thereby show that you blame poor Sergei for what has happened and then you will not only offend our glorious allies but your own family as well."

Nicky shook his head to try to clear it.

"No, uncles, I did not mean that. I do not blame Sergei ..." Catching my look, he added, "And I do not think that is what Alicky meant to imply, either. That's not what you meant, is it, darling?"

I could barely grind out a single word. In fact, that is all I could manage. "No."

Nicky nodded, satisfied.

"Well, there you are, you see. That isn't what Alix meant at all."

His statement silenced the room for a moment and Xenia was the first to respond.

"Nicky, you are the Tsar, and in the end, no matter anyone's private feelings, that is what matters. If the ball were to go on, what about the celebration at the Field? Would that go on as well? Shall we all get dressed and proceed there as planned?"

Sandro and Minnie stared at her aghast, but Sergei nodded firmly, and following his lead the other uncles and Ella nodded in agreement.

Sergei said, "It seems to me that little Xenia here has the right of it. You are scheduled to appear there, Nicky. All these people have come to see you. Why throw the baby out with the bathwater? You must attend the ball and by tomorrow morning all this will be forgotten and life will begin anew. I myself have an appointment for a group photograph with my guardsmen. So, if you will excuse me, I shall see you this evening."

And that was it. With a nod to me and Ella, Sergei left the meeting. Sandro and Xenia watched him go through narrowed eyes; the uncles watched him approvingly; Ella watched him sadly; and Minnie regarded him with a hooded expression that I could make neither rhyme nor reason of.

All she said was, "Then that is what we shall do. Xenia, Sandro, will you lunch with me so we can travel to the celebrations together. No use rushing. I am sure they will hold off commencing the proceedings until we arrive."

Xenia and Sandro nodded, then both kissed me on the cheek before following Minnie out of the door, without saying another word to Nicky. This rebuff seemed to deflate the uncles' former bluster so that they merely mumbled to Nicky that they thought he was doing the right thing and left us without kissing either of us on their way out.

Nicky and I were alone. I did not want to be alone with him just then, so I rose, saying, "I really must dress. I am not in the least hungry, so shall we meet up in an hour to go to the Field?"

Nicky started and held out his hand pleadingly.

"Darling Sunny, can't you stay a minute? I feel so muddle-headed. Was it I who made the decision to attend the ball?"

I did not take his hand, maintaining my steady course towards the door. I wanted to hold my baby, I wanted to see Maria's sensible face, and I wanted to be away from him.

"Sunny!"

I half-turned at the door. "Nicky, please, I do not wish to discuss this. I shall see you at –"

"But you do think I made the correct choice, don't you, if I made a choice at all? Oh say you do, darling. Please ..."

I sighed and faced him.

"How can I both answer you and tell you what you want to hear, Nicky? The sole idea that you raised on your own behalf during the discussion was that you should retire to a monastery to pray. The decision you came to, if you wish to call it that, seems to me to have been to collude with your uncles, or rather to fail to stand up to them."

"Don't, Alicky. You have to stand with me when –"

"Like you always stand with me, Nicky? No, don't ... Let us not go any further. This day stretches out before me like an eternity. I want to spend a tiny minute with my baby and then I have to dress. Let me go, Nicky. After all, it is as Xenia said, all decisions are yours, even when they are not; even when you do not make any decision at all. I shall see you in an hour, my dear. Try at least to look like you are in charge, can you?"

I left him looking small and shrunken. Poor Nicky, he needed so much bolstering, but then didn't we all?

I did just as I had said I would: I rang for my baby and Maria, and spent a peaceful half-hour with them before getting into my costume to visit the Field. I wanted to wear black, but I knew I couldn't. The fuss wearing black would have aroused within the imperial family would have been more than I could have borne, and I had reached my limit already … and all before noon. I chose mauve satin instead, my favorite color, and one that symbolizes half-mourning. That isn't some sort of ironic statement. I had grown up in a family where one of us royals was always dying and most of my childhood had been spent in either mauve or black. That I had learned to love one of these colors does not seem odd to me. I knew even this dress choice would be frowned upon by the Russian imperial family as it would look like I was challenging Nicky's decision to go on as though nothing had happened; and I knew it would not comfort the people either, as I doubt a single peasant would have understood half-mourning. In both these assumptions I was later proven correct, and I ended up having the dress burned.

The smell of Khodynka Field greeted us half a mile before we got to the parade grounds and climbed onto our gaily decorated platform overlooking the festivities. In the heat of the day, the dead had begun to decompose rapidly and the sickening stench was only made worse by the aroma of meat being grilled for the fairgoers, for they were still there, thousands of poor peasants who had doggedly arrived as the carts and conveyances carried away the dead.

They did not look joyful. There was no festive spirit about them. They were there to obtain their small meal and the wonderful, unbreakable cup they had heard others speak of.

They barely glanced up at us on the stage as they made their slow rounds of the Field. They did look at the bodies. There will still dozens of them half-concealed under platforms and even under food tables covered with bunting that had been hastily torn down. They looked and then looked away, and then they took their foodstuffs and shuffled off back to the countryside and their homes. They did not dance to the music of the bands and I do not think that a single one of them paused long enough to hear Nicky make the set speech of welcome that had been written for him weeks before. At least, I hope they didn't.

We stayed upon that platform watching this grotesque scene for nearly two hours. I did not faint, nor did I vomit. I noticed that Xenia did both. I felt dead as I sat there. I felt dead when I returned to the Kremlin to be stuffed into my silver ball gown and paraded down the line of glittering guests for the opening polonaise at the French Embassy. In fact, I did not feel a single emotion or sensation of any kind, save eventually the uncomfortable wetness of my dancing slippers which aroused me from my foggy state.

I was bleeding.

No one had noticed this, so I was able frantically to signal to Nicky and be escorted to an anteroom. I wanted to be taken back to the Kremlin, but there was no time. Dr. Botkin was called and I was carried to the Ambassador's bedroom where I lost my son to the strains of a Mozart air bubbling up from the ballroom. Before they administered the chloroform and my night ended, I recall wondering whether this would forge a deeper alliance with our allies, one written in my child's blood. Further, would the people standing sullenly outside see it as at least some expiation on our part for what they had lost?

There is nothing more to tell of the coronation after that. We left Moscow in a fury of hatred from the people for having danced on the graves of their dead. Sergei became known as the Duke of Khodynka, and I became '*Nemka,*' the German bitch.

Nicky wasn't blamed for any of it, and though he appeared to grieve our lost heir, and said that he was most sorry for how the celebrations had been "somewhat spoiled by the deaths," he rebounded soon enough, and given his naturally buoyant nature had nearly forgotten all of it by the time we returned to Petersburg.

Chapter 8

"Oh, it is magnificent!"

Those were the first words I uttered when I sighted our new yacht, The Standart, and it was magnificent indeed. Laughing for what seemed the first time in weeks, I let Nicky lead me all over it, Olga goggling and chortling in my arms. For The Standart was indeed a ship, and the largest one in private ownership in the entire world, measuring over four hundred feet in length and fifty feet wide, and because of the interior designs I had contributed to it, walking aboard was like entering a floating version of our beloved Alexander Palace.

All the state and family rooms were paneled in mahogany, with silk inset wallpaper in the wainscoting, and I had ordered an entire round gallery of icons downstairs abutting the chapel.

There was a state dining room that could seat fifty comfortably, as well as a private one for when we would dine simply *en famille,* as the French say.

It had several beautiful public rooms, and then it had a replica in both size and décor of our bedroom, another replica of my mauve boudoir, and yet another one of Nicky's Gothic drawing room. I had also ordered a small indoor swimming pool for Nicky's bathing room for days when the weather, or the ship's location, should prove too inclement or inconvenient for him to swim in the sea itself, which he greatly enjoyed.

Despite my having approved every drawing, it was a transporting experience to see my vision realized, and, at least to my eyes, a rather magical thing to have created a *bona fide* floating miniature of our favorite palace.

After all that we had been through, and given my physically debilitated condition – for I had not easily recovered from losing my son – I believed that Nicky and I should be allowed a few scant months to enjoy our new yacht in each other's company, supplying a necessary time of healing, if one will.

However, there is no space for private life allotted to ruling families, or at least not to our ruling family. As I pointed out to Nicky, my own dearest grandmamma had not seemed over-burdened with affairs of state and, as near as I could observe, her time had been her own. Was that too much to ask of our lives? I asked.

Nicky, his arms around Olga and me, but his attention fixed on our yacht, nodded distantly until I poked him impatiently.

"What? Oh yes, time to ourselves." He kissed my neck. "I hate it too, darling, the constant interruptions. I would like to spend all my time with you and our little one, but it is impossible. As it is, Mother says –"

"Oh good, another country heard from ... What does your mother say, Nicky?"

He unwound his arms and lit a cigarette.

"Darling, please, let us not quarrel today. It is our first time on our lovely new yacht and –"

"What does your mother say?"

He shrugged. "She says that we are never seen in Petersburg. You know, balls, receptions, parades – that sort of thing."

I was immediately indignant.

"The court and the so-called nobility of that awful town do not like me. They are rude to me. They gossip about me. So I cannot think why I should display myself back and forth for them like some sort of animal for them to judge."

Nicky, sighed.

"I was merely repeating what Mama said, darling. Do not kill the messenger. At any rate, now that we are here and that we will both be on show for all the world to see at our every port of call, could it be possible that everyone will be happy for a change?"

I wanted to keep discussing this, but the set of his shoulders showed such a deep weariness, and even a defensive hunch, that for a moment he resembled an ogre.

I drew a breath and forced a smile.

"Yes, huzzy, indeed let us show the world our wonderful yacht and our beautiful little girl, and knock them all back on their heels, shall we?"

Nicky looked at me, surprised, and grinned with delight.

"Let us do just that, Your Majesty. Now, if you and her small Highness will indulge me, I shall show you two landlubbers our engine room. It is quite marvelous and I must say that it can hold its own with any engineering feat that the world has yet seen."

I followed him docilely and made all the proper womanly exclamations, even to the point of asking him silly questions about the turbines, which pleased both him and the captain, who chuckled indulgently. Then we partook of tea with the officers, and so it was not until I was in my bath before dinner that evening that I had time to reflect on the forthcoming trip and what, if anything, it signified.

The North Sea only has a certain number of months when it is safe to travel across it. As Nicky had already informed me, there was a silly custom that newly-crowned monarchs should travel about after their coronations to show themselves off to other heads of state. I say 'silly' because every imaginable head of state had already been invited to witness our coronation. Still, when Nicky had ordered The Standart to be finished, I knew he had intended that we should combine this ancient tradition with the unveiling of our new ship.

My pregnancy had scotched those plans as my son would have been born in November, almost on Olga's first birthday, I suddenly thought, tears rising again … Oh, the tears in those days, which came so easily and often …

Impatiently I splashed my face with bathwater. I needed to think this through. When I had lost my son, Nicky, without consulting with me, had gone to his ministers and reinstated the plans for our travels to spend time with other crowned heads in Europe. He had explained it as being really for my benefit, to get my mind off things, and besides, we would get to see dear Grandmamma.

Our journey would begin in odious Cousin Willy's Germany, then we would travel on to Grandmamma, and last, but oh far from least, we would visit our great ally France. I now hated France, the French and all they stood for. I did not tell anyone that, not even Nicky, for I knew that my hatred was irrational.

The French had not purposely thrown their ball on the night of the Khodynka Field disaster simply to make me so upset that I would lose my baby, nor could they be held responsible for the hatred of the people which my reluctant attendance at that accursed evening had caused. Still, I did hate them and I had told Nicky I did not want to go to France, nor to Germany for that matter. Did he not think I had suffered enough? I argued tearfully for us to limit our travels to visiting Grandmamma alone and suggested that we could then cruise peacefully wherever we wanted. It would give me the time to rest and heal, and we could both enjoy our new yacht in such a manner.

As always, my smallest wish was of no account in the great play that was royalty, though Nicky, not wishing to argue with me, had his overbearing buffoon of a Financial Minister, Sergei Witte, explain it to me as though I were a simple-minded child.

"Your Majesty will, I am sure, agree that it would be a most grievous insult to both the Emperor of Germany and the Republic of France if you and His Majesty were seen to snub their countries while making a visit to England alone, which is, if Your Majesty will pardon me for saying so, not an ally of ours at all."

I raised an eyebrow at him, supercilious old goat that he was, and replied, "How clever you are, Minister, and of course it is entirely true that I have no understanding of politics, and nor do I wish to have, but do not the close ties of blood which both His Majesty and I share with the ruling house of Great Britain tend to indicate the presence of a sort of alliance?"

He smiled.

"It is to be greatly hoped so, Your Majesty."

"*Hoped so,* Mr. Witte? It is."

He shook his head slightly and steepled his fingers, clearly enjoying himself.

"Ah, Your Majesty, if only it were so easy, but history teaches us that in times of conflict such familial ties may well fall by the wayside, which is why we seasoned politicians prefer to sign treaties to ensure our protection rather than to assume that such protection will arise naturally from the sentiments of familial duty alone."

I nodded as though impressed by such august wisdom, and then said, "I see. So then, Minister, is it from the lessons of history that you politicians predicate your policies for His Majesty and the country to follow?"

He nodded. "In part, Your Majesty, although other factors may and do come into play."

I mimed clapping. "Then I applaud your course, sir, for history has certainly demonstrated that your selection of France as our principle ally is a wise one. I believe that Emperor Napoleon was surely but one example of the benefits that our two countries could earn from mutual friendship, not to mention their more recent attempt to steal the Crimea from us –"

"Your Majesty will forgive my interrupting you, but my time is rather shorter today than I would wish. I accept your point. It is absolutely true that our relations with France have not always been of the best, but if I may be frank, Your Majesty –"

"Oh please, Minister."

"I thank you. Your Majesty is most gracious. As I was saying, the reality is that Russia has but one European ally. We have not been invited to sign treaties with any other European country. His late majesty, Tsar Alexander, understood the necessity of forming alliances–"

"And why is that, Mr. Witte? Is not Russia the greatest of the world powers? We are much larger than any other nation and –"

"Again, if Your Majesty will forgive me, I shall continue with my explication, although let me answer your observation as well. Russia has size, Your Majesty, great size. We also have a mainly uneducated populace that –"

"Ah, Minister, your opinion of our dear peasants is most touching ..."

He continued as though I had not spoken.

"... And that populace, being uneducated and finding itself perennially on the verge of starvation, does not provide us with a sufficiently large flow of taxes from which to grow our railways and military capabilities –"

"And how does your vaunted alliance with France help in this quest? Although I am only your Empress – so why should anyone bother to inform me of anything? – I would strongly advise you to try to make this clear to me, Minister, for I very much fear that if I continue to fail to see any point in this proposed dog-and-pony show, I might prefer not to go, in which case I think you will find that His Majesty –"

"... Will choose not to go, either. Then, Your Majesty, let me try to be more succinct from the honor of my position as His Majesty's Finance Minister.

France has agreed to loan us millions of roubles to allow us to complete the Trans-Siberian railway. The absence of that railway limits production throughout Russia, for I am sure Your Majesty can easily appreciate the benefit of being readily able to move items from one spot to another. Also, should Russia ever find itself at war again, may God forbid it, we will be able to move our troops rapidly across the country by train rather than having them walk three thousand or so miles to a front, and –"

"And?"

"… And risk dying on the way there. Even if they do get there, Your Majesty, we have outdated munitions and lamentably few of them, and since the great majority of our population is made up of uneducated, barely human, shaggy beasts who have never yet seen a gun, let alone fired one, and that is assuming –"

"To repeat myself, you have a great opinion of our country, Minister Witte."

He looked at me strangely. "Yes, I do, Your Majesty – a great opinion indeed."

"Are you humoring me, Minister?"

"No, Your Majesty, I have no inclination to do that. You asked me a question and I presumed to answer it as honestly as I could. Russia is a great country, but backward, and at risk for that very reason, or perhaps she is at risk because, ever since the time of Peter the Great, we have tried to retain our old ways while simultaneously and necessarily being part of the greater world. We have not managed yet, in my humble opinion, to achieve a satisfactory balance, but possibly we shall. I have great hopes for Your Majesties' upcoming journey."

"Oh yes, I see. During this trip we shall be a glorious and visible symbol of Russia's mighty past, while representing, by say our visit to France, the equal brilliance of our future, one mile of railway at a time, is that it, Minister? You see, I do understand some things, but now I fail to see the benefit of our visiting Germany, or are we asking my dread Cousin Willy for a loan as well?"

I was gratified to see that the great Witte was beginning to look exhausted and I fancied I had surprised him with my easy grasp of matters beyond mere domestic concerns.

"Germany, Your Majesty, has an autocratic system, like ours but not like ours, for Emperor Wilhelm's country is a highly developed one, particularly militarily, and –"

"… And so, although belonging to the same family does not necessarily place us in an alliance, as you have already informed me, you are now saying that we are traveling to Germany to strengthen family ties? I must say, Minister, you seem to be somewhat confused over your own goals while still sending Nicky, I mean His Majesty, and me off to fulfill them."

I was becoming increasingly angry and my head was beginning to pound. Nicky was right: the man was an idiot.

He, in turn, was looking flushed and breathing heavily, and I thought, somewhat savagely, that he might collapse at any minute with a stroke and then we could select a finance minister of our own choosing rather than having to tolerate Nicky's parents' old cast-off one.

I smiled serenely at him, hoping that my conspicuous calmness might have the effect of worsening his condition.

Instead, he continued his lecture.

"No one knows from day to day what Emperor Wilhelm's thoughts and plans are. Possibly not even he does. Given Germany's wealth and growing military might, all of the ministers, myself amongst them, have been hoping that your familial relationship with him might keep him from wondering if he should one day wish to throw some of that might at our country, a country far from capable of fighting back at this moment. One can only pity any country ruled by a leader who does not know his own mind."

With this pronouncement, he bowed and begged to be allowed to take his leave of me, leaving me as confused as I had been when this ridiculous conversation had started.

As I subsequently took my bath, rubbing tiredly at my face with a washcloth as I recalled Mr. Witte's clumsy words, I asked myself why exactly we were being sent to Germany – to find out if Willy was going to declare war on us *for no reason?* As I saw it, and Nicky did not contradict me when I asked him about it, we were supposed to play happy families with Willy and his wretchedly unappealing Empress, enjoy a tiny break with Grandmamma, and then continue on to France, where we absolute autocrats would dance to the tune of a republican nation who had become so by beheading their rightful king and queen on their path to so-called freedom.

Still, I was oddly grateful to Mr. Witte for how he had spoken to me, because it had made me see that the entirety of our success or failure to impress our importance upon Europe had fallen to me. Nicky would not do anything differently. In fact, it seemed to me that Nicky simply planned to enjoy himself and that this was why his boorish Finance Minister had chosen to speak so frankly to me.

I stood up dripping, sighed, reached for my wrap, and then rang for Maria who was once again about to accompany me into unknown situations and distant lands. I felt fractious, but then the crown can lay heavily on one; in fact there is no other position for it. I wasn't just an empress holding the weight of Russia's expectations on my tired shoulders, I was also a wife, and I needed to be especially beautiful for Nicky on this our first night on board The Standart. I had to make him look at me with not just love but also desire, for since losing my son he had not touched me at all.

Oh yes, he had given me cuddles and love pats and comfort, but further than that he would not venture. I could not speak of it, for I knew, if I attempted to do so, he would be both scandalized and repulsed. It was, I knew, wrong even that I should think of it, but I did. How could I not? I had to give Russia a son, for I understood so clearly that all of this – the great yacht, the palaces, the waiting heads of state – they meant nothing, they were only trappings garnered to make us glitter more than others, and that no one alive would see me as a true empress, indeed as anything but a rank failure, if I did not succeed in providing an heir for our throne.

It was not only that, though. Despite my mighty need for a son, I needed Nicky too. There was a magic to our marital love. It took me somewhere far away, where cares and fear did not live, where our differences could not divide us, and where nothing else mattered but the fact of him and me – Nicky and Alix – two people born to love only each other and to rise and fall as did the ocean, surrounded by a rhythm and a place beyond time and every other earthly concern. I needed him – not the Emperor but the man. In him I would become myself again, and together we would face the travails of our lives in love and intact.

So I had Maria dress me in the palest rose silk, a wisp of a gown, and when she began to push diamond-studded pins into my hair, I raised my hand and met her eyes in the mirror.

"Not too many pins, Maria. I want it to be soft and maybe to …" I blushed and looked down.

I felt her gentle hands gather my hair. She chuckled and I looked at her kind face in the glass in front of me and saw that she understood.

"… And maybe set to fall accidentally down, Your Majesty?" I reddened again and might have reproved her for her impudence had she not been smiling at me with such kindness. "You are the most beautiful woman in the world, Your Majesty, not merely the most beautiful queen." she laughed. "That would not be a great challenge, if the Dowager-Empress is an example."

I should have reprimanded her – it is not for a servant to speak of, let alone to judge, their betters – but I liked

Maria. In fact, she was my friend, the sole friend I had in this odd new world I occupied.

So instead I smiled at her and tapped my lips. "Maria you must not say such things. The Dowager-Empress is considered to be a very beautiful woman –"

She winked at me, the naughty creature.

"Oh yes, Your Majesty, all queens are considered most beautiful, even when they are not, though the Dowager-Empress is in truth a pretty enough woman. Old though. And I hear the Empress of Germany looks like a troll. No, I know well enough what real beauty is, even if I am supposed to pretend otherwise. If you will pardon me for saying so, so does his Majesty the Tsar."

She then deftly slid a few pins into my hair, pulled down some long curling strands, arranged them on my shoulders, and after a critical final look, finally let go of my head.

"There you are, Your Majesty. That would do well enough for the angels, if you ask me. Do you want jewels tonight? I would advise against it myself. Why gild the lily –"

"Maria, enough!" I said in what I hoped would sound to her like a much put-upon tone, but from her look I saw that it hadn't. Oh, what did it matter? She had made me feel so much better and unlike everyone else around me, she admired me. She liked me just for me and she really did think I was beautiful, and not simply because I was an empress.

I turned on my stool and impulsively hugged her waist. She stiffened for a moment, sighed and then reached her hand to my shoulder.

"Up you get, then, your gorgeous Highness. Go on, now. There are an awful lot of stars out here on this sea and they can make a person feel small and lonely. Go to His Majesty and I think you will find that you outshine them all."

I nodded against her stomach, rose and walked out onto the deck from my dressing room through the French doors. Maria was right: there were a million stars; no, more an infinity of stars. Even the sea was filled with them, it seemed.

I drew a deep breath of the welcoming salty air and turned. He was there, as I had known he would be, and his sweet eyes locked onto me. I could not read his expression in the dark, but I heard his shuddering sigh.

"Alix! You, my darling, are exquisite."

I did not answer, but merely gazed back at him. I imagined that my own eyes were unreadable in the starlight too.

He came closer and laid a hand on my bare shoulder.

"What is it, darling? Are you cold? Does the ship's motion make you feel unwell? Would you like your dinner now? I think the chef has –"

"I am not cold, Nicky."

His forehead wrinkled. "Oh good. Well then, shall we go into dinner, darling. The others are waiting and –"

"I am not hungry either, Nicky."

"Oh I see,"

Clearly he did not see but I found his confusion sweet and a feeling of ancient power arose in me. Maybe this is true of women and the sea. It must be, for our very cycles are driven by the moon and tide, I had read somewhere.

My thoughts were interrupted by Nicky as he resumed speaking.

"But you see, darling, even if you are not very hungry, mother is on board and they are all waiting at dinner for us. It is our first night and ... Oh, let us go in now so that they can all look at you and enjoy your beauty. Come on, darling, it will be a lovely night, I promise."

He removed his hand from my shoulder and slid it into my own hand, gently tugging me in the direction of the dining room whose lights I could see reflecting on the water. I tugged gently back and with my free hand reached up and pulled out a hairpin. 'Ah, Maria is a genius,' I thought, as I felt my hair spilling down around me.

Nicky gasped.

"Oh no, darling, your hair ... And well, I suppose –"

"I do not want to see your mother, either, Nicky."

He stopped and stared at me for the longest time, and then I sensed his smile growing in the dimness.

He dropped my hand and bowed to me with great courtliness. "Then would you dance with me, Your Majesty? I feel we should open with a polonaise. What do you think?"

I felt shy suddenly.

He smiled more deeply and caught both my hands in his.

"Yes, always a polonaise. Do you know, Your Majesty," he began in a conversational tone, pulling me into step as he spoke. "that many years ago, when I was just a boy really, I danced with ..." He switched us into a waltz and spun me out and back into his chest to hold me tightly with both his arms. "… the most beautiful young girl that I had ever seen." He swept me low and then caught me to him again, leaving me breathless. "And I said to myself, 'My God, if I can but dance once with her, I shall be the happiest man who has ever lived,' but …" He swung me out again. I was dizzy with the dance, with the night, with him.

I waited for him to speak again, and when he didn't, I managed to pant out. "But …? You said 'but.' What happened? Did you change your mind?"

He pulled me back to him in the rhythm of a dance music that only he and I could hear.

"But I was wrong. Once I touched her, I knew I needed more of her … so much more." He stopped and buried his head in my neck. "Ah, Alix …"

I reached out my hand to stroke his face.

"Nicky, my darling, my only love …"

He swung me up into his arms and I thrilled once again, as I always secretly did, to the hidden muscles which only I knew of, and leaned into him as he carried me back through our dressing room to our bed. Then, after gently laying me down upon it, he rose as though to close the doors behind us, but I tugged him back to me.

"No, no one will come. No one would dare. Leave them open. I want to watch the stars tonight."

Chapter 9

Germany was dreadful and not at all as I remembered it from when I had lived there. Of course, that had been in my own beloved, sheltered little Hesse-Darmstadt and this was Berlin, the very heart of old Prussia in Willy's New Germany. I found it dark and depressing, and was bored within minutes by Willy's bombastic need to show off his enormous army to Nicky and me by subjecting us to what seemed a day of never-ending military parades on Berlin's streets.

That evening, as we were dressing in the ugly suite Willy had given us, Nicky, who was smoking and reclining on our lumpy bed, remarked laconically, "Willy's determination to build the largest and most efficient military force in Europe is impressive, I suppose, but I really don't think I understand the point of it all. The world is at peace and has been for a great many years. Who is it, do you think, Sunny, that he fears is going to attack him?"

I smiled at him from my dressing table.

"Oh, he does not really fear being attacked, darling. It is more that he is hoping to attack somebody else. Did I ever tell you the story of Willy at Uncle Bertie and Aunt Alix's wedding?"

Nicky shook his head and sat up, clearly interested.

I laughed. "Well, it was before I was born, but Irene told me about it later. There they all were gathered together at Windsor for the wedding of the Prince of Wales, and of course Aunt Vicky had come and she had brought her charming first-born, Cousin Willy, with her.

He was just little then, but already such a devil that Aunt Vicky was having trouble keeping him still during the festivities. So she asked her brother, poor Uncle Alfred, to help her. He tried, and when wee Willie made too much noise, he told him to hush. First Willie tried to stab him in the leg with his toy sword, and when that didn't work, he bit him, quite hard, Irene said, hard enough to leave a scar, in any case. So you see, darling, that is just how Willie is – awful. He always has been and now he is just a bigger version of that insufferable little boy hoping to bite or stab someone, and that is why he has accumulated his silly old military toys on such a grand scale. It is best to ignore him. We cousins always did."

Nicky laughed again but then shook his head.

"I don't know, darling. That was a long time ago. It seems to me that Willy may have the right of it now."

I was shocked and swiveled around to face him. "Why, Nicky, whatever do you mean? You said that peace was all that mattered. You said that you were going to be just like your father. Silly Wee Willy Winkle will never attack us, and even if he were to run mad and do so, what would it matter? We have General Frost, the one who defeated Napoleon, on our side. You see, I do know my Russian history, my hubby."

I finished by sticking my tongue out at him. I was rewarded by his repeated laughter.

"You do indeed, darling, my brilliant girl, but it is General Winter, and I wasn't thinking of him attacking us. I was ... oh, I don't know ... God, these awful rooms are making me fanciful. Do you know I was quite nervous about opening the door to the bathroom just now? I was afraid I would find Willy's grandfather in there. I swear from the look of this place he must have been the last occupant."

I collapsed with laughter.

"Oh no, it wouldn't be Willy's grandfather. Willie didn't care for him or for his own father very much. If I were you, I would be more worried about your valet opening the wardrobe and finding an earlier ancestor, Frederick the Great, in there, stuffed and hanging, Willy adores him. Besides, naughty one, look at what I have to deal with in this mausoleum ..." So saying, I held up the tarnished silver brush which was still lying along with the rest of the ugly toilette set on the dressing table. "I think it still has some old dead empress's hair in it."

Nicky was laughing so hard by then that it took him a moment to gasp out, "Well, it cannot have been left here by Willy's Empress, darling. I fear that she is as bald as an egg. At least I hope so, because if she is just wearing those ghastly hats of hers to be fashionable, she should be ashamed of herself. The bloody things are so large that she nearly put my eye out this afternoon when she turned her head and one of those stuffed birds that were perched on it pecked me with its beak."

I held up my hand.

"Stop! Oh God, stop, darling. I will burst my stays and then poor Maria will have to start dressing me all over again, and we will be late for dinner, and Willy will go mad and have his army and his navy bombard us from every angle over the first course –"

"... The course being 'stuffed ancestor,' " Nicky gasped out.

Maria, who had just entered the room, stared at us aghast, and as soon as I could stop laughing, I tried to

133

explain the joke to her, which inevitably set us off again. So it took a bit of time for me to explain what was tickling us so much, and as inevitably happens in these situations, the third party doesn't grasp the joke and ends up thinking you have run a little mad, as Maria obviously thought Nicky and I had.

In the end we both gave up and Nicky went off to his dressing room to have his valet prepare him for dinner while Maria finished me off.

I had decided on a gown by Worth in cloth of silver and had chosen to adorn it with a stomacher made entirely of large, uncut diamonds which were accompanied by a stunning heart-shaped necklace, bracelet and earrings set, also of diamonds, a gift from Nicky. I must say that I did like the result, and Maria, always good for my fragile ego, murmured something about a moon goddess and I smiled gratefully at her, and then remembered an errand for her. Gesturing to the ugly old toilette set that had been left in our rooms, I said, "Maria dear, can you find one of Emperor Wilhelm's valets and see that this is returned to them. For all I know, they keep these ghastly rooms as some sort of museum in which to store their ugliest objects. The décor certainly gives that impression."

I waved my hands around to indicate the awfulness of it all and was finally given a giggle as Maria at last understood what I was getting at.

I continued, smiling. "This set, however, has to be given to someone in responsibility for the duration of our stay. It crowds out my own set, and besides, it does not seem quite hygienic, does it?"

Maria carefully picked up the old silver brush and comb, and then attempted to grasp the small mirrors as well, an overly-ambitious maneuver which could only have led to one or more of the items getting broken, for which we would have to apologize to someone. Sometimes Maria's failure to think through even the most menial of tasks could be so exasperating; these Russians were not a practical people.

I got to my feet and moved around her to the bed before stripping a pillowcase from one of the pillows and handing it to her.

"Here, Maria, put all of it in here and find someone to give it to, and then you can go for dinner, though God knows what they are likely to serve here. I am expecting boiled sausage or something equally ghastly for myself. Oh, and don't forget to tell one of the maids to come in and replace the pillowcase."

I was intending to leave but Maria's expression arrested me.

"What is it, Maria? Hurry up and spit it out, because I cannot keep His Majesty waiting, and –"

She curtsied nervously. "Yes, of course, Your Majesty. I was just wondering if maybe I shouldn't just keep this set in my room until we are leaving and then I can put it back in here and no one will know you didn't like it, that's all."

My temper, never far from the surface, unfortunately rose immediately.

"Maria, you do not question my decisions. Just do as I have instructed you. Under your bed indeed!" I huffed and shook my head. "Imagine if it were found there. What a to-do that would be!"

She stared at me mutinously.

"Maria! What in the world is wrong with you? Have you run mad?"

"I don't think so, Your Majesty. What I do think is that you might hurt the feelings of whoever put the set in here as maybe they were trying to be nice, like when people put flowers in a room and things."

I raised an eyebrow.

"Oh, I am sorry, Maria. I sometimes forget that you have stayed extensively as a guest in palaces, hotels, and on country estates, and so have a wealth of etiquette to pass onto me. Well, I am quite displeased with you and I do not want that ugly old set staring up at me for one more second, so please take it out and find someone to give it to, and don't let me hear another word from you about it. Oh, and Maria ...?"

She was halfway to the door, the pillowcase clutched in her resentful arms. Without even bothering to turn towards me, she said over her shoulder in a sulky voice,

"Yes, Your Majesty ...?"

Her insolent attitude served only to enrage me further.

"I have just remembered that my gold toilette set needs polishing. It is covered in fingerprints. I also wish to have the Irish lace here sewn so that it does not slip around on top of the dressing table, which is very annoying. And while you have your sewing kit out, please could you take the opportunity to repair my nightgown, which will need to be pressed afterwards. Once you have completed these duties, you may go for your dinner and retire for the night. I shall ring for one of the other maids to undress me when I return. You are excused now."

At least she remembered to curtsy this time, the uppity creature.

Thanks to Maria, I was in a rather bad mood when I rejoined Nicky to follow one of Willy's cold, stiff servants through the corridors of his gloomy castle down to one of the drawing rooms to gather for drinks before dinner. *Sparing the hosts' feelings indeed!*

Even Nicky, a veritable *impresario* of small talk, found the fifteen minutes with that gathering heavy weather. Willy had not chosen to present himself, so we were compelled to sip whatever it was that Willy was passing off as wine alongside the assorted band of Nicky's mother, Willy's curiously-hatted Empress Augusta, and Willy's senile *chargé d'affaires,* Count Mirenbach.

Empress Augusta, in addition to assailing one's visual senses, was apparently quite deaf, so Nicky's every remark was followed by her barking, "What, what?"

Nicky would then repeat his comment more loudly, which provoked his mother to snap at him in turn. "Dear God, Nicky, must you shout? I am getting a dreadful headache."

She is getting a headache? I thought indignantly. *My headache has its own headache by now.*

Then, just as I was wondering whether or not to pretend to faint to put an end to what promised to be an excruciating evening, both Willy and dinner were announced simultaneously.

The dining room was a perfectly enormous, black walnut-paneled, Gothic monstrosity, whose one saving grace was that it was so dimly lit that I could not see what I was eating or, better yet, Empress Augusta's hat, which tonight was sporting what I believed to be a life-sized elephant eating a life-sized cow, or some such thing.

Willy was, of course, the perfect host, simply filled with great *bonhomie* and joy at our presence. He demonstrated this by asking Nicky not once but several times, before Nicky could even answer him the first time, what he thought of his growing military might. He did not appear to be expecting an answer from Nicky; he simply wanted to take the opportunity to show off to him about how Germany was advancing in leaps and bounds, which he promptly proceeded to do.

"In the time I have been Emperor, Nicky, I have unified Germany into being the greatest world power that Europe will ever see. In addition, we are now running ahead of Britain's industrial growth, for as grows the military, so grows industry. My Kaiser Wilhelm Society for the Advancement of Science discovers new amazements daily. We have provided schools for everyone too. My people are prosperous and happy, my country dominates the world, and I ask myself ..." he paused for breath and a modest laugh. "... 'what can halt the greatness of Germany now?' "

As no answer was immediately forthcoming, he speared a chunk of meat with the fork in his one good hand, chewed it down with a gulp of the ghastly beer that he insisted on serving for himself every meal, and turned his attention towards me.

"Little cousin, you are even prettier than you were when I helped this young rascal secure your hand." In order to illustrate his point, he gestured at Nicky with his fork, accidentally spraying his unfortunate Empress with meat juice, which caused her to spill some of her wine into Minnie's lap.

I smiled tightly.

"Thank you, Willy. It is lovely to see you after all this time and in such good health. Germany, as you say, is such a wonder. Why, it seems almost as though we have taken one of Mr. Wells's time machines back to the Prussia of old. As I was saying to Nicky earlier, it is simply marvelous."

Willy wasn't stupid. He was, without question, vainglorious and overbearing, but he had never been stupid. I should have remembered that.

I saw his eyes ice over while he fought to keep his smile in place.

Carefully setting down his fork, he tapped on the table with his nails. "Why, thank you, my dear. So tell me, does the small princess like Germany, do you think?"

I was startled, and before I could think of an answer, Nicky stepped in, smiling widely.

"Oh, she seems to like it quite well, Willy." He chuckled. "Of course, she does not speak yet, but if her appetite is anything to go by, she is very happy here."

Willy smiled back at Nicky. "That is a fine thing. Ah, a little girl. What a blessing for you. I have been telling Old Dona here ..." He winked at the unfortunate Empress Augusta, whom he nicknamed 'Old Dona' – of course, the rest of us just as unkindly called his sister

139

'Mossy,' but still – who looked back at him nervously, then he lovingly attempted to pinch her on the chin, accidentally knocking her hat off onto Minnie who tumbled to the floor in her attempt to avoid being hit by it.

Nicky rose to help his much-shaken mother back to her feet, as did both the Empress and I, but we women were both exhorted by Willy to stay where we were and to continue with dinner. "No use everyone missing dinner, Nicky my boy. I hope you will join me for cognac and cigars once you have seen poor Minnie to her rooms."

Nicky, a man much to be envied at that moment, stumbled away with a half-fainting Minnie after assuring Willy that he could think of nothing that would give him greater pleasure, leaving Empress Augusta, Willy and me behind.

"I do not think every member of your small family is enjoying our hospitality. Is that true, Alix?"

I was cold, and my head hurt, and I wanted to retire, but I was not afraid of Willy, so I tilted my head at him and smiled curiously.

"What a strange question, Willy. I am German by birth, if no longer by circumstance, and I think that before poor Minnie was assaulted," I threw an apologetic smile at the poor Empress Augusta who seemed to be entirely oblivious to her surroundings, "that Nicky had just finished telling you that even our little Olga was enjoying herself."

Willy made a tutting noise. "Oh, I see. But if so, then why did you have your maid hand over my sainted grandmother's silver toilette set in a damned bag as if it were discarded rubbish?" he roared.

I blushed but did not back down.

"I apologize if my actions offended you, Willy, but I had nothing else to put it in and wanted to return it, so..."

I shrugged.

His eyes narrowed and even the Empress Augusta quailed visibly.

"So, it is not good enough for you, is that right, Empress? What do you prefer – a golden brush? I'll see if I can have my treasurer find you one. Will that suit you better, Alix?"

I laughed back at him without warmth.

"Oh, that will not be necessary, Willy. I already have a rather expensive gold set of my own, designed by Fabergé, I believe."

I heard Empress Augusta stifle her amusement and I grinned back at her.

Willy also turned his head towards her.

"You must be tired, my dear." He returned to address me. "She tires easily. She is expecting again, I believe, and of course," he shrugged, "we have three sons already. As you can imagine, the old girl is exhausted, or then maybe you cannot imagine it yet, Alix ... Minnie tells us that you are usually unwell, even without the challenge of having rambunctious little boys around."

On the instant, I transformed into an empress of stone and Willy heard it in my voice as I rose without permission and stood over him, forcing him to look up at me as I spoke.

"You forget yourself, Willy. You forget that I am no longer your silly little cousin, as I have forgotten that you are no longer the arrogant, clumsy little boy who pined after Ella like a sick puppy when we were young. Oh, forgive me, Augusta," I made a small bow of my head towards her, "I am tired, and if you will both forgive me, I shall say goodnight."

Willy stood and bowed elaborately. The Empress Augusta turned her head away from me.

Willy continued, "Yes, go and rest, your Imperial Highness. But, you know, you are wrong, my dear ..."

I did not want to speak anymore and I sighed wearily to show my boredom with him. "Oh yes, Willy?"

He nodded and smiled into my eyes. It was an unnerving rictus of a grin. "I do not forget anything, Alix. Never. I never forget and I always repay my debts. Maybe you will discover this for yourself one day, who knows? Goodnight, my dear."

I did not see Willy again until our departure on The Standart two days later. He kept Nicky occupied every minute of the day but chose not to put in an appearance at dinner, leaving Mother Dear, Dona Dear (as I secretly now called the Empress Augusta), and the children, of course – Willy's three dreadful children and my small Olga – to fend for ourselves from dawn to dusk.

Willy and Augusta's children had terrorized Olga, much as Willy had terrorized us smaller cousins during our own childhoods, and I fancy that I heard her sigh with relief as I held her against me on the deck to wave farewell to the Kaiser and his family as we sailed safely away.

Nicky put his arm around us and whispered in my ear, laughing, "It is a good thing that you are such a perfectly splendid Empress, my darling, because you would make a dreadful ambassador."

I asked him rather tartly what he meant by that, and he turned my head to face him, kissing the top of Olga's head as he did so.

"Well, you certainly caused quite a to-do, darling, over that silly brush set."

Without giving me the time to answer him, he shook his head smilingly and pronounced patronizingly, at least to my ears, "Never mind. I know old Willy can be difficult, and of course it is hard when you knew each other as children. I think that is why my own uncles are so impossible with me. They still see me as a little boy on leading strings. But we do rather have to try now that we are all grown up, and oh," he chuckled, "running empires and such things, do you not think so, Sunny?"

I stepped back, clutching Olga protectively.

"No, I do not think so. I do not think I should expect that my own husband," my voice broke on a sob, "should criticize me when all the rest of the world already does so. Why do you not just go and fetch your mother too, Nicky? She would love to join you in tearing me apart. Oh God, how dare you bring this up? I did not want to come to Germany. I cannot bear Willy. Now you are attacking me and I did try, I tried so hard. Oh, let us just turn this silly yacht around so that I can take my baby and go home to Tsarskoe Selo where at least I can have a little peace. If I am going to be hated by everyone, I would rather be alone."

Nicky held out his hands imploringly. "Alix …?"

I kept backing away, shaking my head continuously. "No, do not come near me. Do not say another word. Go and visit your mama. You can tell her about this too."

"Alix, please, please, darling, don't be –"

"Be what, Nicky? Be me? Be alive? Be me not as God made me but as you and your horrible mother, and everyone else, wants me to be? No, do not say another word. I will never ever forgive you for any of this and it is all your fault."

With that, still clutching my baby, I stumbled into our bedroom and sat weeping hysterically on the bed, barely managing to ring for Maria.

When she came, I made no effort to halt my crying. I merely handed her Olga and said, "Take her to Nurse. I am too upset to be near her. And ring for Dr. Botkin. Tell him it is my heart, Maria. I think it is about to pound right out of my chest."

I began to sob again.

Maria hesitated and then lifted Olga up into her arms and fled from the cabin.

Dr. Botkin came and gave me a draft of laudanum and everything became hazy. Somehow I was undressed and tucked up in bed, and when I awoke I could see that it was dusk outside. The doors to the deck were partially opened to allow a breeze in and I could hear voices. It took me a moment through my fog to understand what they were saying and then I wished I hadn't.

Nicky, his mother and Dr. Botkin were all talking about me and on the still air their voices carried easily. Nicky asked Dr. Botkin what he thought was wrong with me, and before the doctor could answer, his mother replied, "Hysteria and ill temper is what is wrong with her, do you not think, Dr. Botkin?" She too did not let him get in an answer; she never let anyone answer anything. "Nicky, my dear, it is simply paramount that you take control of matters with your wife. I know she is difficult but look at you, you are a mess, a nervous wreck. All this talk of heart trouble is just nonsense. Alix certainly does not have heart trouble. I fear one must search higher up the body for the source of her problems. What do you think, Dr. Botkin?"

Dr. Botkin was wisely silent.

Nicky tried to stand up to his mother, I'll give him that.

"Mother, I really wish you would not speak like that about Alix. She is not mad, and she is my wife, and I love her, and I am sure Dr. Botkin –"

"Oh yes, Dr. Botkin. Dr. Botkin, do you have anything to say about this case?"

Poor Dr. Botkin cleared his throat.

"Well, Your Majesties, I think the Empress, the Young Empress, that is –"

"Oh, thank you so much, Dr. Botkin, for reminding me of my age. I suppose you think that it is I who am mad, and not Alix, because I am so *elderly*."

"Oh no, Your Majesty, that was not what I meant at all. I consider you neither aged nor mad, nor the Young Empress ... I mean Her Majesty Empress Alexandra. I merely meant to say –"

"Yes, Doctor, what *did* you mean to say? Speak forthrightly. You might find the experience pleasantly refreshing – might you not? – as might we."

I had to stuff the corner of my pillow into my mouth to smother a giggle. In a few minutes, Dr. Botkin might be ready to dose himself with laudanum.

I felt better now and continued listening, eager to hear more.

"No, Your Majesty, I am not having trouble –"

It was Nicky's turn to interject. "Well, what is it, Botkin? What is wrong with my wife? Please do say. Mother and I do not have all night ..."

I could hear the doctor's loud sigh. "Yes, Your Majesties, I am getting to that, but first I must ask a rather indelicate question of Your Majesty."

Minnie snarled back at him, "Is that within your purview, doctor? Do try to remember your place –"

Nicky interrupted again. "No, go ahead, Botkin. It is all right, Mother, if it will help Alix."

"I am most grateful, Your Majesty. I was merely wondering whether the Young Empress might be breeding. You see, at such times –"

Minnie's outraged squawk cut him off.

"How dare you, Doctor? And it hardly matters, for I am living proof that breeding women remain quite sane, despite what you may think, and –"

Nicky again: "Mama, please. It's all right, Botkin, and I cannot say either way. If so, it would be very early days and –"

"Nicky, that is enough! Do not pay any attention to him, Doctor. Now, assuming that my daughter-in-law is not breeding, as you so crudely put it, what else might be the matter with her?"

The doctor cleared his throat nervously and I was sure he must have been sweating even amid the cool night air of the sea.

"I cannot say for a certainty, Your Majesties. The Young ... I mean Her Majesty Empress Alexandra ... is a highly strung young woman –"

"Highly strung? Yes, that has its possibilities, although I was thinking more in terms of a convent."

In my outrage I heard Nicky make a sound of protest but his mother shushed him. "Be quiet, Nicky. It is important that we hear the truth, no matter how unpleasant, and then we will know how best to deal with it."

Botkin shuffled. "You see, Your Majesty, I do not know what the truth is. The Empress Alexandra complained to me earlier today of heart pain. She has never said that to me before, although she has often complained of suffering from head pain, facial neuralgia, and of having a sharp aching in her legs," Minnie snorted, "and these symptoms indicate to me that the Empress Alexandra may be suffering either from genuine pains or perhaps have a somewhat nervous condition which causes her to think she is suffering. This matter with her heart, in other words, may indicate that there is a serious physical problem for us to address or that we are merely dealing with a quirk of the imagination, if you see what I mean."

There was a brief silence and then I heard Minnie laugh.

"Doctor, I doubt that anyone on earth could see what you mean. I must say, even in a profession, if I might call it that, renowned for its obtuseness and obfuscation, you must be its standard bearer. Nicky, take me in to dinner. I am cold and I have decided I would like a large glass of something soothing in my hand right now. Have I prescribed well for myself, Doctor …? Oh, no words, then. Good, I like you better when you are studiously silent and looking like a stuffed animal. Nicky, shall we…?"

"But Mama, I don't think I should leave Alix. What if she wakes up? Also, I think I understand what Dr. Botkin is saying. You meant, Doctor, that Alix may be ill or it may be that her nerves, when she gets upset, make her *feel* ill, and that it really doesn't matter, because the end result is that she *feels* ill either way. Is that right. Dr. Botkin?"

Over Minnie's derisive laughter, I heard Botkin stammer, "Well, I … I … Yes, Your Majesty, something like that. In the end, I suppose, it is simply better to try to keep Empress Alexandra as quiet and happy as possible, and –"

Minnie broke in. "So, in other words, she is half-mad and wholly hysterical at all times, so we must try not to upset her or Russia will never see a male heir. Is that right, Dr. Botkin? Have I summarized the situation correctly, maybe even more concisely than in my son's valiant attempt to do so?"

"Oh, Your Majesty –"

"No, do not say another word. I do understand quite clearly now. Nicky, I would like my dinner. Please take me in."

It was all over. I heard Dr. Botkin still shuffling around outside and then he emitted a sigh before creeping into my cabin, clearly expecting me to be still asleep.

Finding me awake in the dimness, he sighed again. "Your Majesty heard that?"

I nodded and held out my hand to him. He took it gently.

"Yes, Dr. Botkin, I heard all of it. So tell me, do you think I am suffering from hysteria?"

He shook his head.

"No, Your Majesty. I just think that you are suffering. I am not sure of how much help I can be to you, but I will always try, if you will let me."

When I awoke the next morning, it was Nicky who brought me my tea.

He kissed my forehead and said, "You look like you are feeling much better, darling. And I don't want you to spend another moment worrying about anything that may have happened during our visit to Germany or anything that was said last night. You know Mama, she tends to be a little outspoken. Really, she adores you, as I do, as we all do, and just think, by this evening, we shall be in England and you will be showing your grandmamma our little Olga."

Nicky was in luck that morning, for I had awoken vowing to put a good face on all of it. And besides, he was right: We were almost in England, lovely and loved old England, the home of my grandmamma, and my old home in so many ways as well.

Given how awfully I was treated and misunderstood in Germany, I felt quite moved and hopeful of happy times when The Standart entered English waters at last.

When I had last seen my dearest grandmamma, I had not even been a bride yet, and here I was returning to her as a wife, as a mother, and as an Empress. We would be meeting as equals for the first time in my life, and I knew she would be as overjoyed as I was by how my circumstances had changed. After all, wasn't it Grandmamma who had once hoped I would marry poor Eddy and become Queen of England after her one day? She had always viewed me with a special regard and I knew that, unlike Ella and some of her other grandchildren, I had not disappointed her in my choices.

Nicky was almost as pleased as I was to be visiting England. In contrast with our dreadful time in Germany and our up-coming trip to France, this would be a strictly private family visit where we could all concentrate on relaxing and enjoying ourselves.

Chapter 10

I found Grandmamma terribly changed.

I suppose it was inevitable – after all, she was very old – and I tried valiantly to keep her age in the forefront of my mind as she heaped one insult on me after another during our stay.

She was even worse than Nicky's horrid mother, who, I believe, had been poisoning her against me in the course of her correspondence with her sister, Aunt Alix, the Princess of Wales.

First of all, though, she insulted Olga! Within minutes of our initial exchange of kisses and exclamations of pleasure at the sight of each other, I shyly took my baby from Nicky's arms and led her onto Grandmamma's lap. She stared down at her for a moment, patted her head distantly, and gestured to a maid-in-waiting to take her, saying, "So, this little girly is your only one so far. Such a pity, but she is amusing. Her head is rather large like a balloon. Well, no matter, most babies are ugly little creatures and I find they often become more presentable with time. Sit down beside me, my dear, so I can look at you."

I did as she said, but with some resentment at her words. Nicky joined me and smiled at her, filling the awkward silence.

"Dear Grandmamma, you look wonderful. I cannot tell you how much Alicky and I have been looking forward to this visit. Mama too, of course. You will see her later. She has rushed off to be with Aunt Alix, I believe."

Grandmamma batted her thinning eyelashes at him. She had always had a weakness for a well-turned compliment, the dear old dragon.

"Nicky, my dear boy, it is such a pleasure to see you. And you are looking so well. I am so glad. I was just saying to Bertie yesterday that I feared we would find you terribly changed, but I see I was wrong to worry."

Nicky looked puzzled. "Why would you have worried about me, Grandmamma? I haven't been ill a day. Did someone tell you I had been –?"

"No, Nicky, I did not hear that you were ill. I just imagined that after the tragic events of your coronation ..." She shook her head despairingly. "Such an unfortunate impression for the people, and then, of course, your choice to attend the ball that those perfidious French insisted upon continuing with ... Well, we were all so sorry for you and for my poor Alix when we read about it all in our dispatches." She gave a tinkling laugh and continued. "Our papers are so dreadfully salacious, are they not? Why, they wrote of nothing else for days. How fortunate you are in Russia to have censorship. Would that we had." She shrugged. "But what can be done about it now? You are here and I am simply delighted by your visit. But see here, dear boy, why don't you run along and find Bertie? I believe he is most anxious to see you as well and then I can have my little Alicky to myself for a minute before dinner."

Nicky smiled obligingly, rose and took Olga from the nearby maid.

"Of course, Your Majesty. I am most anxious to see dear Bertie and to show off our little girl to him." With a nod to me, he added, "Darling, I shall see you later at dinner, shall I? I will give Olga to Orchie before I join you, unless you want her to be brought back to you first?"

Grandmamma tilted her head.

"Nicky dear, I think Alicky can go a few hours before seeing her baby again. Why, when I –"

He laughed. "No, Grandmamma, I meant since Alix nurses her and our little one might not choose to wait for her dinner."

I gestured behind Grandmamma's back that he should not broach this subject in front of her, but it was too late.

Grandmamma's laughter rang out again.

"Oh, you really do do that still, then, Alix? I was hoping the letters I had received from Minnie were mistaken, or at least that you had stopped doing so in the hope of having more children." Her eyes narrowed. "Your mother nursed all her children, too, as I may already have told you. I do not approve. It is not right for royal women to stoop to such a thing like they are wet nurses. I named a cow at Windsor after your mother. I called it Princess Alice."

She chortled to herself at her wit.

And so the niggling went on for five days of endless lectures on how I had failed my country by not producing a son; on how I had failed my "dearest" mother-in-law, Minnie, with my coldness; and on how I had failed the court by my insistence on living "some sort of bourgeois hausfrau life in seclusion."

The latter complaint nearly made me choke on my stewed tea. Hadn't Grandmamma spent some forty years doing just that? I didn't say so, though. Instead, I kept the litany of, 'old, old, she's very old, this might be the last time you see her, stay the course,' in my head and I think I was right to have done so because while the elderly tend to lose their grasp of things, they do insist on voicing their opinions regardless. What else do they have to do?

On and on she went again: I had offended every single German citizen with the great brush incident; I wore too much jewelry but not a tight enough corset; my coloring was bad; I should be resting more, then maybe I could have a baby. On other days she would contradict herself by announcing that she had heard that all I did was rest, and that maybe if I took some exercise I could have another baby.

Nicky did not fare much better than I did. Uncle Bertie had taken it upon himself to drag Nicky out hunting every day and it hadn't stopped raining once. Then, at dinner, Grandmamma would regale him with lighthearted stories of British monarchs who had failed in their duties and subsequently – indeed *consequently* – lost both their crowns and their lives, and if the British examples were insufficiently convincing, she reminded us both to ponder carefully the fates of France's last ruling couple while we were visiting that country.

If Nicky and I hadn't both seen dark humor in the whole ghastly visit, we would have gone mad. Instead, at night in our damp, cold chamber, we held onto each other in mutual mirth before submitting ourselves to the passion which arises within two people who are completely in sympathy with one another.

I have, however, looked back with pleasure all of my life on our last night in England. It was the night of the 'Ghillies Ball,' a funny event that Grandmamma staged each year at Balmoral which the servants attended as well and where they were even permitted to dance with their masters. Some unkind wag once suggested that the Ghillies Ball only existed so that Grandmamma could dance a quadrille with her servant John Brown. I don't know about that. I despise gossip, and, anyway, I loved the balls as a child and had so much been looking forward to attending one with Nicky.

I even had a tartan ball gown specially made for the occasion. Since I seldom wore any colors other than mauve, pink and white, Nicky's eyes nearly fell out of their sockets when he saw me, although it has to be said that he looked rather astounding himself. Grandmamma had made him an honorary colonel of her beloved Scots Greys, and to honor her and them, he was wearing a kilt in their colors. He always had the strongest and most heavily muscled legs, and I will confess that my own legs trembled a bit at the sight of him as he grandly swept me out onto the floor.

Using a moment in the dance to bring me to him, he whispered in my ear, "So, my darling, you make the most beautiful daughter of a constitutional democracy tonight."

"Speak for yourself, Your Highness. Never has a Tsar shown the leg quite like you," I sparkled back at him.

He grinned delightedly and spun me terribly, the naughty thing.

When I was close to him again, he laughed and asked, "And are you ready for more evenings of *liberté,*

155

egalité and fraternité such as this in France, Your Highness?"

I laughed back loudly enough to attract Grandmamma's disapproval, but I didn't care.

"Oh yes, Your Majesty. *Vive la République!*"

"Spoken like a true autocrat, my precious," he replied and kissed me right there on the dance floor.

Because of her endless hectoring, it was with a lighter heart than I had anticipated that I was able to kiss Grandmamma goodbye the next morning. Nicky shook Bertie's hand enthusiastically and thanked him for the hunting and, humorously, for the cold he had caught in the process. Best of all, Minnie decided at the last minute to stay on in England with her sister, Aunt Alix, so we sailed over to France in real anticipation of enjoying ourselves, I even more so than Nicky as I had felt ill that morning, but not in an unfamiliar way.

I say all of this to show that I entered France with every intention of trying to be as pleasing to everyone as possible. My gowns and hats had been designed by their great couturier, Worth, and my jewels had been oh-so-carefully selected to provide that touch of grandeur that I believe people enjoy seeing, while avoiding the risk of intimidating the wives of the Republican ministers and other officials we would meet.

At first it went beautifully. The President and his wife met us at the quay and ushered us into an open carriage. She was a plain woman but complimented me rapturously on my pink *crêpe de chine* traveling gown and on our baby as we rode down the Champs Elysées between rows and rows of cheering people who screamed loudly, *"Vive l'Empereur. Vive l'Impératrice,"* and most touchingly, *"Vive la bébé."* That night we were accommodated, as I had requested, at Versailles and I was able to sleep under the same canopy as poor Marie-Antoinette. On our second day we were fêted at the Elysée Palace and I was presented with an astounding Goeblins tapestry and a painting of the last French Queen. So, despite what was now developing into a rather debilitating morning sickness, I was feeling most contended with our trip. The French newspapers were filled with compliments as to my clothing and appearance, and Nicky proudly read them to me over breakfast.

Then it all went wrong again.

Nicky and I had been invited to a private tour of the Louvre, with a luncheon to follow. I had dressed very carefully for it and, despite my nausea, I fancy I looked rather well. However, when we arrived, our hostess was a French countess to whom we had not been previously introduced. She curtsied deeply to Nicky and me, but I saw it as a test and merely inclined my head. Nicky then spoke to her in his habitual charming way in fluent French while I remained silent, not being sufficiently conversant with the language to attempt a conversation. Worse was to follow. When we had completed our long tour of the works of art, I was beginning to feel faint and my legs were aching, as was my head, and my stomach was running away from me, so I whispered to Nicky that I felt too unwell for luncheon and wished to return immediately to the Elysée Palace where we would be staying that night.

Nicky did not even answer me. He merely shook his head and the hand he placed on my arm as he escorted me in for lunch felt more like a manacle than a support.

Given my state of health, my usual shyness, and the fact that every single lady at that ghastly luncheon was some sort of leftover from the *Ancien Régime* – being a countess or a duchess or a princess, all title and no land – I can hardly be blamed for being unable to speak to them, let alone touch a bite of food. Moreover, every woman there had seemingly been embalmed in thick, cloying perfume.

I could not endure a second more of this, and, with or without Nicky, I was determined to make my exit. I rose shakily and murmured a cursory apology, which the French ladies pretended not to understand, presumably because my halting French was unintelligible to their refined ears. Nicky had no choice then but to hurriedly make his own apologies and rush me out towards our carriage.

Unfortunately, even on the ride back we were not left in peace. Oh no. A French minister was awaiting us at our carriage, and brushing aside Nicky's rather stiff request that we be allowed to return post-haste to the Elysée Palace, insisted, "But *non*, Highness, it is eempossible. We have notified the papers that your majesties will be riding down the Champs Elysées once again, and the people have been gathering there since dawn to see you one more time before you leave. Surely you would not wish –"

"I surely would, Minister," I replied. "I am feeling most unwell and will have no part of any parade you may have arranged without consulting me, and –"

Nicky looked horrified.

"Minister, please forgive us. My wife, Her Majesty, is, as you can see, feeling poorly, and while I appreciate the gesture, it might be better if –"

The minister, who was by then eyeing me with barely cloaked contempt, managed a smile for Nicky.

"But, Your Majesty, look, we are already here."

And indeed we were. Our open carriage had turned onto the Champs Elysées, where once again tens of thousands of cheering Frenchmen and women were gathered.

I could not help my instinctive reaction, which was to put my hands over my ears. The noise was causing my head to implode. Nicky was almost as aghast as the minister at this and actually tried to pull one of my hands away, but I jerked my body sideways and squeezed my eyes shut in rage and denial at the torture I was being subjected to.

After that, it only remained for me to be formally sentenced, having already been tried and found guilty by the French press, without the benefit of a proper hearing. Marie-Antoinette would have understood my predicament. The papers wrote that the young Russian Empress seemed half mad at best, and it was to be hoped that she was mad, since what else could explain her rudeness to her elegant hostesses at the Louvre, the crazed scene she had made in her carriage, and possibly, worst of all, that she had not even noticed that silk blossoms had been wired into the trees just for her pleasure? And while they were writing that, they thought they might as well mention at the same time that Monsieur Worth had been interviewed and he wished it to be on record that the clothes I had worn while in France had been so tastelessly altered according to my errant whims that he could no longer recognize his own designs. I was not so *soignée* after all, seemed to be the verdict.

Nicky barely addressed a single word to me during the entire trip home, which was just as well as I was extremely ill, even fearing for my life as the pain in my legs, head and face became nearly unendurable. I sent messages through Dr. Botkin to the ship's captain to complain that we were going too fast and that it was causing me more nausea, and I felt the engines slow as I lay there on my bed of pain. Dr. Botkin liberally dosed me with laudanum but none of it helped as I was too far gone in illness for any relief, and too sick to my very heart that my own husband no longer seemed to care for me or for my well-being.

Chapter 11

Upon our return to Tsarskoe Selo, I took to my bed.

I had experienced discomfort, quite a bit of it, during my pregnancy with Olga, but that was as nothing compared to what I can only remember as a time of utter illness and agony with my second full-term baby. Dr. Botkin explained that the infant was lying upon my spine. I suppose this understanding helped him, and maybe Nicky as well, but it hardly mattered to me as the knowledge proved to be of no assistance to Dr. Botkin in the treatment of my horrendous pain. I just could not get comfortable: If I turned, the sickness overwhelmed me; if I tried to sit up, my back would spasm; and if I moved my legs, they would cramp in agony.

I came to forgive Nicky for his callous treatment of me on our return voyage as he was the only one I could bear to have near me during my illness. Indeed, I insisted on his keeping close by me at all times. He was as good as gold about it, too. He was terrified for both me and the baby, and spent all his waking hours sitting beside me in my darkened rooms – for I could not bear any light – gently holding my hand or conferring in whispers with Dr. Botkin and the other surgeons whom he had called in to try to find relief for me.

All that endless winter I suffered the tortures of the damned with Nicky dutifully by my side. It drew us closer than we had ever been, and I believe he learned the very essence of marital love and commitment by being forced to watch what I had to go through to give him his heir.

By springtime, my health had not improved, and by now Nicky and Dr. Botkin – and I think even my mother-in-law – seriously feared for my emotional state as I had become quite depressed in my dark, cold, pain-filled isolation. So, after much consultation, it was decided that I could be oh-so-carefully moved to the nearby palace of Peterhof where the cleansing sea breezes might prove beneficial to me.

Nicky himself carried me to the train, and though the motion of it increased my sickness, I immediately felt better once I was installed at Peterhof, so much so that one day I even allowed Nicky to put me in the new wheeling chair that had been built for me and to push me up and down the paths skirting the great fountains laid out in the gardens.

Then it came, the day of delivery, during which I nearly died, for once again I was weeks overdue and totally wasted from having been unable to move for nearly a year. Chloroform was finally administered and when I awoke I saw Nicky's face and knew there was no point in asking after the child. I turned my head and looked at the play of the sun on the water instead.

As if from a distance I heard him say in a careful voice, as though I might shatter otherwise, "Another beautiful little girl, darling. She looks just like you."

I said nothing.

He tried again. "I was thinking that maybe we could call her Tatiana, as we did with Olga, from that Eugene Onegin story and –"

"That is fine. Name her that. Could you take her to Orchie now, Nicky? I really ... I must sleep for a bit."

162

"Of course, darling. Yes, you rest, and then ... and then ... well .... well .... yes ... I mean I ... I should go and send telegrams and notify people."

I nodded tiredly.

I did not rest, though, not until I heard the cannons fire ... ninety nine ... one hundred ... one hundred and one, and then no more.

I let the tears come then.

A year later I was pregnant again. I had no choice; I had to submit to the will of God and to that of the Russian people and do my duty.

It didn't matter. I hadn't really recovered from Tatiana's birth, but no one cared at all for me by that point. I was reminded, both subtly and not so subtly – by Nicky's mother – each day that all that was really required of a Russian Empress was to produce an heir. Once she had done so, she would be beloved of her husband, of her family – which, of course, was really *his* family – and of the country. Until then, she was an object of suspicion, and, in my case, of disappointment. That I was given to prolonged and excruciating pregnancies and that I had delivered two enormous babies was of no concern to anyone, Nicky included.

Oh, he pretended otherwise. He told me that he adored me and our beautiful little girls. He said that if we never had another child he would still consider himself the luckiest man alive. He told me my health was far more important to him than any son we might or might not have. He said all of these things, and perhaps I would have believed him except that he always finished by reminding me that, should we have no son, his tall, handsome younger brother Michael would "make a fine tsar, do you not think, darling?"

Her son – sweet, beloved of all who met him, tall and attractive, Grand Duke Michael, 'darling Misha' as he was known in the family – even I could not resist his charms, and I had more reason to than most, but, for all his virtues, all I could ever think of when he was near me was *her*, Nicky's mother, the Dowager-Empress of Russia, the thorn in my marriage, the woman who on every public occasion led the way on the arm of my husband, who glittered and chatted and danced and enchanted all who saw her, and whose legend remained firm in the Russian land and the European courts.

No, I would not fail in my desire to have a son. I would not sit by while she stripped me of my honors and of my social position, and smugly accepted congratulations for being the mother of not one but two emperors. If I were to allow this to happen, it would only be a matter of time before people would begin to say openly what I knew they were already discussing in whispers: that I was no good for Nicky, that I kept him from the court and the ministers, locked up with me and our useless little girls in some sort of endless tea party at Tsarskoe Selo; that I couldn't be an Empress, and I couldn't have a son, and so maybe I should be put away to see if matters could not be improved upon; and that if Nicky still wanted to be with me, then Michael should be made Tsar. Nicky, after all, was little admired himself. People said he was indecisive and nearly invisible, and hadn't he even said he didn't want to be Tsar?

Well then, why not Michael ...?

... Because not one of Minnie's schemes, or of anyone else's for that matter, was going to come to fruition. As Nicky had once said to the representatives of the zemstvos, "Let go of your senseless dreams." I would have a son and I would thereby become the sole empress in the hearts of all.

So I endured my fourth pregnancy, my third to go to full-term. I went back to bed at Tsarskoe Selo, back to my wheelchair for outings, and back to all the misery I had yet to recover from ... and at the end of it, exactly as before, I was taken to Peterhof and brought to childbed with chloroform, and delivered of yet another daughter.

This time, however, when I awoke, Nicky wasn't even in the room. He had gone off for a long walk, "to give thanks to God, Your Majesty, for your safe delivery of a daughter."

I received a letter from Grandmamma, congratulating me on my safe delivery but regretting "a third girl, for the country's sake," as though I didn't know what this meant: another endless pregnancy, more waiting, more hoping, and more fearing.

I thought that maybe I was not going to be able to rise to this challenge again, and I certainly never wanted to see Nicky's mama or hear her thoughts on the matter of "my strange bareness," as she called it, then we received a telegram that Nicky's younger brother, his dear Georgie, had died following an ill-advised bicycle ride. Poor Georgie, who had suffered a long-drawn-out martyrdom from his consumption and who had lived all alone in the Caucuses to try to improve his health, was gone.

Nicky was devastated and pathetically read to me little notes he had saved from his childhood. He had always enjoyed Georgie's wit and had taken to writing down things Georgie had said so that he could quote them later. I stroked Nicky's dear head as he recited them.

Minnie was also devastated, of course. She had lost her son, her child, and I was fully inclined to be wholly sympathetic to her – I meant to be, I wanted to be – but then she made the villainous decision to use her terrible loss – Nicky's loss, too – to demand that he proclaim Michael as Tsarevich.

Nicky would have done it too, had I not stopped him.

"Nicky, if you do this, if you issue a formal proclamation that Michael is your heir, you will in effect be killing me."

He looked at me. "How?" his voice sounding far less concerned or startled than I had been hoping for.

I spoke through choking sobs. "If you declare Michael your heir, you are in effect saying that we have no son –"

"Alix, we do not have a son –"

"… And that we will never have a son, or at least not by me. Oh, I see now, that is it, isn't it, Nicky? You have finally chosen to see things your mother's way. Yes, of course, let us declare Michael as heir, then you can find a way of putting silly Alix and her useless little girls out of the way."

I was crying so hard that I had begun to choke on some of my words.

Nicky tried to interject but I raised my hand to stop him and gasped out, "No, no, don't protest. It is what all

166

of you want. Please go ahead, then, Nicky, and proclaim Michael your heir, and the day after you do so you can announce my death, for if you take my one hope away from me, the hope of bearing you a son, of bearing Russia a son, which is what God brought me here to do, my tired little heart will cease to beat. Go on, go tell Mr. Witte to write it up and have it published for all to hear. What are you waiting for?"

Nicky rose from his chair and walked heavily to the door.

Alarmed, I cried out, "You are, you are. That's just what you're going to do, isn't it?"

He spoke without turning.

"No, as you well know, that is not what I am going to do. What I am going to do is nothing. That is what I do best, after all, isn't it, Alix? That is what Mr. Witte, and mother, and you think too."

"No, I didn't say that. I didn't mean –"

His shoulders rose and fell, and he gave either a stifled chuckle or a sob – I couldn't tell which – since he refused to look at me as I suddenly desperately wished he would.

"It doesn't matter, Alix. Really, darling, do not upset yourself. I am doing exactly as you have asked of me and I am afraid that will have to be enough for you for now. I have just lost my brother. Now I have to betray the only other one I have left, and in so doing hurt my mother in her time of grief. But I am doing what you wish, so let us both try to find comfort in that, shall we?"

Before I could answer, or cry again, or throw something at his head, or hurl myself at his feet, he was gone and I couldn't follow him. I couldn't do what any normal wife in my situation could do, to rise out of bed and chase him down and finish our words. I wasn't dressed and there was a huge Abyssinian man standing right outside our door, one of four of them who had no other function than to open doors that Nicky and I wished to walk through. Oh, it could, and had to be, overlooked that these gigantic, cumbersome creatures doubtless overheard, and then discussed, every word of our private family life – that was simply to be expected. What could not have been overlooked would have been the sight of me, their Empress, running past them down the corridor in my nightdress, calling for Nicky.

I was locked, once again, behind the iron wall of Russian etiquette. I couldn't be alone, though, not feeling like this, so I rang for Maria and asked her to tell my maids to lay out a driving gown and to order the carriage. If I had not a single friend in the Alexander Palace, I did have some in Petersburg, and I was determined to see them immediately.

The Montenegrin princesses, Stana and Mitsia, who had helped me prise the crown jewels out of the Dowager-Empress in time for the coronation, had recently reached out to me again at a time when I was feeling most alone.

The princesses were known as the 'black peril' by the court. This charming appellation had been accorded them by Minnie, who unreasonably disliked both of the sisters because of their interest in the occult. I found her attitude quite backward and ridiculous, for my own grandmamma and mama had both been very committed to communicating with those who had passed beyond this plane of existence.

The sisters were the daughters of the King of Montenegro, a mere pinprick of a country that every crowned head in Europe habitually paid court to owing to its strategic position near the Balkans. Their elder sister had married the King of Italy and the two younger princesses had come to Russia to attend school at the Smolny Institute for Young Ladies. They were both very pretty – probably another reason why Minnie disliked them – and had, upon coming out, caught the eyes of Nicky's cousins. In Stana's case, she had married Prince George of Leuchtenberg; Mitsia had married Grand Duke Peter Nikolaevich, generally considered to be a bit of a nonentity but the brother of Nicky's colossus of a cousin, the Grand Duke Nicholas Nikolayevich, who commanded all of our armies.

I had never forgotten the sisters' earlier kindness and interest in me, so it was with genuine gratitude that I took up their invitation to tea at Mitsia's palace so shortly after the birth of Maria.

The ladies made a great fuss of me and said they were simply dying to see my little girls whom they had heard were creatures of great beauty and charm, and they couldn't compliment me enough upon my decision to nurse my babies personally and told me that in the Balkans, and in Italy as well, being a mother was considered a woman's highest calling.

I must say it felt perfectly heavenly to be the recipient of genuine praise for once. Also, I had not had any meaningful female companionship since my arrival in Russia and found it really wonderful to speak of new fashions in clothing and embroidery and to hear a bit of harmless chit-chat about some of the more scandalous behavior of the young ladies of the nobility.

Both princesses asked when Nicky and I were going to begin entertaining again at the Winter Palace and I hesitated before answering.

"Oh, I am not certain when. I mean, in the light of the way people in Petersburg regard me, I wonder if it is worth my going to all that trouble for them. Do you know that you two are the sole ladies of the court who have ever even thought to reach out the hand of friendship towards me?"

They gasped in unison and Stana said, "But Your Majesty –"

"Oh please call me Alix. I should so like that."

She smiled, delighted.

"Then Alix it is. As I was saying, there is not a person in the entire city who would not be honored to have the opportunity to meet you, but of course we all understand so well why you have been unable to put on entertainments for us all. You have been so busy having babies."

I nodded cautiously. "Yes … but … well, you see …" I blushed and looked down at my hands.

Mitsia jumped in.

"What is it, Alix? Is there a problem? Oh do tell us. We are all friends here."

"Well, you see … Oh this is a dreadful thing to say, but my mother-in-law, the Dowager-Empress that is –"

Their charming giggles halted me.

Stana said, "Minnie, isn't she simply appalling? Why, I do not know how many times Mitsia and I have been simply shocked at her ludicrous need to take precedence over you –"

Mitsia interrupted her. "And everyone knows that she tried to be placed in front of you on the prayers, and there was that crown jewel incident the last time we met, and –"

"And, really, isn't she the most dreadfully interfering woman in the world?" Stana finished for her.

I was astounded, invigorated and delighted. I had imagined that everyone adored Minnie, at least that is what Ella had always told me, so after that revealing exchange my life was immediately altered. If I wasn't visiting Stana and Mitsia in Petersburg, they and their own little ones were with me and the girls at Tsarskoe Selo.

Nicky, poor boy, was even more delighted that I had friends than I was and said as much that night in bed. My head was on his chest and we had been half-dozing to the sound of Maria's little snores, for she was still sleeping in our room at that time to make night nursing easier for me.

Stroking my hair, he said, "Precious one, I cannot tell you how light my heart is now that you and the pretty Montenegrins have become firm friends. I have been so worried that my girly has been lonely and I have been blaming myself for it. I am always so occupied by these cursed and relentless demands upon me and you are always left all alone. It has been terrible for you, I know, my darling."

I was so pleased to hear this that I teased him a bit.

"*Pretty Montenegrins,* naughty one? I see that I am going to have to watch you tomorrow evening."

I felt his chest rumble with laughter under my cheek.

"I suppose you are," he chortled. "It is difficult, you see ..."

"Difficult?"

"Well, yes. I mean, of course you are wondrously beautiful, but, after all, we have been married simply forever, and –"

Whatever he was going to say after that was cut off by my playfully punching him, followed by a bout of wrestling breaking out between us, so it was not until the next morning over the breakfast trays in our bedchamber that he brought up the sisters again.

"So, we are going to pay a visit to your friend Mitsia's tonight, but not for dinner. What is the occasion, Sunny?"

I was all too eager to tell him.

"Oh Nicky, you see Stana and Mitsia meet the most interesting people and they have a new friend whom they think we will like very much as well. His name is Msgr. Philippe Nizier-Vachot and he is both a doctor and a seer. He has come all the way from France, and –"

"What do you mean a *seer,* darling?"

"He can speak to those who have passed on, darling, and according to Stana he can do other things too."

Nicky put down his cup and eyed me sternly.

"I think speaking to the departed is quite remarkable enough, assuming, of course, that he truly can."

"Oh, it is true, Nicky. Why, Stana said even your cousin Nicholas has spoken to him and that he contacted his father, your grandfather, on Msgr. Philippe's behalf."

"Really? Nicholas Nicholaevich has met him? I must say, I am most surprised."

I hid my smile in my cup. Grand Duke Nicholas Nikolaevich – known familiarly as either 'Nikolasha' or the 'Dread Uncle' – stood 6'6" tall, had a voice like thunder, and was a boyhood hero of my still worshipful Nicky, and so Nicky was undoubtedly going to be impressed by Msgr. Philippe Vachot if he already had Nikolasha's approval.

"Sunny, what did you mean when you said Msgr. Nizier-Vachot could do other things?" Nicky asked.

I shrugged.

"Oh well, I do not know personally, of course. I mean I have not even met him yet …" I laughed, Nicky didn't, so I finished in a light voice, "Now, do try to keep an open mind, naughty one. Both Mitsia and Stana have told me that they know of women in his native France who have gone to Msgr. Philippe when they were pregnant and that he was able to change the sex of the child inside their wombs. Not only that but he can intercede with certain powers when a woman –"

Nicky was shaking his head. "Don't, Sunny. Let us not speak of this, darling. I thought we had agreed –"

I couldn't let him finish. I knew what he thought I had agreed to, that we would take precautions for a few years. Dr. Botkin did not feel I should attempt another baby for a long while, but I hadn't agreed to that, I just hadn't argued about it. Now I wanted to avoid a quarrel. I wanted Nicky to go with me and meet the man Vachot, and letting loose my anger on him would not help me achieve that. Nicky could be terribly stubborn when he set his mind against things.

So, to his obvious surprise, I smiled at him.

"Darling, I wasn't speaking for us, good heavens. I am far from ready to try for another baby." I snorted derisively. "I just think it is interesting, that is all. Mostly I was thinking how nice it would be if Msgr. Philippe could help me to contact Papa and Mama. I mean, wouldn't you like to speak to your own darling Papa?"

Nicky looked troubled.

"I often wish I could, but then, well, I remember that Papa never thought much of me, and anyway," he smiled adorably, "I hardly need to talk to his ghost when Mama does such a fine job of telling me what he would think if he were here. Why, it seems as if every other sentence out of her mouth starts with, 'Your father would have done this,' or 'Your father would have done that,' or whatever."

I broke out laughing, and then so did he, and both our fine moods carried us right through the day until the evening, when Nicky suggested that we take a sleigh ride into Petersburg as it would be "much more romantic."

So, as we entered Mitsia and Peter's palace to meet the man who would forever change the course of our futures, we were in the very best of spirits, which was appropriate enough considering the purpose of that evening,

Chapter 12

I am not sure what Nicky thought about our first evening with Philippe, as he had asked us to call him, but for my own part I was as one entranced.

Philippe didn't look at all as I had expected. I don't know why, but I always expect Frenchmen to be small and neat, and he was large and a bit shaggy, but compelling, oh so compelling, with his black piercing eyes and the firm, almost stern, way he had of delivering his sermons and guidance. I have to call them sermons because Philippe did not speak in ordinary ways, rather he made pronouncements on various far-ranging topics.

He told us that people who suffered from fits were actually speaking in tongues and could, if listened to carefully, reveal the will of God. He said that he had invented hygienic methods for women to give birth and had been given an honorary certificate to practice medicine by an American college, although his own country had not similarly rewarded him because, as he said, they preferred to embrace filth.

That at least made Nicky smile. He had been somewhat tense up until then because, as Philippe had insisted that we not call him 'Doctor,' so, in return, he had insisted on dispensing with our "cumbersome titles." Titles of all sorts, he intoned, weighed one down and kept one from behaving *naturally*. Nature was a great theme with him.

"If people behave with utter naturalness at all times, they will discover that God is speaking to them through trees, and grass, and even through their food. If they would only listen, then the entirety of the power of the natural world might then be imparted to them. For example, last week I became a blade of grass and found it so enjoyable that I might have remained in that state indefinitely, save that I feared being trampled upon."

I took my cue from Stana and Mitsia and their somewhat idiotic husbands, and laughed pleasantly, but Nicky was rather judging when he asked Philippe, "Are you saying, then, sir, that at any time you could become a bird, or a tree, or a cow, if you so wished?"

Stana tittered but she was quickly silenced by Philippe's fierce glare, before he answered Nicky with the utmost seriousness.

"I have at times been all of those and more, Your Majesty. If I may call you Nicholas –"

"You may not."

"Yes indeed – Nicholas. I have seen all the animals of the earth through their own eyes. I find that to do so broadens my knowledge, my understanding and my appreciation of them. Have you yourself never dreamed of being other than you are, or do you find that being Tsar is all you have ever wished for?"

Nicky, appearing momentarily stunned, replied somewhat hesitantly, "Well, I have always thought I might like to be a farmer. And no, it was never my wish to be the Tsar. But, you see, Msgr. Philippe, God rather foisted that upon me. Well, He and my father, so –"

"Yes, I have spoken to your august father many times, Nicholas, and he assures me that he is most pleased with your work as Tsar. As for being a farmer, you are that too. As the Father of all the Russian people, you till the soil of their lives and care for them as your crops. You are indeed a great farmer, sir, for one has merely to observe your peasants to observe that your crop flourishes."

I could see that Nicky had many questions but I wanted to talk to Philippe too and so asked him eagerly, "You have seen our peasants, then, Philippe. You have traveled through Russia, then? What did you like best?"

"I have not traveled throughout Russia in my corporeal body, Alix. I have done so through mind projection, which is a very freeing form of travel. Practical, too. I have many people to care for throughout the world and I am often called upon to heal them or to perform services for them, and I cannot just cross the sea willy-nilly at the drop of a hat, as the Americans say. But by knowing the secret of soul casting, I can be in Paris for breakfast, in Rome by luncheon, and in Siberia by teatime."

We all breathed a collective sigh of admiration and then Philippe stared at me with his black, probing eyes and leaned very close.

"You have this power in you too, don't you, Alix? You've always known it. The power to see into places and situations that you have never been a part of, to see, I believe, even into the souls and minds of others. You are no ordinary human being and indeed would be far from ordinary in any incarnation you might adopt, whether as Empress or as an eagle."

I felt transformed by his words and also oddly naked, for I had long suspected that I might have held a sort of power to recognize and see what others could not, although I did not answer him, not then. Nevertheless, he saw in my eyes that he was correct and I knew that we would subsequently discuss it all at greater length in private.

That wonderful evening ended all too soon and I, who was often too exhausted even to stir out of my bed on some days, found that I was filled with energy and a new awareness of the world around me. I shared this with Nicky on our sleigh ride home and commented to him that even the stars seemed nearer – did they not? – and wondered aloud if our new friend Philippe had ever visited any of them.

Nicky shifted uncomfortably beside me.

"I don't know, darling. Doesn't it seem to you that one might say or claim anything if one wishes, without making it so? I mean, I found him an interesting enough fellow, although I don't like his disrespectful form of address to us at all, but I am highly skeptical about his having ever spoken to Papa. I mean, Papa never said he liked anything that I did while he was alive. In fact, he often called me a muttonhead. Can death so easily have changed his point of view? Anyway, that blade of grass story seemed ludicrously far-fetched to me. Really, I think –"

I jerked as far away from him as the small sleigh allowed.

"Isn't that just like you, and just like all of your family, Nicky? If I like something, it cannot be right. I have friends for the first time since I have come to your ice house of a country, but your mother has declared them to be mad. I find a man of God who speaks of things beyond all the dreary disappointments I have suffered, and you poke fun at him. Well, I like him and I

178

want to see him again, and often, if what I like still matters to you even a little."

I couldn't help beginning to cry then. We'd had such a lovely time and he had ruined it all.

That night I asked him to sleep in his dressing room, and while I lay in bed alone, I tried to imagine myself as the eagle that Philippe had compared me to.

To be able to fly was so marvelous, and to be able at times to be anyone or anything I wished other than me seemed a gift beyond measure. I couldn't quite manage it, but there was a funny flutter in my chest that I had never experienced before; not pain this time, something else, something almost birdlike.

I fell asleep thinking 'maybe,' and that in itself was miraculous, for usually in those days I couldn't sleep at all unless Dr. Botkin had dosed me.

In the morning, Nicky was all contrition, and to show me that he was sincere, he announced that he had already had word sent to Stana and Mitsia and their husbands to come to the palace that night and to bring Philippe with them.

He finished by saying, "I have asked Mama to come too, darling. You are right and I am wrong. He is a special person and I am confident that she will concur. And if, through you, she meets a man who can enable her talk to Papa again, she will be very grateful to you and maybe you can finally be friends. I would like that so much."

"Oh Nicky, I don't know. Your mother is always so judge –"

179

He sat down on the bed and looked at me so searchingly that I couldn't bring myself to continue. I just shook my head and to my horror his eyes filled with tears. I reached out for his hand but he didn't give it to me, which was the first time he had ever ignored me in that way.

In a broken voice, the kind I hadn't heard since his father had died and certainly didn't like, he said, "Can't you try for my sake, Alix? I do everything you ask. You do not like the court, so we always stay here. You haven't invited Xenia here for ages because you say her boys are too rough. I do not see any of my family but Mama, and there is always an argument. I know she can be difficult at times ..."

I started to speak but he shook his head at me with uncharacteristic fierceness and I fell back on my pillows, aghast at his behavior. He could see this, but continued talking anyway.

"I love Mama, Alix, and I like to be with her. I miss her. You want Philippe and the black sisters, fine, of course, whatever pleases you. But why can't Mama join us too in the fun and then I can see her and –?"

"All right, Nicky. For heaven's sake, pull yourself together. Of course your mama can come. I don't know that she will have quite so much fun as you say, but include her. Have her come early to dine with us and then she can see the girls, too. I am sorry that you have been so upset by this."

He was immediately overjoyed by my capitulation and returned happily to his study while I went off to the bath Maria had drawn for me, rather less contented than he.

I had no guilt at all about my determination to maintain some level of family life and keep mostly to Tsarskoe Selo when we were not at Peterhof or on The Standart. I had been ill and I was not wrong to believe that I was forever the object of malign judgment. However, I did feel some guilt for my recent treatment of Xenia and that was why I had agreed to Nicky's request with regard to his ghastly mother. I loved Xenia, and I liked her husband Sandro too, and I knew that Nicky adored them both, but I simply couldn't see much of her. Xenia and I were always pregnant at the same time and now she had two sons and little girl while I had two more daughters and no sons. It was too much to ask of me to stare our different fortunes in the face. Besides, I truly did consider that her boys were ugly little brutes who were far too rough around my girls. That was indeed the case, but the less pretty thing was true as well, and so until I had my own boy, my feelings on the subject were unlikely to change.

If entertaining Nicky's horrid mother was the price of peace, then I would try. I did love him, I loved him utterly, but I wasn't happy, I had long known that. What I hadn't known until this morning was that he wasn't happy either and I found that this disturbed me a great deal. Nicky had to be happy with me. If he wasn't, it would mean that I had failed him as a wife, in the same way that it seemed I had failed him as an empress and as a mother, too. For though I loved our girls and took pride in nursing and caring for them myself, I knew no one else shared that pride. They called me the old woman who lived in a shoe; they called me bourgeois; oddly, they also called me barren, for having no boy was to most intents and purposes the same as having no children at all.

I had thought Nicky felt differently but now I saw otherwise and for a moment I considered simply letting myself slip underneath the scented water of my bath. Then I remembered that things were different now – or could be. There was Philippe. He had been sent to me and he was going to show me things unseen and he was going to do more for me: he was going to help me conceive a son. I knew he had sensed this too; a palpable connection had been established between us.

I sat up firmly and rang for Maria. I no longer felt tired or defeated. With his help I would show them all what I was truly capable of.

That evening proved to be a complete disaster, as it happened, though it started out better than I had hoped.

Minnie arrived an hour before dinner and made, for once, a proper grandmotherly fuss over the girls, and even held my baby Maria on her lap for a while. Whether she had been primed by Nicky to make an effort or she had decided to do so on her own account, I cannot say.

Minnie could be charming when she so wished, and she was the complete mistress of rippling small talk, and, to my relief, on this occasion, she forbore to say anything rude about Stana or Mitsia, or even to make a single mention of her upcoming meeting with Dr. Philippe, under which title I had decided to introduce him to her. Therefore, I allowed myself to relax over dinner and even to hope that the Dowager-Empress might also wish for our relationship to improve.

Subsequently, she greeted Stana and George graciously, and Peter and Mitsia, all of whom, I noted, seemed overwhelmed with delight to see her, despite their private avowals to me of disliking her.

However, she was visibly less accepting of Philippe and of the strange guest he had brought with him, to the extent that she immediately eyed him with suspicion and stared with open, shocked horror at the poor armless woman whom he was holding by the shoulder. When he failed to bow and asked her whether he could address her as 'Minnie,' as everyone else was doing, the Dowager-Empress I knew all too well was quick to emerge.

"You certainly may not. And what is that …. *thing* you have brought with you, Monsieur?"

He stared at her sadly.

"This is Matriona, Your Imperial Highness, a holy woman who sometimes works with me. I have brought her tonight so that all of you may hear the voice of Christ."

"How disappointing! I have, of course, always hoped to hear our Lord's voice, but I have never imagined that it would come accompanied by the sound of urination, which I see is occurring at this moment."

Horribly, Minnie was correct. The poor creature had indeed lost control of herself right there upon my prized Aubusson rug. I began to ring for a manservant, but was halted by the screams of the woman who had fallen over and was rolling back and forth in her own waste and deafening us all with her shrieks.

Minnie began to laugh hysterically.

"Oh, this is delightful. Thank you, Alix. Things are so terribly boring in Petersburg these days. Nicky darling, I'm so glad you included me and –"

Against all etiquette, Philippe interrupted her energetically.

"This is a very good sign, Alix. Matriona is in contact with Christ now. Please, Minnie, do be quiet so we can hear what she has to say."

I never admitted it, not to a still-cackling Minnie as she left, nor to a tight-lipped Nicky, but I hadn't really been able to understand the presence of Matriona either and it was all I could do not to agree with Nicky when he turned out our bedside light, saying, "Darling, this was most certainly a memorable evening, although next time I may fortify myself with a vodka or two beforehand, for I fear that one needs nerves of iron to withstand the company of that idiot, and of Philippe as well, for that matter."

Chapter 13

I hated to keep secrets from Nicky. We had yet to descend to any such compromises in our marriage, but I felt that I had no choice other than to do so now. I needed to see Philippe and Nicky did not wish me to see him. Worse, he made fun of him. That was Nicky too: he did love me but in his nature two opposite poles warred. I knew that he always loved me, but oftentimes his love was useless, for he also cared about pleasing his mother and so many others that it was said of him that he listened to all, but that he only ever heard the last person who had spoken to him.

I could even understand such a thing when it came to his bellowing uncles and the silly ministers, for with so many people talking at once, it would be very easy to seize upon the final argument and say, "There, it is going to be this way. Begrudge my decision if you will, but this is my final say." Yet I was his wife and I found it incredible that he could listen to anyone but me on matters regarding our personal lives and it surprised and hurt me anew each time that this happened.

So I do not blame myself for starting to tell Nicky that I was off to tea with Stana and Mitsia, while failing to mention that Philippe would always be there too, a lie of omission more than of commission, I suppose, although, if I had been forced to, I would have lied to his face, for Philippe was changing things utterly for me and I needed him.

"Alix, I have had a dream about you. Last night I saw you surrounded by your sons."

"Alix, I received a powerful vision on my way here. There was a great wave of trouble throughout Russia and you alone rose to save it. All hailed you as the greatest of the Russian rulers."

"Alix, last night I was visited by my spirit guide. He said to tell you that you must wait to conceive a child. The greatest of the Romanov tsars shall come from your womb, but he must be born with the new century firmly established. It is great ill luck to be born within this century. I do not know precisely why this should be so, but it has been revealed to me and so must be obeyed."

So naturally I had an urgency to see him and to listen to him. He had been sent to me by God – he had told me so himself – and if that were not true, then how did he know such things? Even Mitsia and Stana were reduced to silence in awe at his pronouncements and unselfishly did not spend any of our times with him to ask after their own futures.

As Stana said, "You are the Russian Empress, the Mother of our people. What Philippe says to you is of far greater importance than anything I might wish to know."

I knew, as did all of Russia, that her husband, Prince George, was unfaithful to her and that their marriage was a poor affair at best, and I can imagine that she would have very much liked to have known if a brighter future lay ahead of her, but she was right to choose to let Philippe concentrate on me. I never saw myself as much in and of myself, but what I represented mattered to all and Philippe helped me to lighten this terrible burden.

Dear Stana, she was indeed my good friend then.

Oddly, Philippe was not offended at Nicky's withdrawal. Indeed, like the man of great holiness that he was, he urged me to try to help Nicky carry his own burdens as he, Philippe, helped me carry mine, attesting that, "The Tsar's aura is clouded. I believe that he is a man carrying the heavy weight of his ancestors. Only a pure and enlightened spirit like yours, Alix, can help him in this present incarnation to achieve greatness. It all lies within you."

I protested that Nicky always wished first and foremost to prostrate himself before the will of God, but I learned from Philippe that to wish to serve God, even with one's whole heart, may not be enough. "No, I fear that in this case, the Emperor, by wishing to give into the will of God on all matters, is in actuality defying God who made him Emperor so that he could rule, and that he should not, as it were, abdicate his will to lesser mortals, if you see my point."

Sometimes when he spoke he would so lose himself that he would even lay his hands upon me. While I was unused to being touched, I did not find the sensation wholly unpleasant, as Philippe seemed to carry an odd sort of electricity which would pass through my own body at such times.

Nicky, who did not know that I was still seeing Philippe, did however notice how well I was that winter, he and our girls being the unwitting beneficiaries of my sessions with Philippe, for he made me strong and happy and unafraid of the future.

Because I felt better about myself, I felt better about all of them, and so I worked very diligently to make that Christmas, our last of the old century, a very beautiful one. I had a tree placed in nearly every room of the Alexander Palace, and even in the upper and lower servants' gathering rooms. The one I ordered for the day nursery I decorated all by myself, with tiny dolls and candies, and when I had my girlies brought in to see it, their little faces shone with wonder, and my baby Maria's great eyes went as round as saucers.

That was the Christmas when I started to observe the tradition of letting them sleep by their tree for the season. At four, my Olga was already quite the big girly and a year out of her crib and into her own camp bed, and I think my big little one might have missed her nice soft crib at times, but the camp bed was an inviolable and extraordinarily stupid Romanov tradition which I was powerless to change.

Long ago, some girl-child-hating Russian tsar had proclaimed that no Russian grand duchess must ever sleep in a soft bed until she was married, and that, in addition, she must begin each day with an ice cold bath. Nicky, being an ardent ancestor worshipper, insisted that this routine be upheld and so now my little one slept, or attempted to sleep, in a soldier's camp bed with a hard pillow. She seemed finally to get used to it, thank the heavens, and no longer tortured me with reproachful looks as she tried to make her tiny body comfortable in that silly contraption.

Tatiana was just two, and as Nicky said adoringly, a remarkably beautiful little girl. I thought so too, but I did not like to admit it openly, given her resemblance to me, which was striking, and not just in appearance.

Olga was obviously very intelligent and was already banging out little tunes on her miniature piano and had a very large vocabulary of words in which she expressed herself quite clearly. Tatiana was quieter than her sister but I fancy that she understood everything she saw and heard just as well as Olga, but, like me, preferred to keep her own counsel. The pretty little thing liked nothing better than to lean against my knees at every opportunity, and Nicky and I joked that we each had our very own shadow, for at the sight of him Olga would squeal out "Papa" and run after him as fast as her little legs would carry her.

Our baby Maria also promised to be quite a beauty as she grew. She had enormous eyes and the sweetest smile I had ever seen. The "big pair," as I had started to call them, were on occasion terrible to her, pushing her away from their toys after she had laboriously crawled over to join them and calling her "fat baby, bad baby" and such. I reprimanded them whenever I saw this and had instructed their nurses to do the same, but Nicky simply laughed and called it "nursery hierarchy," which he said would serve all of them well in later life.

I loved them all exactly the same, of course, though I can say with a small amount of shame that it was somehow easier for me to have Maria's bassinet taken upstairs to the nursery than it had been for her older sisters.

I never held their sex against them. I loved them absolutely, just as I loved Nicky, and we had a most joyous Christmas that year, and if I wasn't looking forward to the upcoming ball to greet the new century, then I wasn't dreading it either.

I had ordered a perfectly sumptuous gown from Worth which I fancied would set the ladies of Petersburg back a bit. It was in a heavy cream satin, covered from shoulder to toe with dark green beading, and with it I planned to wear my emerald set.

I even teased Nicky a bit about our opening polonaise.

"Now, darling, don't you dare put your hand on my waist. I have little confidence in Mr. Worth's seamstresses and I don't want beads scattering all over the ballroom. Can't you just hear now what everyone would say. 'The Empress made all of the ladies slip on her beads and break their ankles.' "

Nicky roared with laughter and pulled me close to him, holding me tightly.

"I had better get my hands on your waist now then while it is still safe for everyone else, Your Majesty."

Nicky was marvelous when he was happy, and when I was happy, and when our girls surrounded us there in the nest I had made for us. We were, I am certain, the most contented family in all of Russia, if not in the entire world.

Yet the world intrudes on ruling families, and so we gave our great ball on the last night of the century at the Winter Palace and, predictably, it was a disaster.

Count Fredericks was responsible for overseeing all the details and had issued two thousand invitations, all of which had been accepted. I chose, naively, to see this as a positive sign, a sign that the nobility had accepted me and wished to dance away the end of the old century with their revered imperial family.

I had even written about it to dear Grandmamma who had been rather cool towards us since our visit to see her three years previously, and she had happily written back to me.

> *Dearest Alix,*
>
> *I can't say enough about how terribly pleased I was to receive your dear letter telling me about your Christmas festivities with your dear Nicky and sweet little girlies. I am glad too, more than you know, my dear child, that you have returned to the Winter Palace for the season. You know I have long been concerned about your withdrawal from the court and the subsequent withdrawal of your husband. It is not good, Alix. One must remain near one's people.*
>
> *I know that if you were here you would say to me, "But Grandmamma, have you not kept to your own ways all these years since*

you lost your dear one?" If you were to dare to say such a thing to your old grandmamma, I would call you an impertinent girl, my child, but either way remember, child, that our cases are not the same. England is a stable country with a parliament, and it has a Prince and a Princess of Wales in place. I have not always been glad of Bertie, but the fact of his existence has, I will acknowledge, allowed me to live a much more private life than would otherwise have been possible.

You see, my child, what I am saying to you is that, beneath it all, beneath all the grandeur of our position, there lies an older and deeper duty known to queens alone.

I fulfilled that duty to my people and to my husband within the first year of my reign. Your dear mother-in-law did the same. Having fulfilled her duty, a queen may then decide upon how she wishes to be. Almost all ways are acceptable after that. However, until that time comes, my dear, do try to please both your people and dear Minnie.

My own dear daughter-in-law Alix has almost always been a comfort and not a disappointment to me in my later years, providing both me and the Empire with a son who has now had sons of his own, and this assures me that all will go well for us in the future.

I do not have long now, dear child, and I can say in all truth that I can begin to move happily towards that other world where my dearest Albert awaits me, with no qualms at all save for my concern for you, my sweet little Alicky. If I can move on with a glad heart and know that my own people live in a peaceful and prosperous country where the reign of my own family will continue for generations, could you, my dear, say the same were the moment suddenly to come upon you?

I know, my child, that this letter from poor old Grandmamma may not be what you might wish to read, and you may say to yourself, with great justification, that I am old and you are young, and all the world belongs to youth – and a great deal of it does indeed belong to the House you have married into. However, God, my child, He who in His wisdom decides the fate of both kings and paupers, has often surprised me and may surprise you too. The state of Russia is very bad, my dear, and at times I feel quite glad that I will not live to see

*much of what I fear may be a terrible new
century.*

*If you feel that you have tried your best,
your very best, Alicky, in the elevated
position in which God and fortune have
placed you, then ask yourself this: Is it
enough? Can I do better? What if I have
no son? What can I then offer my husband
and my people?*

*Try, my child. Try to be good to those you
rule. Try to show Minnie greater kindness
and the respect which is her due.*

*I am tired now and must rest before our
own great century ball, which I have
decided to attend despite the bleating of
the doctors, for I wish it said of Victoria
Regina that she did indeed try her best. I
wish it said of you too, beloved child.*

I remain your loving grandmamma,

Victoria R.

Oh I did love her so and I did take her words to heart.
I kept that letter with me for the rest of my life, and the
night of the ball I was aflame with an almost righteous
desire to show myself as the great empress I could be,
the granddaughter of the greatest queen the world had
ever seen.

I remember walking down the Jordan staircase at the Winter Palace and smelling the roses I had ordered from the Crimea and feeling the heat of ten thousand beeswax candles warm my bare shoulders.

Nicky's arm was firm under my own and his eyes were ablaze with love and pride, and when I saw the enormous crowd of titled and entitled nobles awaiting us, I did not flinch but proudly inclined my head and tried to smile confidently at them.

Their eyes, though, were like the glittering eyes of jackals. I could see their terrible malice, their dislike of me, reflected in their every smirking grin. I sensed their disdain for me as they passed by us in a reception line that seemed to stretch for a hundred miles.

"Your Majesty," a bare touch of cold lips on my hand, a half-curtsey, a stilted bow.

Not for Minnie, though, not for the woman who was standing right next to me, as ever in between me and my husband, and between me and the affection and reverence that was my due. For her and for Nicky, the men bowed until their noses practically dragged the marble floors and the ladies' curtsies were so deep that the old ones had to be helped back to their feet. Oh, the bright chatter and compliments that were so gaily offered, but not to me, no just "Your Majesty" to me, and then they dared to look at me expectantly as though I could think of something personal to say to them or to ask them, as though I could remember their names, let alone their titles, at that moment.

They all spoke in French that night and I could not understand them and I could not smile back at them because I was frozen with fear, and yes, with shame, for there is no feeling worse than to know one is disliked but not to know why. Except maybe that one does know, that it is because of one, the very essence of one, and how can one counteract that?

The room began to sway around me and I began to feel sweat gather at my forehead and under my breasts and arms, and Minnie hissed at my side in a whisper loud enough for those gathered near to hear and titter at, "You are all over blotches again, Alix. What in heaven's name is wrong with you?"

I couldn't answer, and suddenly all the people in line were gone, but I didn't remember having seen them pass me by, and Nicky was looking at me with concern and saying, "It is the polonaise, darling, our dance … They are all waiting."

I couldn't feel my feet, and I was collapsing against him, and he practically had to carry me past their ugly, strained, staring faces to a small anteroom off the great ballroom where he summoned Dr. Botkin.

I reached for Nicky's hand but he had backed away from me and was standing pressed against the wall as though he wanted to melt through it.

"Nicky?"

He placed his hands behind his back and shook his head.

Dr. Botkin rushed in. He looked funny in his tails and I managed a smile for him; I was already feeling better.

Nicky addressed him. "Dr. Botkin, I thank you for coming so promptly. Her majesty is ill. You can see that she is ill. Everyone saw … Well, I must return to the ball. Mother is waiting. They all are, you see. I must

196

return now. You'll see that her majesty is … is … returned, yes, but to her rooms. I must return –"

"Nicky, what is *wrong* with you?"

He wouldn't look at me directly. He would only face Dr. Botkin as he addressed me.

"I am sorry that you are feeling unwell, Alix. I think you had better let the doctor attend to you as I must return –"

With little concern for Dr. Botkin, who was an unwilling witness to this, I stood up and moved in front of Nicky practically to scream in his face.

"Yes, Nicky, you must return. You have made yourself quite clear. Which is a nice change for all of us, I am sure."

I saw Dr. Botkin flinch, but Nicky didn't. His eyes met mine and he smiled coldly. He had never smiled at me like that before.

"You seem better now, Alix. Maybe you would like to return with me, to the ball, to our court?"

I felt myself falling again. Nicky did not reach out for me, and if Dr. Botkin had not done so, I would have hit the floor.

Dr. Botkin uttered the words, "Your Majesty!" but whether he did so out of concern for me or out of disapproval of Nicky's callous behavior, I could not say.

What I can say is that I was all alone in our chamber at the Winter Palace when I heard the orchestra strike up for midnight and the bells began to toll from the cathedrals to celebrate the new century beginning.

Nicky cruelly insisted that we remain in Petersburg for another week as he said he wanted to meet with the ministers and wished also to attend the ballet, and that since we were going to have to be there for the sixth of January and the silly Blessing of the Waters, why inconvenience himself by traveling back and forth constantly?

The Blessing of the Waters was another anachronistic tradition instigated by that fool Peter the Great, whereby the Tsar approaches the edge of the Neva, where a hole in the ice has been carved, and gives his solemn blessing of the waters with all due pomp and ceremony, waters which the people will not actually see for months as Russia is locked down in her endless winter and will remain steadfastly so until May, or even later.

He made this decision without consulting me, saying only, "It seems to me, darling, that if you are going to remain in bed for weeks to recover from the ball, then there is a bed here as well."

We were at war, the two of us, and it was in this mood that I openly summoned Philippe to the Winter Palace to meet with me in my boudoir. This, of course, set off talk all throughout Petersburg, which was solely Nicky's fault, as if we had gone home to Tsarskoe Selo, I wouldn't have been obliged to behave so recklessly.

People – and by people I mean the lazy nobles who dwelled in Petersburg all season, sleeping till noon and dancing till dawn – had begun to gossip about Philippe.

It had all started when that idiot Yusupov, a nobody who had married Russia's greatest heiress and leading society figure, Princess Zenaida, had been taking his daily sleigh ride down Nevsky Prospekt and had waved to Mitsia and her passenger in their passing sleigh.

Mitsia, who had been riding with Philippe, declined to return his greeting, and that night, at one of the endless balls, Yusupov asked her why she had cut him, to which Mitsia foolishly answered that when she was with Philippe she was invisible.

Naturally that idiot Yusupov repeated this story to his wife, and by the next morning it was all over Petersburg, instantly creating a fashion for everyone to greet one another wittily by pretending to wonder whether they were indeed seeing the person standing right there in front of them.

I asked Philippe about this when he came to me and he shook his head in irritation.

"Alix, Mitsia is a foolish woman who did not listen to what I told her. What I said was that when she was with me, her thoughts were invisible to others, and that she was free to think what she wished about them and they would never be revealed. I did say that sometimes, when I am cloaking my own thoughts, my earthly body also vanishes from sight, but that is never a planned situation and not to be counted upon. At any rate, let us not speak of this nonsense, for I have had a vision and must impart it to you."

"Oh, Philippe, what is it?"

He stared at me so deeply that I felt he was reaching right into my soul.

"It is time for your son to be born, Alix. The Tsar, the great leader, he will come this year, or possibly next year, but the time is here and we must begin to prepare you physically for your blessed state."

Chapter 14

Philippe was very exacting in my care over the next few months.

After Petersburg, I was so distant from Nicky that, in order to placate me, he quickly returned to his previously loving state and argued on my behalf in front of his mother, in front of my interfering sister, Ella, and in front of his own sister, Xenia, who happened to be pregnant yet again, this time with the child who would doubtless be her fourth son, that I should be allowed to see Philippe. Indeed, he even agreed to my request that Philippe be given a set of apartments in the nearby Catherine Palace so that he could minister to me more easily.

Philippe's treatments were two-fold: At times he would insist on Nicky joining us and on the three of us seating ourselves in a darkened room in a precise geometric orientation that varied according to the vibrations that Philippe was sensing at the time. We would then hold hands and envision our son while plaintively invoking the help of our ancestors. At other times, Philippe, more pragmatically, used his medical knowledge to administer to me foul-smelling drinks while rubbing seaweed unguents upon my face and arms and insisting that my maid Maria add clams and kelp to my baths.

Maria, who clearly thought, as did many of the unenlightened, that Philippe was a charlatan, did not dare to come right out and say so, but took to sniffing theatrically whenever I was coated in his potions or whenever the seafood baths were prepared.

I attempted to explain it all to her, although why I bothered to do so, I do not know.

"Maria, the sea is the source of life for the entire world, and Philippe ... Doctor Philippe ... is helping me, as the mother of the future Tsar, to harness the power and might of the sea through these devices."

She shook her head and opened wider the window in my boudoir.

"Your Majesty will forgive me if I ask how a child can be conceived in a room that smells like a fishmonger's stall."

I was utterly shocked at her impertinence.

"Maria, you will apologize to me immediately, and, if you value your position with me, or indeed do not wish to end your days in Siberia, do not speak that way to me again."

She sullenly murmured an apology but the sniffing and eye rolling on my special treatment days did not end. I think maybe Nicky felt the same, but, if so, he was sensible enough to keep his thoughts to himself.

His patience and mine were rewarded, for on Christmas Day I was able to say to him, "He is coming now, dearest. I am pregnant. Our boy is here, my darling."

Naturally he was overjoyed, as everyone was. I think even Minnie and Ella felt that this pregnancy was the one. I felt it too, for I was completely well, in marked contrast to the trauma of pain and nausea that had accompanied my earlier pregnancies. Dr. Botkin said I was a veritable advertisement for the glowing mother-to-be, and it was true.

My pregnancy should have been spent just as Philippe had ordered, to be a time of serenity and blissful thoughts, but then, like a thunderbolt out of nowhere, I received the awful news that my grandmamma had died and I felt as though the world had shifted upon its axis. What could England be without her Queen and what was I but suddenly, once again, that wee orphaned child who was all alone in the world, save for the kindness of my dearest grandmamma? It seemed impossible to me that she was gone.

I must say this was also one of the rare instances where Philippe's wisdom failed to comfort me when he stated sonorously, "The great queen's death, coming at the beginning of this new century, foretells of a time of the greatest terror for the people who will live through it. There will be a blood-soaked time of inhuman cruelty and it will leave the entire human race with a new and dreadful knowledge of itself. I shall not be here to see it, I feel and know this, but there will be millions who will and who will envy those, like myself, who have passed over before them."

This was such a depressing statement that I felt, if anything, angered by it. I had just lost my dearest grandmamma and I did not need doom-laden predictions of worldwide catastrophes to come; I needed comfort.

Comfort was thin on the ground, though. Nicky declared court mourning for a month, which I felt was terribly short considering she was my own grandmamma, but he explained that it was the longest possible time that one court could "indulge" in mourning for the head of state of a foreign land. I was displeased and vowed to wear mourning for at least eighteen months in memory of her. A *Te Deum* was held at the cathedral in Petersburg and, to my embarrassment, I broke down utterly for the first time in public, whereupon not a single hand was outstretched to me or a sympathetic gaze thrown my way.

In fact, Mitsia later told me that she had heard that my mother-in-law was saying that if I could not manage to control myself in public, it was better after all that I "choose to remain hidden away crocheting doilies at Tsarskoe Selo."

I had so wanted to go to the funeral in England, if only to see and kiss her dear old face once more, but I was forbidden to travel because of my pregnancy, and so once again I was imprisoned by my position and by the dictates of others. I saw that I would never come first and I can admit that, at the time, I envied my perennially childless sister Ella her freedom of movement. It wasn't just my position or my pregnancies, it was that, over and under it all, we were surrounded by the most stifling rules imposed on us for reasons of protocol or security that at times they seemed more set up to monitor Nicky and me and to keep us from independent actions than to protect us.

I had fallen into a dark season in this pregnancy, this all-important pregnancy, the one which Philippe assured me would end with joy for both ourselves and Russia. I wanted to believe him, and at times I did, but at other times I felt lost and uncertain, and wondered what had become of me.

Worse, I had begun to wonder who I was. Everything seemed to happen so suddenly and in such unexpected ways. I remained Alicky, didn't I, my grandmamma's beloved childy? Yet she was gone now and I was still living in these rooms in this so very foreign ice-shrouded land where I was Empress in name but in truth of no significance whatsoever to the life of the country. I was the wife of the most powerful man on earth, but he had proven to be a small, frightened creature as overawed by his strange circumstances as I was, and worse, afraid of them. I was the mother of three children, but they were all little girls and no one, besides myself and Nicky, seemed to think that was a worthwhile thing at all. I lived quite alone and isolated, while millions of my subjects speculated upon my every thought and move, while knowing nothing about me at all.

At times I felt as though I were in a waking dream, or nightmare, and although Dr. Botkin and Philippe counseled me to be cheerful and to think only of the coming baby, I found it difficult to follow their advice.

Then none of my grief or confusion mattered one bit because my Nicky fell ill and his very life was threatened.

At first the useless doctors were too afraid to tell us the truth. They said he was suffering from a chill and from overwork, the cure for both being that he should go to the Crimea for a rest. I shouldn't have listened, for wasn't that the self-same thing they had told Nicky's poor father when he had fallen ill? Still, when one is frightened, one clings to doctors and to any advice, really, that might suggest a way forward.

205

So off we went on a long, excruciating train journey during which Nicky shook with fever chills and hardly seemed to know where he was. I was terrified, especially when I realized that it would be far preferable for me to lose my own life, for without him what would become of me and our poor little girls?

When we arrived in Livadia in the Crimea, Nicky's health was so obviously at a crisis point that the doctors were forced finally to admit that he had contracted the deadly disease typhus and, moreover, that they did not expect him to live.

The funny thing about Russia is that everything is a secret, no matter how inconsequential, and yet nothing is secret. So, within a day, the dreadful uncles began to arrive in Livadia, bringing with them that most pompous of ministers, Sergei Witte, mainly, I think, that he might be on hand to drive home their points lest their bellowing alone proved insufficient, their point being that Michael, Nicky's silly young brother, should be proclaimed Tsarevich and heir to all the Russias as soon as possible.

I received these terrible men, Minister Witte included, in the small anteroom just outside Nicky's bedchamber and they were so eager to have their way that they dispensed entirely with tact and personal consideration in their dealings with me, perhaps having decided amongst themselves that I was a person who merited neither.

Witte puffed away, swollen as always with self-importance.

"You must see, Your Majesty, that to leave the country in such a state of uncertainty with regard to its future would be unwise, as one might say, to the point of recklessness. The Emperor's illness, which his doctors inform me is of the most serious nature, is creating a crisis, or more precisely will create one forthwith should his heir not be named now. While, naturally, Grand Duke Michael is the *de facto* heir and Tsarevich to the Tsar, no formal proclamation of his position has ever been made, a situation that must be remedied immediately by this document that I have brought with me."

He then had the effrontery to proceed to extract this offensive document from among his papers and offer it to me as I struggled through my exhaustion and fear to find self-mastery and to harness my rage instead.

'Enough!' I said to myself as I threw out my hand to block these noxious papers, causing them to flutter across the floor. The looks of shock that shot across the faces of all present at my reaction caused me to laugh, if only in bitterness.

"Your words, Minister, make no sense, as I am certain that the Tsar's august uncles will agree."

I eyed them in turn – Uncle Vladmir, Uncle Paul, and my own brother-in-law Sergei. Not one of them would meet my eyes. Then I raised my eyebrows at them as if amused by something they had yet to grasp, although inwardly I was trying to stifle a rising scream.

"No, you do not agree, gentlemen? You are in fact in agreement with Minister Witte here?" Not giving them a chance to mumble out some two-faced namby-pamby answer, I continued, drawing myself up to my fullest height and lacing my words with a cold smile. "Aren't you all the most forgetful of messengers, then?" They rustled uncomfortably and I felt my confidence grow.

At last Sergei Witte, who seemed to be the most courageous of this Judas group, spoke.

"In what way are we forgetful, Your Majesty?"

I smiled back at him, this time in triumph.

"Well, in case you have chosen to forget her, there is Her Imperial Highness the Grand Duchess Olga Nikolaevna and –"

"Alix, don't you know that Salic law forbids –?" Sergei began.

I shook my head to silence him and continued.

"… And there is the son I carry in my womb."

I placed my hand protectively over my protruding belly and smiled with what I hoped was radiance, but my legs were shaking badly.

Grand Duke Paul seemed to recognize this and moved to my side as he addressed the others.

"Her Majesty is overwrought from caring for the Emperor. Here, Alix, please sit down," he said, gesturing to the only chair in the tiny room.

I did not want to sit down, which would mean having to look up at them, but neither could I keep to my legs a moment longer.

As I sat down, I felt the air thin in the room and found that I could barely breathe.

I would not look at them. I would not look up at these men, but neither could I cover my ears.

Witte began to address me again.

"While I speak for all of Russia, Your Majesty, in wishing you a safe and happy outcome to your present state, the baby's eventual sex can have no effect on the succession, should the Emperor ... should he ..."

He fell silent and Sergei finished for him.

"What old Witte here is trying to say, Alicky, is that if Nicky dies, God forbid, then it will not matter if you subsequently have ten boys. Michael will still be Tsar."

The room tilted around me as I struggled against the onset of a great darkness, yet I would not fall at their feet. To my added misery, my voice, when I could speak, came out high and querulous.

"Sergei, what do you mean ...? My baby is a boy. I know it because ... but no, that is not what I meant to say. I meant ... well, you see ... it is Nicky's boy ... so surely, when he is born, if Nicky isn't here ... I mean, then, Michael ... he will just be Regent for him ... and ... and ..."

I couldn't go on and I felt Sergei's hand on my shoulder. Silence surrounded me; no one, it seemed, wished to speak.

I heard someone clear his throat, but I kept my hands over my face. They would not see my tears, my terror.

It was Uncle Paul who eventually broke the silence while trying, I could tell, to be gentle with me.

"Alix ..."

My head jerked up and I heard, as if it were coming from another woman, a crone's howl.

"I am not Alix, not to you, not to anyone but Nicky. I am your Empress, and you will not ... you will not ... you –"

Uncle Vladimir finally entered the fray with his booming awfulness.

209

"Yes, Your Majesty, you are indeed the Empress, and it is wrong for us to address you with over-familiarity." I could swear I heard someone mutter "madness" under his breath, but maybe it was only my nerves playing tricks on me. The ghastly Uncle Vladimir continued as I forced myself to listen to him. "You see, Your Majesty, should the Emperor die, Michael will immediately be proclaimed Tsar of all the Russias. There has never been a protectorate for an infant in Russia's history and –"

"That is not true," I shouted wildly at him as I found my feet and stood up to face him. "Emperor Paul was –"

Vladimir had the effrontery to interrupt me. "… Deposed by his own mother who became Empress in his stead. Are you perhaps planning to organize a coup, Your Majesty, to gather the army behind you and to ride to the capital? If so, I can only point out to you, given … how shall I put it delicately? … yes, given your great popularity with the court and the Russian people, that this may not be an endeavor best suited to success. But then," he shrugged and smirked infuriatingly, "I may be wrong."

At that he bowed to me.

I held out my hand to Sergei. "Sergei, help me back to Nicky. I feel unwell."

He took my hand, but grudgingly.

"I see that you are unwell, Alix, and of course I shall take you back to Nicky, but you must understand that –"

I snatched my hand back from his.

"What I understand is that you are all my enemies, each and every one of you. That is less to my bad fortune than to yours, for I shall not forget this, nor shall I ever forgive it. Nicky is not going to die and I am carrying his heir, a boy, who will be the greatest Tsar this stupid, backward country has ever seen. He will be raised by me, gentlemen, his mother, your Empress, and he will hear how I was treated by you and he will remember it when your sons come looking to him for favors. Oh well, not your son, Sergei. You have no sons, do you?"

My speech was met with more shocked silence. I did not care.

Shakily, but proudly, I edged around them to the door of Nicky's sickroom and eased my way through it. Then, as I slid down the other side of its paneled surface, obscured from their view, I reached behind me and bolted the door shut with a distinctive ratcheting sound that they must have heard in the silent chamber I had just left in which they were no doubt lingering foolishly for a while before gathering themselves to depart for a larger chamber better suited to their plotting.

I watched Nicky from my place on the floor. He looked so small and pale that it was if he were dead already. I was too weak to get to my feet, so I crawled over to his bedside and clasped his hot hand against my face. He burned like a furnace and in that heat I felt the strength of his life force. My son happened to move inside me at that moment as well and I suddenly knew that everything would be all right: Nicky was not going to leave me … leave us … not then.

I knelt beside him and moved his limp hand over to my stomach. "Feel, darling, feel our son. He wants to meet his father. He needs his papa. I need you too, my love, my one-and-only. Come back to us. Please, Nicky, please, my dearest one."

He sighed and murmured my name. I looked quickly at him but his eyes were still shut. Still, he knew. He had heard me, and from that moment on, no matter how much the doctors repeated their dismal prognosis for his survival, or how hard his mother and sisters cried and wrung their hands, I knew he would get well. I knew because I wanted it and Nicky could never deny me anything.

I was right, too, for within a week he had begun to rally. Oh, they all feigned the greatest delight at his recovery, throwing around such sentiments as "It is God's will" and "Our prayers have been answered," but I knew that what they had really been praying for was his demise and I made sure that Nicky knew that too. He hung on my words as I sponged his dear face and as I fed him healing broths. I let no one else near him. Then, as his strength returned, his gratitude towards me grew and, if such a thing were possible, so did his love for me.

It was during those weeks, I think, that he finally began to understand that there was no one other than me he could trust, no one else who truly cared for him and who loved him in the way he so badly needed to be loved, for himself alone

He said as much on our long, slow train ride back to Tsarskoe Selo.

"My wify, she is hubby's only joy and truth. You saved me, my darling, my angel. They wanted me to die so they could have Michael as their tsar. You were right, Sunny. You have always been right, and poor hubby has wronged you if I ever thought differently. It is all changed now, darling. I know whom to trust. We are all alone in this world but for our girls and the little boy you will give me, but God is on our side and that is all that matters. You and God are all that matter to me now, Sunny, and I shall never change."

We had returned to Tsarskoe Selo in the spring and every lilac bush greeted us with its glorious rain-wet scent that filled my beloved rooms. We would not travel this summer, Nicky decreed. Our son would be born at the Alexander Palace in the same room in which he himself had been born thirty-three years before. All there was for me to do, he said, was to rest and to await our son.

I did just that, but it was different for Nicky. His illness and the events surrounding it had changed him somehow. He was harder and more suspicious of people than before. He had never liked Witte but now he openly detested him. He had always feared his uncles, and perhaps still did, but now he began to refuse to receive them, giving instructions that they must make appointments for audiences with him through Count Fredericks who was ordered in turn to refuse them.

Witte was frightened because he saw his power beginning to wane. The uncles were enraged, but what could they do? Minnie, I fancy, was beginning to become unsettled by this as well, for in truth Russia could only have one Empress and I was the wife of the man who ruled Russia, and that same man had learned that there was only one person in the whole of this vast land who loved him, and I was that person. Moreover, it was I who was going to give Russia her heir, so that Minny, for all her plotting and planning, would soon be retiring to the shadows.

Chapter 15

In late May we decided to move to Peterhof after all. The heat at Tsarskoe Selo was stifling and, deprived of a beach, the girls had become terribly restless and disruptive, and their constant whining was driving me mad in my condition.

Nicky too was bored with our little house, I think, although he tried not to show it, and had become nearly as prickly amidst the heat and the boredom as the girls were. So I felt that, since we had foregone our annual cruise and our customary summer retreat to the Crimea, we should decamp to Peterhof as a sort of holiday anyway. As I explained to Nicky, our son could just as easily be born by the sea as in the park.

He seized on this idea so eagerly that I felt somewhat annoyed with him, but then, with an effort, I reminded myself that no man can understand the sanctified feeling of impending motherhood and that even the mother of our Savior was forced to travel far in the latter stages of her pregnancy. Thinking of Mary cheered me considerably as we made the arduous shift of an hour south to the coast, for hadn't she had the happiest of outcomes following her difficulties? Moreover, Msgr. Philippe, who continued to provide me with great solace and wise counsel, assured me that this move would create for Russia an even stronger heir, one who would one day rule the seas as well as the land.

Philippe seemed to settle into life at Peterhof nearly as well as if he had actually been born there, explaining to me that it reminded him of the South of France and was therefore a place of joyous familiarity. He seemed to feel this familiarity rather excessively as far as I was concerned, for he tended to spend the days pursuing his own interests and often did not join me on my chaise until late afternoon.

Two days before giving birth, I summoned him to my balcony to relate to him a disturbing dream of the night before. I had dreamt that my child was a girl and, more bizarrely, that she had been born as a fully-formed young woman, with streaks of blood upon her face from the womb she had crawled out of. Upon leaving my body, she had stood over me and held out her stained hands imploringly with a look of terror upon her face. I had woken up, gasping, and it had taken me hours to fall back to sleep.

He listened quietly as we sat together overlooking the deep blue gulf, but his face was troubled when he spoke to me.

"Alix, our dreams are things sent to us, not by the subconscious as that madman Dr. Freud in Austria would have us believe, but by either God or the Devil. We must accept this, and if we accept this, we must examine our dreams carefully in the fullness of our spirits. Your dream is one in which many things are being foretold and in many ways."

I revered the great Dr. Philippe, I really did, but at times the vagueness of his statements drove me to distraction, and this was one of those times, so, a tad impatiently, I snapped at him. "Yes, well, you see, Philippe, that is why I summoned you, so that you could untangle the dream and explain it to me so that I could cease to worry about it."

He sighed and closed his eyes for a long time, then his breathing grew into rasps and he began to rock backwards and forwards. Just before I rang for Maria to fetch Doctor Botkin, he fell back against his chair and exhaled loudly, his eyes bursting open in an alarmed way. He turned to me and abruptly seized my wrist, his eyes wild. Involuntarily, I tried to jerk back from him but his grip was like iron, and cold, despite the sun.

"Alix, did you tell Nicky ...? Did you tell him about Serafim?"

"What? ... I ... Who is Serafim? What do you mean, Philippe? And please do not call the Emperor 'Nicky.' You know he doesn't like it."

Philippe stared at me as if it was I who had run mad.

"*Who is Serafim?* May God help us in our dark hour, Alix, because –"

"No, Philippe, you mustn't say 'dark hour.' You promised ... my son ... my ..."

He shook his head and released my wrist. Turning his eyes towards the sea again, he spoke heavily.

"Serafim of Sarov was a great holy man, a worker of miracles. I have all along been asking for his prayers and help for you to give birth to a son, but I see you have ignored my request that he be honored by canonization through the Orthodox Church, and those who turn their faces from men of God turn their faces from God himself and cannot expect His help at such times. Oh Alix, I fear you have not been faithful to our contract."

I fell back with a gasp, my heart beginning to skip. What did he mean? I had never heard the name Serafim before in my life, and I told him so.

217

"Philippe, this is madness you speak of. When did you ever tell me of this supposed holy man, and –"

His voice thundered at me, "In your dreams, Alix. I have spoken to you of nothing else every night. Why have you ignored me?"

I was thrown into confusion.

"But, Philippe, I do not recall any dreams about –"

He leapt out of his chair and paced before me, wringing his hands.

"You do not recall them or you have ignored them? Yes, that is what I now understand, and that is why the young woman in your dream was crying. She saw, too. She was doubtless a messenger from the Holy Mother who grieves at your lack of faith in her chosen ones. I cannot predict what will happen now. It is doubtless too late to have Serafim canonized and so, Alix, you must prepare yourself for the possibility that the child inside you has been transformed from male to female as a warning that you must always heed my words."

I began to shake as if with ague and stared up at him pleadingly.

He sighed again, sat down heavily beside me, and took my hands, gently this time.

"Yes, it may be so and we must prepare ourselves for the eventuality. But do not lose all hope, Alix, for if God is not too angry, you will still have a son and then of course you must immediately canonize Serafim, as I have been asking you to do. If the child has indeed been turned, then you must heed this and do as I have said, and He will give you a son one day."

I couldn't speak for fear and disappointment, and yes, I will admit, anger too, but as I sat there shaking, I had to ask myself at whom my anger should be directed – at my true friend and healer Philippe for not trying hard enough to penetrate my dreams or at myself for closing myself off from his messages?

Philippe, as he always did, seemed to sense the drift of my thoughts and his fingers began to toy softly with mine.

"Alix, you cannot, and must not, blame yourself. Could it be perhaps that one who is closer to you even than I has sown in you the seeds of doubt, of skepticism?"

He meant Nicky. It could only be Nicky, Nicky who had indeed made slighting remarks about Philippe, remarks that I knew had been inserted into his mind by his dreadful mother who told all and sundry what a charlatan my friend was and what a credulous fool her poor son had married. I understood all then, but out of loyalty to my husband I did not share my thoughts with Philippe. I merely nodded before rising and ringing for Maria to prepare me for bed, for I was tired far beyond mortal exhaustion. Once again I had given over my body to bring forth Nicky's heir and had suffered great physical and mental anguish in so doing. Yet, despite my selfless sacrifices, the smallest props which held me up were being scorned by everyone around me and pulled from beneath me.

I confronted Nicky when he came to bring me my tea, recounting to him the entirety of my conversation with Philippe. To my everlasting horror, he laughed, and actually spat out his tea as he did so.

"Pardon me, darling, but you must realize this claptrap is the most ridiculous attempt at self-justification anyone has ever heard of. Please assure me that you do." Not giving me time to answer, he smiled complacently at me. "He reminds me of Witte, actually. If all goes well, all credit goes to him. If, on the other hand, we face failure, it is because I have apparently forgotten some key piece of advice of his and therefore I am the one who must shoulder the entire blame for whatever fiasco he has dropped me in. Ah Sunny, it seems that we are forever to be targeted by all and sundry. Fortunately –"

"Fortunately nothing, Nicky. How dare you compare that stupid old politician of yours and your mother's to Philippe, a holy man and my only friend in this world?"

I couldn't continue for my sobs.

There was a long silence, which surprised me somewhat, and when I looked up from my pillow, Nicky hadn't moved to comfort me. He was merely staring at me with an expression I could not puzzle out.

"Why are you looking at me that way?"

He shook his head a little. *"Your only friend,* Alix? Am I not your friend?"

I couldn't bear it, I really couldn't. Was I to be accused and wrong-footed by every living person I came across that day … and so near to my time? I was simply not up to another wrangle, and as soon as I realized this, I felt my heart begin to jump jerkily about in my chest.

I clutched at it and stared helplessly at Nicky, unable even to cry for help.

This time Nicky looked properly alarmed, fearing no doubt that he had killed me, as he so nearly had. He

220

jumped up and rang the bell, and then, too panicked to wait for a response, he threw open the door and shouted for Dr. Botkin who came right away and administered a soothing potion to me and doubtless a stern warning to Nicky.

When I awoke late that night, Nicky was all concern and love, and when I asked him to contact the Metroplitan as soon as possible to discuss the canonization of Serafim of Sarov, he could not consent quickly enough, whereupon I felt a peace and calm stealing over me and realized that now I was in God's hands and must prepare myself to await the results of His verdict.

That verdict came two days later in the form of my fourth daughter. Nicky chose the name Anastasia for her. I was far too ill to care one way or another.

Chapter 16

Nicky told me that he could not have been more pleased. Xenia, who had just delivered her fifth son, told me that she envied me, as she despaired that she was ever going to have another little girl to be a companion to her Irina. Olga, Nicky's younger sister, told me she envied anyone with any babies at all. Mitsia and Stana asked to be Anastasia's godmothers, a wish I granted without interest, and Philippe told me that we must now seriously address ourselves to the canonization of Serafim of Sarov, for he saw that my son was seated in heaven, awaiting this event, before being willing to appear in Russia.

I think, given all this, I might have abandoned all hope, if it hadn't been for Nicky's darling mama deciding to pay me a visit, although from my vantage point her magnanimous gesture appeared to provide her with an opportunity to gloat more than anything else. There again, it has been said that one man's bread is another man's poison, so I suppose I should not judge her too harshly; I will leave that kind of judgment to her.

The Dowager-Empress bustled in, all rustling in her black silks. She wore black a great deal, not necessarily for mourning, but because it suited her dark eyes and hair so beautifully, making it all the more ironic that she insisted on referring to my only friends Mitsia and Stana as "the black peril" for sharing her coloring, but that is neither here nor there, I suppose.

I smelled her before I saw her, as I had decided beforehand, if possible, not to open my eyes during her visit. Minnie tended to adorn herself with a strong attar of roses, which she mistakenly believed reduced the smell of tobacco which clung about her as she was a chain smoker, a rare accomplishment for a woman of her class and times, but then Minnie was a rare woman indeed.

As soon as she entered my bedchamber I felt my head begin to pound, but whether it was from her odor or her presence I cannot be certain, and my sad little defense of pretending to be asleep was summarily ignored.

"Alix, I have come to congratulate you on the birth of yet another daughter. You have now produced more daughters for our House than nine or ten of the previous empresses combined." I shuddered involuntarily. "Ah, so you are awake, then. Good. I shall ring for some tea, shall I?"

I didn't answer or open my eyes but I heard her taffeta rustling and then, within a minute or so – as the maids all revered her and responded with amazing quickness when she was about – I recognized the sound of the tea cart being wheeled in.

I waited, still trying to keep my eyes squeezed together, head and heart pounding, as she gave directions to the maids and then shooed them out.

I sensed her leaning over me and smelled tea and felt heat.

"Here, Alix, I have poured you a cup of tea. Let us please stop this pretense. Sit up and take the cup. I am not leaving until we have spoken, so the sooner you join me, the sooner we can end this *tête-à-tête*, if your mastery of the French language stretches that far."

I opened my eyes and reached up to push the offending cup away, which caused it to spatter her with hot tea.

She didn't even flinch.

"Good. You are up. Let us speak."

I couldn't, I simply couldn't. I shook my aching head, which caused the room to tilt.

"No, Mother Dear, forgive me, but I am too ill. I am most grateful that you came to visit me, but —"

"Yes, of course you are ill. You usually are, aren't you, dear? Pity. Well, I shall speak and you may listen."

I shut my eyes again.

"I will take that as your assent, Alix, and if you have anything else to add, you can simply rap your knuckles on the bedstead, once for yes, twice for no. That is how those of you in the spiritualist community communicate, if I am not mistaken."

I didn't answer but I'm sure she noted my reddening skin.

"I am not here, Alix, because I want to be. Do not assume that you are the only one here who is uncomfortable. I am here because there is no one else left who is in a position to speak to you frankly now that your grandmamma is gone and you have terrified my son into catatonia."

I roused myself.

"*Your son? Your son?* Your *sons*, don't you mean, Mother Dear? Surely this visit is really about your wanting to bully Nicky into naming Michael as his official heir as I have no sons, and you, of course, have so many."

She met my gaze squarely.

225

"I have two sons, Alix. One is the Emperor, and I worry for him daily. The other is young and untested, and I do not, despite your implication, dream of the death of one of my remaining children in order that the other may rule Russia. You do realize, don't you, that that is what you imply when you say such things?"

Feeling a rare sense of shame, I looked down and twisted my hands nervously.

"I am sorry, Mother Dear, I did not mean that –"

She waved off my half-hearted apology.

"Oh, I'm sure you didn't, Alix. And please call me Minnie. We are far beyond pretense here, are we not? I do not believe you mean to be cruel, Alix. I do not believe you have meant any of the things that have befallen you. The problem is that you simply cannot see beyond your immediate wishes to the larger picture you are painting for our country, and that picture is looking grimmer by the day."

"This is because I haven't had a son, isn't it?"

She looked at me with genuine puzzlement.

"Of course not. Who cares if you have a son? My elder son is only thirty-three and he has a surviving younger brother. His uncle, Grand Duke Vladimir, and his wife Miechen have produced … what … five sons. His brother, Grand Duke Paul, has one … and, oh for heaven's sake, Alix, the one thing the Romanovs are not short of is a male heir. They positively grow on trees, the family tree in this case. A son … good God … I mean, of course it would be nice for you and Nicky to have a son, but the existence or lack of a son born to you does not threaten the dynasty, whereas your actions do."

This was too much even from her. I sat up, despite the pain to my skull as I did so.

"And how, if you do not mind me asking, have I done this?"

She smiled thinly.

"I am delighted that you are willing to hear me out, and remember you did ask." She settled herself comfortably and I felt horrified, but what could I do? I was actually trapped in my own bedchamber. I, the Empress of Russia, was powerless, and only she, the dreaded Minnie, could make me so.

What an odd realization. There was not another living person on earth, including my own dear husband, who would ever dare to say a single thing I didn't wish to hear, no one alive who had the rank to do so, except Minnie. If Minnie were gone, this could never have happened and I would be safe.

This thought made me ponder this welcome circumstance even as I was forced to hear her erroneous opinions, couched of course, as such things always are, as caring advice.

"Your decisions, Alix, and let us not pretend that they have been anyone else's, have driven my son as far away from his court, and necessarily therefore from his people, as one could imagine, save if you had actually persuaded him to move to Hesse-Darmstadt. Although I must say," she paused to look about my room with obvious distaste, "you have certainly created here a charming approximation of a German hausfrau's idea of domestic heaven."

I hated her, she knew that, so there was no point in saying a word.

She acknowledged both my emotion and lack of reaction with a tilt of her head.

"Nothing to say, then? Fine. I shall continue. You see, my son, as your husband, and possibly even as your servant, which would of course be all fine and good if he were indeed the German burgher which you have turned him into –"

This was too much for me tolerate, even from her, and I spat at her, "Minnie, you seem to be somewhat overheated and a trifle confused. I think you will find that no one alive sees Nicky as anything but the Tsar and Autocrat that God has made him. Your comments are ridiculous at best and treasonous at worst."

She merely raised an eyebrow.

"Ah well, Alix, if so, perhaps you should persuade him to send me to Siberia. That would surely only increase your popularity."

"You see, Minnie, this is where you and I differ. I do not, as an Empress, feel the need to pander to popular opinion, whereas you, as a *Dowager*-Empress, clearly do."

She laughed and my fury was such that I felt my heart begin to pound in what was obviously a truly life-threatening manner. I nearly put a halt to our encounter by ringing for Botkin, but somehow she knew what I was thinking, like the old witch she so truly was.

All false concern, she asked, "Are you about to have one of your spells, Alix dear? If so, do not worry. I shall wait until you feel more yourself again. You see, the threat of your hysterics does not cause me to run away in fear as it does my poor son."

I sat up in agitation.

"Yes, that is right, Minnie, *your son*. If you see Nicky as some poor, weak-willed little boy masquerading as a man who hasn't a thought or action in his head that I did not put there, then whose fault is that? Who is the one who taught him to be so easily dominated by a woman? It is in fact untrue that he is, but if it were true, shouldn't all that be laid at your feet?"

Her face became serious but not angry, and she leaned forward.

"You are not asking me anything that I haven't asked myself, Alix, and maybe you are right, I don't know. Sasha, Nicky's father, was such a powerful presence in the lives of all of our family, and Nicky was afraid of him, and I did often step between them to protect my son, and I wonder now whether, if I had not, he would be more able to face arguments and stand up for things he believes in."

I was too angry to find her admission softening.

"I see. Well no, I don't, actually. You are speaking in riddles, Minnie. What does Nicky not stand up for that he believes in?"

"Duty to his country first, above duty to you, Alix."

"Duty to his country by your estimation, Minnie, which, if I understand it, means opening the Winter Palace for the season and holding and attending balls, which is, of course, the God-given demand an Emperor and this consort, by which standard Nicky and I can only be deemed to have failed, but –"

"Oh but nothing, you silly girl. Is that how you really see it, because –?"

229

"Of course that is how I think you see it, Minnie, but Nicky and I share a faith in God and know that the real Russians, the peasants, love and revere us and –"

"No, they don't, Alix. They do not know you, and yes, the balls and receptions matter because Nicky needs to see and hear from the people, and, unfortunately or not, depending on your viewpoint, the Autocracy is made up of people who hear from lesser people, who hear from the least, and it is all filtered terribly by the time it gets to us, but at least it is better than pretending there are no people in the world other than yourselves. And as for God –"

I felt I was on much firmer ground here than my frivolous mother-in-law.

"Yes, and as for God, Minnie …? Do tell." She stood up and began to shake out her skirts. I raised my eyebrow curiously. "Ah, then you are leaving? May I take this as an agreement that when it comes to matters of faith –"

She shook her head dismissively.

"No, you may not, Alix. Unlike you, I do not view God as my personal assistant, as a sort of secretary who spends all of His time deciding who and what is best for me alone. I am an Empress, as are you, because long ago some ancestor was either handed the crown by a pandering nobility or had the temerity to pluck it off the head of his predecessor whom he had no doubt just defeated in battle and butchered. God watches over us, I guess, but no more so than over the sparrow in the field. Nor do I believe he will intercede if hubris brings us to our knees. He may see all but that does not mean he will choose to do much about what he sees."

I was shocked.

"You are impious, Minnie, and moreover you are silly. My own grandmother did not show herself to her people for decades, but when she did –"

"… When she did, they undoubtedly enjoyed the free food and drink, and then forgot all about her existence for another decade or so, I imagine."

"That is not true, and –"

Minnie pulled on her gloves and reached for the door, but one of the Abyssinians, who I think must have spent their lives with their ears pressed to the wood, anticipated her and opened it, standing there large and impassive. Minnie nodded at him and smiled, and I fancy that I saw him blush with pleasure even under all that black skin.

She did not let his presence deter her from a parting insult.

"It is true, but it does not matter anyway because the English people know that no fortune or misfortune that befalls them comes from their Queen or the King. They are just figureheads and pictures to them. Blame and approbation fall upon the government. Russia does not have a government, save the Emperor, so you work it out, Alix. Whom do you think the people blame when things go badly wrong for them? No, don't say another word. I have wasted my time here and I shall now complete that waste of time by stopping in to see my son, who will no doubt ignore my advice as well. I will say this though, Alix. I have picked up an invaluable idea from you."

"Oh yes?"

She smiled brightly at both me and the, I am certain, embarrassed Abyssinian.

"Yes, I have decided that when I return to Anichkov today, I shall feign a heart attack and take to my bed with brandy and sal volatile indefinitely."

She giggled girlishly on her way out and I swear that I heard the stupid black man chuckle, but then I comforted myself with the impossibility of that. He couldn't have understood. None of our people could, nor did they seek to. Minnie was, as always, wrong-headed. I understood that, and so did Nicky, and most importantly, so did God.

Oddly, instead of pushing me further down into my depression, Minnie's visit galvanized me. Over the next few days I began rising and dressing and joining Nicky for lunch again. This pleased him greatly, although I know he was worried about me. I would catch him casting me covert looks when he thought I was otherwise occupied.

I did not address this with him. I felt no need to reassure him about my renewed mastery of myself. Soon enough he would understand.

For while I did not agree with a word Minnie had said to me, what I did see was that my prestige as Empress was at an all-time low, otherwise how would she have dared to speak to me in such a manner.

It has always been my way to disregard what others say about me and to look to the reasoning behind why they have said it. Philippe had noted this ability in me early on, and a few days after Minnie's visit he came to see me and I shared with him the whole of the indignity I had suffered.

As was his way, he did not speak at first but only stared off into space, drawing his spirit guides to him for answers. Finally his face cleared and I knew that he was back with me. He turned towards me, his dark eyes burning in his oddly attractive face.

"Alix, do you understand what the Dowager-Empress was saying to you?"

I shrugged, for I did of course, but I preferred to hear his interpretation before answering him.

"The Dowager-Empress is so clearly jealous of you and of her own son that she has decided to try, with the help of the evil men and women in Petersburg, to depose you and her son, and to take power for herself. We must not judge her in anger, but rather in pity, for she has fallen slave to pride and hubris. She hopes to discourage you from having a son of your own, to make you see your husband as a weak king, and to allow matters to drift along until her moment comes when she will wrest the crown from your hands."

Philippe had so neatly echoed my own views of Minnie's motivations that I was momentarily speechless with astonishment. Philippe was indeed a man of unique gifts.

Not bothering to hide my admiration, I beamed at him in pleasure.

"Yes, what you say is true, Philippe, but I find myself at a loss for I do not know how to counter the malicious gossip in Petersburg and I am uncertain of what to say to Nicky regarding political matters, for though I of course have opinions, I have no experience and –"

233

"You do not need to look at questions of ruling yet, Alix. In fact, I foresee that your entry into the political sphere would be greatly resented at this time. Even Nicky, the Emperor, might not wish for it as he is, I fear, feeling put upon by the judgment of others and would treat your offering him advice as more of the same. No, your sole role at this moment is to give him a son, which will increase his confidence in his autocratic powers and divinity, and which will, at the same time, grant you the popular confidence of the people, which will allow you to take all the power you wish for yourself."

Oh, I knew he was right but how I hated knowing it. I did not even want power. All I really wanted was to be left alone to try and have some sort of happy family life with Nicky and our little girls. Moreover, I utterly dreaded the idea of another pregnancy.

I was thirty years old in that sad year of 1902 and I had endured five pregnancies. They had given me four daughters and a miscarriage. My health was ruined, my figure had become, I feared, permanently matronly, and after all my suffering and illness and struggle there was not a single person alive who had said to me 'Well done, Alix. Look at that lovely family you have created. Thank you for these beautiful children for Russia.'

Other women were allowed simply to be happy in their motherhood, to enjoy their labor of love. Not I. I alone was forced to lay in bed, exhausted, time after time after time, and shudder at the sound of the gunfire welcoming my children into the world. One hundred and one shots. So many and so loud, but not nearly many enough.

No, the world, and yes, my own sweet husband waited for the hundred and second shot which would indicate two hundred more to come, which would mean that I had finally done something right and worthwhile, and knowing this made me hate my life and myself, and still, most pitiful of all, to long to accomplish it. But how? How does a woman have a son, or more to the point, how could *I*?

I stared at the portrait of Marie-Antoinette that I kept in my boudoir beside the one of my mother and grandmamma – three women of ruling houses. Marie-Antoinette had given her country a son, but late, too late to regain public approval. My mother had produced sons, but one had died from the terrible bleeding disease that ran throughout our family, the disease that two of my sister Irene's boys had, sons that were flawed. Was that worse than having no son at all?

Could I finally have a son, only to see him ...? No, if I could ever have a living son, God would not be so cruel as to give me one like that, unless that was why He was withholding one from me now. If that was true, there was never going to be a son and it would maybe have been better if I had never married Nicky and come to Russia, and maybe, best of all, if I had never been born, and no, I could not allow myself to follow this drift ...

I rose and rang for Maria.

Carefully gowned that night in Nicky's favorite pink, and wearing my rubies, I can admit freely that I had, if only temporarily, regained all of the beauty and charm which had once chained his heart to mine.

He gazed at me, smiling, as he came to my boudoir to escort me down to dinner.

"Darling, you look exquisite. I feel positively underdressed. Do we have some awful dignitary joining us from some place I haven't yet heard of and I have forgotten him?"

I laughed and kissed him.

"No, precious one. It is just for you."

"Ah, then I am, as always, the luckiest of fellows."

I leaned into him as we made our way down the hall to the Maple Room where I had ordered dinner to be served that night.

A funny feature of our little home was that, unlike the great palaces, it had no official dining room, so we had taken to eating in whichever room caught our fancy, unless there were guests, in which case the great round hall was turned into our banqueting area.

I adored the Maple Room. It had been wholly designed by Ernie and was a jewel of art nouveau corners and palms and pretty rounded seating areas. That night we chose to sit in a far corner on a banquette so that, if we wished to, we might brush up against each other discreetly without the nosy servants seeing us.

Over dinner, I kept the conversation light, asking Nicky about his new Collie dogs and whether or not he thought the hunting would be good for him and Ernie in Poland in the fall. Occasionally I leaned towards him to let my perfume waft his way and it all worked beautifully, because by the time I rang for coffee, his eyes appeared glazed with contentment.

As soon as the servants had withdrawn, I put my hand to his face and stroked it lightly.

"Nicky darling, I think I want to try for another baby soon."

He sighed and closed his eyes.

"Is this is what tonight was about, Sunny, not you and me but another baby?"

I held onto my temper and managed a tight little laugh, which I hoped sounded more tinkling than angry.

"Well, dearest, that is oftentimes what comes of you and I ... isn't it?"

My bawdiness surprised him and he opened his eyes and peered at me curiously.

"I ... well, yes."

He blushed deeply and this time my laugh was genuine.

"Nicky ..." I breathed.

"Alix, darling, my angel ..." he breathed back at me.

Our faces were inches from one another's and I leaned still closer.

"Alix, should we retire?" he asked cautiously.

I shook my head, smiling.

"No, darling, there is no need. No one will come back here now, but lock the doors if you wish to."

I let my hand caress him in secret places and I felt him grow under my touch, his entire body shivering with the desire I alone could arouse in him.

"Alix, darling ..."

"Nicky, my angel, my one-and-all, will you do a tiny thing for me?"

"Yes, Sunny, anything. I will give you a baby and the world, if you want it."

I kissed him deeply and we inhaled from each other.

"Thank you, my precious one. Will you make a saint of a good man for me?"

He was breathing shallowly.

"Yes, a saint of anyone, darling. A saint and a baby. Is there anything else you want? Feel free to ask for the moon. I shall have it brought to you and –"

I stopped him with my kisses.

"Just one more thing, my Nicky. Make me happy now."

We were as one.

Chapter 17

We six, our family, spent a quiet summer and fall at Peterhof and returned home in late October. We had a lovely, quiet Christmas just to ourselves, and at the beginning of the year I was able to announce to Nicky that our prayers had been answered and there would be a new baby, a boy, coming to us in August.

This would have been a time of near-perfect happiness for me but for the terrible news from Hesse-Darmstadt. My dearest brother Ernie had written to me in a shaky hand that his wife, the selfish Ducky, had left him and their little girl and was demanding a divorce so that she could marry Grand Duke Cyril, Nicky's cousin, son of the odious Uncle Vladimir and Aunt Miechen.

I felt I might die of shame, and for once Minnie and I were in accord when she stated that it was better to be dead than to endure the ruination of divorce.

Ernie, the innocent victim of a reckless, adulterous wife, was beyond devastated because, in an effort to clear herself, the ghastly Ducky was spreading the vilest slanderous lies about goings on she claimed had taken place between Ernie and a stable boy. Naturally, no one believed her and she was consequently shunned by every European Court. Nicky hardly needed me to remind him that no marriage would ever be permitted with Grand Duke Cyril.

In an effort to cheer up Ernie and to show our complete support for him, Nicky had invited him to meet us in Poland in the fall for hunting and I had insisted he plan to bring along his little girl Elizabeth. She was of an age with Olga and I felt the poor child must be feeling nearly as bad as Ernie and missing her mama, treacherous creature though she was. Ernie had agreed and we were all looking forward to the trip.

However, before I would see Ernie again, there would the spring and the time for our departure to Peterhof; then we would board The Standart and visit the Crimea, before returning to Peterhof, from whence we would embark for Poland by train, which meant that I had at least one piece of business to conclude before our long time away.

I therefore summoned the Metropolitan of the Orthodox Church, who was a silly old man named Metropolitan Anthony, from Moscow to inform him that Nicky and I had discovered a holy man, Serafim, whom we wished to have canonized as a saint of the Orthodox Church as quickly as possible.

We met in the red drawing room and I immediately sensed that the meeting would not go well, for the poor old thing was clearly half out of his mind, spending an unseemly amount of time staring at our Abyssinian servant and chuckling to himself. It was not an auspicious beginning and things went further downhill from there.

"Your Majesty," he began, sighing and steepling his hands, "the great honor that you show an old man by asking me here has nearly overcome me. What a tremendous blessing it is. Will you join me in prayer, Your Majesty?"

I nodded rather impatiently.

"Yes, of course, Metropolitan, but I do not have much time. We are setting off for the Crimea shortly and we shall then be going on to our palace in Poland. The whole palace is at sixes and sevens in preparation for our travels, so you see –"

I was interrupted by the shockingly noisy entrance of all four of my girls and their new governess, a Miss Eager, whom I had recently engaged from England. Olga and Tatiana stared at the Metropolitan with awed interest but Maria immediately asked him why he had a beard and a dress, and baby Anastasia pulled upon the former and made faces at him.

I threw an exasperated look at Miss Eager, who merely shrugged helplessly.

"I am that sorry, Your Majesty, but they would insist on coming to see their mama and I am badly outnumbered by these little Indians."

Maria found that statement quite funny and whooped as though she were indeed an Indian, and I saw the old Metropolitan wince visibly as Anastasia tugged ever more fiercely at his whiskers.

I didn't like to send them away as it was the time of day when I usually had them with me, so I nodded at Miss Eager and addressed the girls collectively.

"You can stay, girls, but I want you to play quietly while Mama speaks to Metropolitan Anthony. Maria, stop making that dreadful noise. Anastasia, leave the Metropolitan alone. Oh no, Miss Eager, do detach her from his poor beard."

Anastasia was duly removed and I watched with no little amusement as the Metropolitan rubbed at his chin. Olga and Tatiana, my big pair, were quite used to seeing their mama receiving strangers and so occupied themselves with peppering Jim, the Abyssinian, with questions about his family. The Abyssinians were traditionally taught to remain silent and impassive at all times, much like the Guard at Buckingham Palace, but Nicky had waved this ruling if the girls wished to speak to them, as they were doing now.

Olga, who was quite fond of Jim, had just asked him when he was going to go home for a visit and he had rumbled out that he was planning to do so as soon as our family had left for our holiday. This so startled poor Metropolitan Anthony that he goggled openly at him, looking quite foolish, and sounding more so when he said, "He speaks English. How is that possible?"

I shrugged, uninterested.

"I suppose it is because he is from America. His name is Jim. There have to be Abyssinians, you see, Metropolitan, since there always have been Abyssinians here, but they are apparently quite difficult to find, so any black man who is large enough will do, I suppose. Might we get to the matter at hand?"

He managed to tear his gaze from Jim long enough to nod helpfully.

"Oh yes, of course, Your Majesty. What can I do for you on behalf of our mother church?"

"I need you, Metropolitan, to begin whatever proceedings you people need to go through to canonize a holy man of whom his Majesty and I have become aware. His name is Serafim of Sarov. Really, the sooner it can be done the better, although since in this case his Majesty and I plan to attend the ceremony ourselves and obviously do not wish to be trapped by bad weather, well that, and with our travel plans, we would like this done in the spring or early summer of the coming year."

I chose not to share with him that Philippe had been quite adamant that Nicky and I bathe in some pond in which, according to him, Serafim had baptized animals. I thought that was a private matter and unnecessary for him to know. The idea of bathing in ice-covered waters was not pleasant to me, although I knew Nicky wouldn't mind it a bit as he enjoyed swimming in any sort of temperature. For my part, I feared catching an ague, which is why I preferred a summer canonization.

The Metropolitan's face was twitching disconcertingly. I was already bored of him, and the girls were making a terrible racket, and I had a million things to do, so I fear that I was less than polite when I said, "You seem to be unwell, Metropolitan. Perhaps you should go and rest so that you can work on setting in train these proceedings in the morning. I would appreciate it if you would keep Count Fredericks apprised of your progress while his Majesty and I are traveling. I am most grateful that you came to see me. I shall ring for someone to see you out, shall I?"

He didn't move and I sighed in obvious exasperation.

"Is there something you wished to discuss further, Metropolitan?"

He jolted upright and tried, with an obvious effort, to gather his dignity about him. He didn't seem to have much dignity in the first place, so he failed but spoke anyway.

"It is rather impossible, Your Majesty, for me to promise such a thing without due consideration of such a case by my fellow bishops. To be in a position to canonize someone, that is to recognize the sainthood of a person, requires certain –"

243

I waved him off and rang for a footman to lead the old man away

"That is the business of the Church, Metropolitan, and none of my concern. Please see that it is done. Working through the hows of it is why you hold your office. The Tsar and I wish this to happen and I think you will find that all things are possible if the Tsar wishes it. So let us say no more on the matter. I shall simply expect a speedy confirmation that it will be possible. It has been a pleasure to meet you, but as I have said, I really have many things to attend to, so…"

With that I rose and Jim hurriedly jumped out from behind the curtains where he had been hiding at Olga's instruction to bow and open the door.

The girls and Miss Eager did not follow me, nor did the Metropolitan. I could still hear their laughter and his odd mumbling as I slowly ascended the stairs. I say 'slowly' because I had grown quite heavy with my new pregnancy and seemed to be fat all over rather than just in my tummy. Nicky teased me unmercifully about this but I only laughed along with him, too contented overall to care overmuch for my appearance, not that I really ever have. Vanity is not one of my sins.

Our son would be born at Peterhof, as all our babies had been, in the late summer. Given Ernie's planned trip to Poland to stay with us and hunt with Nicky in the fall, the baby and I would, depending upon the state of my health, either travel with Nicky and the girls to meet Ernie in Poland or we would meet up with them back in Tsarskoe Selo in the early winter.

Oddly though, I felt certain that the tiny Tsarevich and I would indeed be joining the rest of the family in

Poland, for this pregnancy did not feel like my earlier ones. I felt quite well. I had no illness in the mornings and my legs, although a bit swollen, were not sore and aching badly as they always had before.

This pregnancy was different in many ways as the boy had been made by Nicky and by God, but he had also been made under the protection of Philippe's treatment and prayers, and in gratitude I had done what he had requested of me. I had arranged for the canonization of Serafim and made Philippe a Russian count. There would be plenty of time to bathe in the icy pool in the spring or early summer to, as Philippe called it, "baptize" my boy while still inside me so that he could receive the special powers and prayers of Serafim.

Dr. Botkin bustled about me in a most annoying way for I had dispensed with his services, feeling too well to be bothered by any other physician than Philippe, who in his role as both my spiritual guide and my doctor was overseeing my diet and had even ordered me to follow a light exercise regimen. This was, of course, quite different from my earlier pregnancies during which I had been too unwell to take any exercise at all and was consigned to strict bed rest besides.

Nicky was naturally delighted by the prospect of the new baby, although he refused to discuss his name. I tried not to let that annoy me as I was aware that he had absolutely no faith in Philippe, although I could not for the life of me understand why not. However, he was certainly attentive to my needs in every other way and regularly ceased working at two in the afternoon so that he could take me for either a stroll or a drive. We were closer than we had ever been before and I saw this as a promising omen in its own right of the baby's sex.

A day later, Nicky, myself and our girlies were happily installed at our cottage at Peterhof. For once I was in such a contented mood that I hardly noticed the endlessly irritating presence of the rest of his family who all insisted on gathering there to mark each visit. This was an unfortunate result of policies devised by previous emperors who believed strongly in keeping the large and unwieldy, not to say troubled and argumentative, Romanov family as closely in sight of them as possible. Nicky had explained this to me with the amusing saying that one should keep one's friends close and one's enemies closer. Having myself come from such a warm and supportive family, I found this sentiment to be sad and its reality truly irksome.

In furtherance of this policy, earlier tsars had therefore gifted over time a cottage here and there to various grand dukes and grand duchesses, so that their descendants inevitably flocked to the palace in droves the second we appeared.

On the other hand, the presence of Xenia, who was by that time pregnant with what would be her sixth son, did not upset me as much as on previous occasions, for I was secure myself in the anticipation of greeting my own son before long and I found her usual sweet, if somewhat dimwitted, enthusiasm not unpleasant.

Xenia was not by nature of the disposition to spend a lot of time examining much of anything, and while we could not discuss books or politics, she could be rather entertaining in her long diatribes about the plucky Boers

246

of South Africa who were fighting the English for the right to retain their lands, their rights and their servants. I was silently on the side of England but I didn't really care enough to argue the point.

Xenia was utterly submissive to both her husband, Sandro, a man who loved to hear himself speak, and to her mother, the horrid Minnie, who suffered – and made others suffer – from the same habit, and I did enjoy watching Minnie and Sandro trying to outshine each other in front of Xenia to see whom she would pay the most attention to. It is possible that this is why Xenia's children were such little beasts.

Irina was a pretty, if dull, little girl, but Xenia's huge brood of ugly little boys was a positive danger to my girlies, and keeping my girlies from being drowned by Xenia's boys kept Miss Eager in constant motion that year.

While Minnie had been invited to join us at Peterhof, she had not been invited for the further leg of our journey on The Standart as we headed for Finland, nor to be with us in the Crimea, so, in a display of absurd extravagance, she had decided to have The Polar Star, the previous imperial yacht, redecorated and brought to Peterhof solely so that she could travel in style to visit her father, the aged King of Denmark instead. Really, the entire clan behaved as if diamonds were like grains of sand. They disgusted me. This was not how I had been raised, and nor was I raising my girls to live in such a careless manner, but even this brought down further disapprobation upon my head. "The frugal grand duchesses," they called them. "Next she'll be teaching them how to sew their own dresses."

So I was amongst the happiest of women when I boarded our lovely yacht The Standart and waved a cheerful goodbye to all of them. I think that The Standart and the days we spent on board her were amongst the few, oh-so-few, days of real peace that we and our children ever had. The rest of the time, it seemed as though we were always fighting for clear time together. At Tsarskoe Selo the demands on Nicky were ceaseless and often we could only be together at lunch and tea and dinner, and in the evenings. The rest of his time was taken up by silly papers or by ministers, or his stupid uncles, or court officials paying him court. I too was madly busy with embroidery and answering letters and organizing the girls' clothes and other such activities, and even at Peterhof and Livadia our responsibilities seemed to follow us. It was only on our yacht that we truly found the peace we so craved.

The girls adored The Standart, for on this ship they were able to see their papa and mama at all times. They also adored the sailors who danced and played with them and taught them how to aim their slippers with ever greater accuracy at the ship's resident rats, a problem that we never could resolve. Nicky joked that the rats were actually his ministers in disguise.

However, all good things must come to an end, and all too quickly, as I have found, and so it was with that summer's cruise, for soon we were docking at Yalta and heading for that grim so-called palace in Livadia.

I adored the Crimea itself. It was a veritable paradise on earth, resembling a great deal the South of France, without the necessity to be plagued by swarms of French people, or by much else at all, as Nicky's papa had forbidden development in the region by anyone outside the Russian aristocracy in order to keep the environs pristine for the Imperial Family. All the great Russian families, including the Romanovs, had estates there. The Yusupovs, the richest of them all, owned the spectacular Archangelskoe, while Sandro and Xenia had the utterly beautiful Ai-Todor. Grand Duke Nicholas and his brother had an almost equally fine palace, and only Nicky and I were stuck in the dreadfully damp, small, dark, wooden palace of Livadia.

Anything less like a palace I could not have imagined and it was only referred to as one because a tsar had built it. Nicky's papa, though undoubtedly a fine man, had a strange affection for small, dark, poky houses. This was particularly odd given his enormous height and girth, but that is what he liked and that is what he had built both in Livadia and in Poland. This preference of his for terrible places was so marked that even in Gatchina, the enormous suburban Petersburg palace that he preferred to live in, he had forced his family to occupy the servants' quarters. Grandmamma had once said that the Tsar preferred low ceilings as they kept knocking sense into his bull head. This was, I am certain, both unkind and untrue, but it cannot be denied that this predilection of his was unusual and I did not enjoy the residences he had constructed. No one but a bat could have done.

The palaces at Livadia and Poland were in fact so dark that the electric lights had to be kept running all day, but Nicky tended to demur when I shared my distaste of these residences with him. In regard to Livadia, he said, "But darling, dearest Papa died here. How could we ever tear it down?" As for the one in

249

Poland, he adored the place. His father had constructed an indoor swimming pool there, entirely appropriate to a palace surrounded by swamps. Nicky adored the swimming pool so much that he had it copied everywhere we lived, except in Livadia where he had the sea for bathing, and besides, the damp and rotting wood of the place could never have supported a swimming bath.

Fortunately, in order for our boy to be born at Peterhof, our time in that miserable old place was limited to a mere fortnight before we reboarded The Standart to return to Peterhof so that I could give birth, although the voyage back was not to be the calm and joyous trip we had enjoyed earlier, at least not for me. While previously I had positively exulted in reclining on my chaise on the boat deck, watching my girls playing and beaming at Nicky as we shared that special anticipatory joy that the imminent arrival of a much-wanted baby brings, I felt differently now. Something was wrong; the baby wasn't moving. In fact, now that I thought about it, I could not really think of a time when he had. Before this I had not let myself get frightened. He had, after all, been growing steadily and Philippe had said that he was spending his time resting and thinking inside of me. I had never let Dr. Botkin examine me and so I didn't feel right asking him what he thought; nor did I want to mention my fears to Nicky, for this summer's travels had nearly succeeded in erasing every line from his face that the stress of the last few years had added.

While I did not wish to dwell on all the ways in which this pregnancy had been different from my earlier ones, there were too many for me to ignore. At first I had seen them all as blessings, as assurances that Philippe was right, that this was my boy at last, but why had I not been sick even once? Why didn't my legs and back and head ache? Had he died inside of me and that was why I felt so well? God help me, but oh how I began to beg for God's mercy in my prayers.

Hiding my secret terror from Nicky and the girls made it that much harder, and so it was with much relief that I disembarked at Peterhof and immediately took to my bed, thereafter summoning Dr. Botkin and my obstetrician, Dr. Ostrosky. Nicky was not alarmed by this. He thought – well, I suppose anyone would have – that it was simply past time that I had them check on me and the baby.

They were all there again, his family, all there and waiting.

We were all waiting, but we did not have to wait long. For, you see, I was not pregnant, not any longer – nor had I ever been. Call it what you will: a hysterical pregnancy, or as the good doctors chose to term it, "an interruption in my flow brought about by anemia." That at least was what the bulletin in the court circular reported. What people concluded, on the other hand, oh well, that is always a very different thing, I find.

Lying in my bed, agonized with shame, I managed to laugh bitterly and say to my stricken Nicky, "Well, at least we shall be spared the one hundred and one shots. That is all to the good, isn't it?"

Then my tears began. They lasted so long, and comprised such soul-tearing sobbing, that even Minnie, who had come to gloat yet again, merely patted my shoulder and said, "It doesn't matter. You are young. You are both young. Do not carry on so, Alix. You will hurt yourself," as if there could be any injury in the world greater than this. In fact, if someone had plunged a dagger into my heart, I would have thanked them in all sincerity.

After that there is nothing much to tell. Nicky ordered Philippe back to France; plans were made to resume our trip to Poland; and Ernie and a great quiet surrounded me. It was a veritable conspiracy of silence, *Do not upset her; Do not speak of it,* that was the mantra, but underlying it I could hear so clearly the whispers of, *She's mad; She'll never have a son; Poor Nicky.*

Poor Nicky, indeed: *Sweet, silent, long-suffering Nicky,* that was what everyone thought, my own sisters included. He, of course, never said he was sad – he simply did not say anything at all – and so it went on during those thousands of miles we travelled across Russia by train, past the cities, then the villages, then the empty Steppes, and finally into a dark forest of never-ending silence.

Did he still love me? Did I still love him? Or were our respective silences so filled with mutual blame and unspoken recriminations that, like the forests of Poland, all you could see were thick, dark trees devoid of either light or space, where it seemed as though, no matter how hard you looked or how far you might choose to walk into that vast forest, you would never come out on the other side; that this was all there was and all there ever would be.

Chapter 18

We arrived in Poland and proceeded to Spala. Despite my recent trauma, I found real joy in seeing my beloved Ernie, although I found him sadly changed by his recent trials with the dreadful Ducky. I fear he must have thought the same about me. Still, after years apart, we seemed to have wordlessly colluded on the decision to rise above it all and simply enjoy one another's company.

Nicky and Ernie always got on well and so from Day One things began to improve equally between Nicky and me as we learnt to relax and laugh and talk together again.

Ernie's one great happiness in life now seemed to be invested in the beautiful little girl that he and Ducky had created together during happier times. My niece, the small Princess Elizabeth, was indeed an enchanting child and, oddly, her makings seemed to be all of our family and not one inch of Ducky's. It was as if the angels themselves had fashioned her from everything that was best and kept back any ugliness. My girls adored her, and though she was younger than Olga, she had a natural leadership about her. Baby Anastasia was nearly always to be found in her arms.

Nicky, wishing to share his passion for hunting with Ernie, was eager to take him hunting each day in the stocked forests around Spala, so poor Ernie, who did not enjoy participating in blood sports, was continually dragged away from my side where he was happiest.

Meanwhile, Ernie and I had a most wonderful secret project we were working on and we hadn't had such fun since back in the old days at the new palace in Darmstadt when Ernie used to sketch out art nouveau rooms and show them to me. Ernie, who possessed the most refined of tastes, was as appalled as I was by the silly old Polish hunting palaces at Biezlova and Spala, and we spent hours giggling together, pretending to be startled as we came across all the dead stuffed animals scattered about in the dim rooms.

Ernie suggested that we tear down everything we didn't like and start again. I didn't like Poland enough to want to bother with all of that, but I told him that if he had any ideas for that horror of a palace in Livadia, I might be able to persuade Nicky to change it. This more than anything began to bring Ernie back to his former high-spirited self and he started sketching away like a madman until, within days, he was able to show me pictures of the prettiest white marble palace imaginable.

I was determined to have it and was just getting ready to charm Nicky into the idea when Miss Eager requested an audience with me.

She was quite flustered but then people from her part of Britain, which was either Ireland or Scotland, I couldn't remember, are always rather excitable.

"Your Majesty, I'm that worried. The little princess, Miss Elizabeth, she looks terrible poorly."

I started in surprise. I had seen all of the children together the previous night in the makeshift nursery as they had said their prayers and I hadn't noticed that my niece was ill. I said as much to Miss Eager but she shook her head stubbornly.

"That's as may be, Your Majesty, but she's sick now. I think you and His Highness Duke Ernie had better come and look at her. After that, you'll want to send for Dr. Botkin, I'm quite sure."

Naturally, I rose to follow her, sending someone off to find Ernie. He must have been nearby for, in memory at least, I see us entering the small room to which Miss Eager had moved Elizabeth. She did look a bit pale and seemed listless, but when Dr. Botkin arrived he said that she merely needed rest, although he cautioned us not to move her back in with the other girls quite yet. Quiet, he said, was all that she needed.

Ernie, however, was deeply concerned and wanted to stay with her. It was I – and I cannot shake this fact from my mind – who insisted that she was fine. I had four children of my own and could perfectly well tell the difference between an ill little one and one who was simply overtired.

I said, and I wish I could forget having said it, "Ernie dearest, she's fine. She may even be shamming a bit so as to avoid having to carry Anastasia around all over the place. Let us leave her to sleep now. Nicky has accepted an invitation for the three of us to go to a nearby house for dinner and view some sort of droll play that their servants are putting on. We really should go as it is too bad to keep you all locked up in this dreary old place."

I said that, I who hated entertaining or being entertained or meeting strangers.

When we arrived back later that evening, Dr. Botkin was pacing outside on the carriageway, the furrows on his face clearly visible in the torchlight. I think I already

255

guessed at what had happened, but I couldn't speak of it to either Ernie or Nicky. Ernie, it seemed, could not bring himself to ask either, so it was my Nicky who grew inches in my estimation by taking control of this strange tableau.

"Botkin, what is it?"

"Your Majesty, I ... well, I –"

"Spit it out, man!"

"It is the little Princess Elizabeth. She is much worse and she is asking for her mama. I think she may be ..." He trailed off and looked down, and that was when I saw the tear tracks on his face shining in the light of the torches.

My own heart nearly stopped and Ernie, in his haste to exit the carriage, would have fallen were it not for Nicky's steadying arm.

Nicky said calmly, "Well then, someone had better telegraph Ducky. Even if the little one is only a bit ill, she should see her mama if she wishes to." Turning to me he said, "Darling, will you see to it that a telegram is sent? Call Fredericks, he will manage it. I am going to go up with Ernie now. Yes, here Ernie, keep my arm and we shall just go to see her, shall we? Botkin, you accompany us."

Oh how I hated to summon Ducky but I did as Nicky had asked, wondering all the while how I would ever be able to remain civil with that serpent of a woman. Then I made my cumbersome way up the stairs, the weight of my fear making my legs feel sore and leaden. As soon as I saw Elizabeth, I knew Dr. Botkin's tears had not been precipitate and I wished instead that I could give Ducky wings to fly to her child.

256

Elizabeth died an hour later, without ever regaining consciousness as I watched from the corner of the room, my hand pressed to my mouth to keep from screaming as Ernie fainted into Nicky's arms. Afterwards, during those terrible days while the small waxen form of my niece was laid out in the parlor awaiting the embalmer, my brother remained unmoving at her side, looking nearly as ethereal and unearthly as his child.

Had this all happened because of me? After all, I had wanted to see Ernie and it was only because of me that he had agreed to come to this terrible, dark forest and stay in this awful, ugly house. My girls were all still healthy, for which I thanked God on my knees, but Ernie's little one had also been healthy when she had arrived here and now she was dead, and Dr. Botkin said that he feared it had been typhus and that the dread illness had caused her heart to stop.

I needed to be reassured that no one blamed me, but Nicky was much too preoccupied arranging for all of us to leave Poland as soon as possible and he was even decidedly brusque with me on occasion.

As for Ernie, he was no help to me or to anybody else. When I approached him that morning, he silently stared at me without appearing to recognize me at all, and then, in a disassociated voice said, "I received a telegram from Ducky."

I waited, but since he said no more I was forced to ask, "Oh yes, I see. Is she, is she coming here to be with you and Elizabeth?'

He shook his head.

"No, Alix. She says that we – you and I, that is – have murdered her little girl. She will meet the train in

257

Petersburg and she is planning to accompany us back to Hesse-Darmstadt for the funeral. She is bringing Cyril with her."

I couldn't think what to say. I hated Ducky and now she had made a foul accusation against me. Besides, how unimaginably cruel it was of her to think of bringing her filthy paramour to Hesse-Darmstadt.

I wanted to rant on about her, but then Ernie looked as if his mind had been blasted away, so I merely nodded.

"Yes, of course, Ernie, if that's what you think is best."

He looked at me.

"What I think is best? No, Alicky, I don't think it is best. It is just that I do not care anymore. You see, what was best was my little one and now she is dead. I, sadly, am not dead, but I wish I were. Do you think that is best, Alix – that any of this is?"

Ella came in. She and Sergei had arrived the previous day after receiving my telegram. She looked beautiful, as she always did, and unexpectedly serene. Great tragedy, I noted, seemed to bring out the best in our sister.

She moved gracefully to Ernie's side and put her hand lightly on his shoulder. He looked up at her gratefully. She smiled beatifically at him and sighed as she spoke to me.

"Alix darling, I do not think that this is the time for you to air your grievances against poor Ducky to Ernie. They have just lost their only child and I think –"

I could not bear to suffer another one of Ella's lectures. My head and heart began to pound, the room turned a crimson red, and Ella and Ernie's heads suddenly looked enlarged and distorted to me. I gasped in fear.

Ella, who had been on the verge of launching effortlessly into a litany of my failings, moved towards me urgently and Ernie rose to his feet, their expressions of confusion so curiously alike and comical that I began horribly, without any volition on my part, to laugh at them.

They hesitated as they gaped at me. I tried to stop laughing but I couldn't, and then the room was swaying around me. I staggered and grabbed for the back of one of the chairs around Elizabeth's little coffin, but it fell, and then I fell, and then I heard, as if from a far distance, Ella screaming like a Banshee for Nicky, for Botkin, for anyone, to provide assistance and I closed my eyes.

Later, in the dank small room that Nicky and I shared, I woke up and looked about me, disorientated. It was always so dark there that one could never tell whether it was day or night.

I tried to raise myself up and call out but I found that I couldn't. My body seemed to have become enormous and monstrously heavy. My head pounded in a way it never had before, not even during the worst of my headaches. I moaned and felt a blessedly cool hand stroke my forehead. It was Maria's hand.

"Sssh, Your Majesty, don't move. Here's a glass of water, but don't drink it fast or you'll be sick again. I'll get Dr. Botkin now."

Sick again? What did she mean? I hadn't been sick, just dizzy, and Ella …

I must have muttered her name because Maria hesitated at the door.

"Do you want your sister, Your Majesty?"

I tried to shake my head for no, but the pain the movement caused me made me groan.

Maria shook her own head.

"Don't, Your Majesty. Don't move. Don't speak. I'll fetch Dr. Botkin and inform His Majesty that you are awake. He has been so worried."

She left me and a moment later returned with Dr. Botkin who looked very grave. He pulled out his stethoscope and bent over me. I shivered and he nodded.

"Yes, that's the fever, Your Majesty. I fear that you have contracted your little niece's typhus and we need to take very good care of you. Do you think you can go back to sleep without medicine or should I –?"

"Nicky. I want Nicky," I moaned.

Dr. Botkin straightened himself up and sighed heavily.

"Your Majesty, that would not be advisable. The Emperor and the girls are much better protected if –"

"I want him. Nicky, Nicky!" I tried to scream out his name but my throat was so swollen and sore that only a cracked whisper emerged.

I squeezed my eyes closed in pain and desperation and heard a rustling at the door. Through my swollen lids I could just make out the extraordinary scene of Nicky standing at the threshold of our room being pulled back by Sergei. I tried to call for him but my voice failed me.

Sergei was virtually shouting at Nicky, "Nicky, stop this! You cannot go in to her. She is infectious. Jesus

God, man, think for once in your life. Try to have a little sense. What about the girls –?"

I heard my darling answer him and my heart lifted despite my experiencing such heat, such pain.

"Unhand me, Sergei. You go too far. The girls are already in the train with Miss Eager. If I have to, I shall ride in a different carriage, but I am going to be with her."

"You can't, Nicky. What if you become ill? You do not have a son and Michael is not ready for this. Can you really take this responsibility upon yourself now?"

My God, even now that I might be dying, I was less than nothing to these people, having failed in my duty to provide Nicky with a son. I would die unforgiven by Nicky and then be forgotten, while all his family and Russia as a whole would consider it all to have been for the best.

I heard a scuffle and miraculously Nicky was beside me, his dear face twisted with concern and love.

"Sunny, my little darling, hubby's here. I won't leave you, my precious one." Then, over his shoulder, he added, "Damn typhus and damn you too, Sergei."

I tried to raise my hand to touch him but I couldn't manage it. Nicky noticed my feeble attempt to do so and understood; we two always understood each other.

He laid his precious face beside my burning one and I closed my eyes into sleep.

Of course, Nicky couldn't stay, I understood that. He had to return to Tsarskoe Selo in order to govern Russia and who else could take care of our girls away from me if not he? I was in quarantine and would have to remain

261

so, completely alone save for Ella and a few doctors and whatever servants Nicky left behind.

I had not wanted Ella to stay. In fact, I had asked for my sister Irene to come and nurse me, but she had cabled back her regrets. Her oldest boy, Waldemar, suffered from the terrible English disease and he wasn't well. So there I was, left with Ella.

Ella did not seem much more pleased about the situation than I was. She said that her dresses were developing mold on them from the damp, and as soon as I had passed the crisis point of my illness, we began to argue about anything and everything, including how cold it was in my room.

"Alix, you have been terribly ill and you really must let me order up a fire for you here. I can see my breath and you are as like to catch pneumonia as not in your current weakened state, For heaven's sakes, I might well catch it too from just being in here with you. Here, I am going to ring for someone to lay one this instant."

I scowled at her.

"Oh no you won't! I cannot bear a hot room. A fire will exacerbate my fever. Really, Ella you are too weak. Don't you remember how Grandmamma never allowed any of her houses to be heated and she lived to a ripe old age."

"Yes, Alicky, I remember all too well freezing at Osbourne, but I think even Grandmamma would have heated the rooms if she had ever come to Russia, or to this Godforsaken Polish forest for that matter. There is snow outside and you are either going to let me ring for a fire or I am going to have to leave you all alone here. I cannot even feel my feet any longer."

She then stamped her feet around to make her point, which struck me as funny, so I giggled. She looked at me, surprised, and grinned in return. I hadn't seen that smile on my sister's face in years and maybe she thought the same because she stood and, making an elaborate show of shivering, pointed at the empty side of my bed, Nicky's side.

I threw back the covers and she scampered into my bed just the way I used to jump into her bed when I had been a little girl in Hesse-Darmstadt, scooting up next to me and pulling the covers up to her chin. She exhaled, which did indeed make her breath show in the icy air of the room.

She noted me watching her and laughed.

"There, you see, we are going to freeze to death in here and they will find us in the spring looking like snow queens, and then you will be sorry."

I laughed with her.

"Well, I don't know that I will, since presumably I shall be dead and beyond mortal concerns. Ellie ..." I began tentatively, calling her directly by her old nursery name.

She shifted onto her side, her crinolines rustling and our faces only inches apart.

"What is it, Alicky?"

"Do you believe we will all go to heaven?"

Her smooth forehead wrinkled a little.

"Well, yes. I mean, that is what we are taught. It is why we must be good and why we must know that our life here on earth is one of –"

I put my icy feet against her legs. She shrieked at the cold of them and jumped and pushed at me.

"Alix, you are a horrible child. Take those freezing lumps away!"

I giggled but then became serious again.

"No, those things you were saying, they are what we are told, but I want to know what *you* believe. Or no, that is wrong. I want to know if you ever think about it, I mean if you ever doubt what we are told." She became still beside me and her eyes closed. I touched her shoulder. She sighed and opened her eyes, which to my dismay were filled with tears. "Oh never mind, Ellie. We don't have to talk about it. I think I'm just getting all full of fancies lying here in this ice house without having anything better to do than think."

I said this but I was truly enjoying a return to our old intimacy.

She shook her head and reached for my hand, which I gladly gave her. Closing her eyes again she spoke brokenly.

"I do think of it, Alicky. I think of it all the time. It is why I …"

I felt her body quake next to mine and I inched closer to give her warmth. Speaking almost in a whisper, for these were secret things, I proffered, "It is why you have stayed with Sergei, isn't it, because of the fear of Hell?"

She nodded tightly and I put my arms around her. Now it was I who felt myself to be the big sister. I kissed her temple. She smelled wonderfully of lilies, our mama's old scent. It touched me that she wore it.

When I saw that she wasn't going to talk anymore, I felt free to continue.

"Ellie, you know I feel like that sometimes –"

Her eyes flew open.

"What, you with your darling Nicky, who worships you, and all those lovely little girls, and you are the Empress of Russia, you ...? Oh God, Alix, you don't know, you couldn't know, what it is like to ... to ... No, I won't talk of this, I can't. What am I doing? I shall get up and we shall get a fire going and you can have some soup and –"

I pulled her against me and stroked her hair while she sobbed against my shoulder. When all that was left to be heard were her heartbreaking little gasps, I spoke again.

"I know, I know, I have so many blessings that you have been denied, but in the end it is much the same for me as for you."

She sniffed and sat up in the bed, pulling at her clothes to straighten them. I felt suddenly cold as much from the withdrawal of my sister's warmth as from the covers being pulled back.

"Ellie, don't. It is so nice to talk freely like this, to be real sisters again, and –"

"No, I don't want to talk about it. Talking never helps anyone and it never changes anything, and you of all people should know that."

I sat up too and watched with narrowed eyes as she struggled out of the bed and nearly fell over her skirts.

"What does that mean, Ella?"

Finally releasing herself from the bedclothes, she moved quickly to the door and did not look at me as she said, "Well, who talks more than you do, Alix, to the Montenegrins, to your stupid quack Philippe, to Nicky? Oh always to Nicky. *Do this, don't do that, I want this, no I don't want that.* It hasn't got you what you wanted at all, has it? You might as well be as barren as I am,

Alix. You don't even care about your little girls, or your sweet husband who worships the ground you walk on, and you don't care about Russia either, or you wouldn't have made Nicky disappear from everybody's sight. No, all you care about, the only thing you care about, is having a son, and no one else in the world cares whether you do or do not have one, but as long as Alix, Princess Alix, Empress Alix, doesn't have what she wants, then no one else in this world is going to matter, are they?"

Good heavens. I had never suspected that such a putrid well of bitterness existed in my sister. I had always known she was mad with jealousy, but this …

I laughed angrily.

"As always, Ella, you are wide of the mark. Yes, I want a son, but I want a son for Russia, not for myself. I have never cared about myself one bit. I am not a stupid, selfish, vain shell of a woman who spends my life thinking about dresses or making up silly face creams to try to retain a youth that has long passed me by. And I do love my girls. You are not a mother, and never will be, because of that sad, twisted imitation of a man you chose to marry. And why was that exactly, Ella? Why Sergei? Oh yes, he was rich, wasn't he, so rich, and you love that, don't you? Well, I am far richer than you shall ever be, Ella, and I don't mean that in terms of stupid money, although I have more of that too. I am rich in love and in children, and I will have a son, and you will see, as will everyone else, including your precious friend Minnie, that not one thing I have ever said or done has been a waste of my time. Can you say the same?"

She turned around and curtsied to me.

"No, of course not, Your Majesty. What a shame that the Russian people so dislike you. What a silly lot they are. Why, just imagine if you did not seclude yourself away on the pretext of real and imaginary illnesses. They could have the pleasure of really knowing you as your family does. I am sure then they would all adore you, just as we do."

With that she left the room with a swish, just managing to dodge the bedside vase I weakly threw towards her departing back.

Nicky responded to my desperate telegram for help and deliverance by not only sending the imperial train to collect me but also by accompanying it himself.

To avoid Ella, whom we were dropping off in Moscow, we remained closeted in my car. I no longer burned with fever but I burned for and with Nicky across those endless frozen miles. While Ella lay cold and alone in her car, I lay warm in Nicky's arms. So loved and loving was I that I could almost find it in my heart to forgive her. Almost.

Chapter 19

We had such a lovely Christmas at Tsarskoe Selo and our recently having been separated as a family for the very first time made our reunion especially poignant.

Nicky gifted me with a veritable Aladdin's cave of new jewels, all of which, as I laughingly pointed out, I would never be able to get through even if I changed my set daily.

His smile gleamed at me like the candles on the tree.

"Well, darling, you can start by showing some of them off next week in Petersburg."

He said it, I think, innocently, but being reminded of the coming miseries made the bright jewels turn into cold stones in my hands and I dropped them back into their casket and sighed deeply as I turned away from him.

During my illness, while deprived of my company and guidance, Nicky had been at the mercy of his mother, and his uncles, and the various gold-corded court functionaries – who, despite their nominal role as functionaries had no actual functions to perform during the winter season unless the Emperor was in residence – all of whom had been assailing him in unison with repeated demands that, as soon as I returned to Russia, we should move to Petersburg for at least a month and host several receptions and at least one great court ball in the imperial style.

Finally, Nicky conceded.

I would have been upset enough as it was at the prospect of facing that dreadful, cold palace and the even colder people whom I would be forced to receive, but Nicky's air of anticipation about it made me despair all the more

I couldn't resist asking him.

"You are really looking forward to this, aren't you, this so-called season in Petersburg? Don't you mind even a little that they will all be staring at me and whispering behind their hands about what happened to us last summer?"

"Alix, I am not sure that you are wholly correct, darling. Don't you think it at all possible that no one is much interested in us at all? In fact, Mother says that if we don't start showing ourselves off every now and again, everyone will forget we ever existed in the first place, and that is not –"

"Oh don't be ridiculous, Nicky. We are the Emperor and Empress of Russia, and we are all the people – the real Russian people, that is – think about. They venerate us and I doubt they care one bit whether or not we get dressed up in fine garments and parade ourselves about like zoo animals for people to gawp at."

He smiled sadly.

"I think you will find, darling, that one of the main purposes of royalty is to do exactly that, to make oneself readily available to be gawped at." He smiled at me so mischievously that I could not help but return his grin, but I still did not want to go to Petersburg and told him so.

"I see, naughty one, that no matter what I say, or how I feel about it, we are going to have to endure this awfulness, but Nicky, I would feel a bit better about it if

I at least thought you minded terribly how it will be for me."

He sighed.

"Yes, dearest, I do know that you hate it and that saddens me, but I cannot help wishing that you didn't mind it all quite so much. After all –"

"After all, *what?*" I snapped back, instantly defensive.

He tried to take my hands but I pulled myself away from him.

He shook his head, looking almost ridiculously beaten down, and I wondered if this was the expression he habitually wore in front of his ministers and his uncles, which would go some way towards explaining their barely disguised contempt for him.

"Nicky, you know they all hate me because of your mama's endless gossiping about me. If you were treated that way by them, you would despise them all too."

He stood up.

"Alix, no one has ever treated you with any less than the respect and dignity that you, as my wife and their Empress, deserve, at least not that I have witnessed." He shrugged. "If there is gossip, and there most probably is, that is an inevitable feature in our lives. People have always been interested in the lives of their betters, and particularly in the lives of members of the Imperial Family. As Mama says, it is when they stop being interested in us that we will know that we are in trouble. Nor can I control the thoughts and whispered opinions of my subjects."

I didn't like it at all when we were not at one on matters and I tried to appeal to him again.

"But Nicky, don't you want me to be happy and contented?"

"Yes, of course I do. It is the most important thing in the world to me, but I am not just your funny little hubby, Alix, I am the Emperor of this vast land and I have certain responsibilities to our people, as do you, darling, hate them as you will. And there are compensations, are there not?"

He lifted an eyebrow and I stared back at him, confused.

"Compensations?"

He laughed.

"Well, yes. I mean, aren't you looking forward even a little bit to our costume ball. Your costume will make everyone gasp, you know it will, darling. I even find that I am quite excited about my own costume. After all, you know how much I have always admired Tsar Alexei."

Oh for the love of mercy, he was talking about our getups for the ball we were holding for Petersburg society on the first of January. Having had no interest in attending it at all, I had absentmindedly agreed to his request that we turn it into an event with a historical theme, the theme being the court of the ancient Muscovite tsars, and in that spirit Nicky had decided to dress up as his favorite ancestor, Tsar Alexei, Peter the Great's father. From the little I had heard about him, he was such a hapless idiot that even the ascension of the somewhat insane Peter the Great came as a considerable relief to everyone. One of the incidents I heard about was that after Tsar Alexis's devoted Tsaristsa, Maria Miloslavskaya, died in childbirth while bearing his thirteenth child, he held a bridal fair of the daughters of

272

the nobility so as to pick the choicest one as his next wife. That he was Nicky's favorite ancestor had always struck me as being completely absurd, but at that moment I found no humor in my situation.

I do, however, usually have the wisdom to know when I am beaten, so I merely inclined my head.

"Yes, of course, Nicky, what could be more fun than dressing up as a long-dead corpse for an evening? I do hope I can bring glory to the memory of poor Empress Maria amid the agonies of my exceedingly uncomfortable costume. Still, it will no doubt prove to be a most memorable occasion."

He smiled at me uncertainly before returning to his study and his endless paperwork, or whatever it was he did in there.

When he emerged again, it was to announce that he had received "a rather troubling letter from Mama."

"Aren't they all?" I quipped.

"No, it's not about us, Alicky. It is about poor Uncle Pavel."

"Your Uncle Paul? Why, has something happened to him?"

I rather liked Nicky's Uncle Paul, which is to say that I found him significantly less offensive than his brothers, and I felt sorry for him. He had lost his young wife a few years earlier and had been left widowed with two small children. Eventually he had remarried someone called Olga something-or-other – these Russian names! – who was, sadly and scandalously, not of royal birth, during a morganatic ceremony in Italy, and that was the trouble Nicky wished to discuss with me.

"Mama is still most upset by his marriage. I suppose I shall have to banish him from Russia altogether."

"Why? That was over a year ago."

"Well, you see, darling, Mama was at a ball last week and Uncle Pavel was there with his so-called wife. The odious creature was wearing Uncle Pavel's mother's necklace, and so of course Mama ordered her to leave, whereupon Uncle Pavel brazenly opted to leave with her and he hasn't written to Mama to apologize for, or explain, his outrageous behavior. In fact, he went quite mad and took his ill-bred bride and boarded a train to France, of all places. I am so fond of Uncle Pavel but I really see no other way than to write to him to notify him that he may never return to Russia."

I didn't say anything for a moment, tempted as I was to interfere in this dilemma and take on Minnie with a show of my power. But no, I really couldn't. It had been terribly wrong of Uncle Paul to flaunt his silly wife in front of the Dowager-Empress. Indeed, she was hardly a wife at all – more of a mistress, really. As everyone knows, a morganatic marriage is just a sham, a way for those who are not – and never could be – noble to worm their way into families where they do not belong. That any priest would ever preside over these ceremonies seemed entirely wrong to me. Then Uncle Paul had exhibited the additional temerity of letting this woman wear his mama's necklace, his mama being Nicky's grandmamma and once a ruling empress …

Nicky lit another cigarette from the one already in his mouth.

"Alicky darling, do you think I should perhaps show him mercy by not banishing him?"

274

I shook my head and patted his shoulder.

"No, you have to banish him, darling. Much as it pains me to say this, I agree with Mother Dear on this one, God help me."

He laughed a little at this and then I thought of something.

"Nicky, what about Paul's little ones, his children? Will he send for them too, do you think? I know that they have been staying with Ella and Sergei a great deal, but surely –"

"Oh, I know. It is all quite painful with the children, of course. Sergei has asked me to award him permanent guardianship of them, and –"

I sat up sharply.

"But surely you cannot do that. They are Uncle Paul's children and they must love him very much. And what sort of parents would Sergei and Ella make? I cannot see it. Why can't you just tell Uncle Paul to divorce that woman and come home? In time we can find him a –"

Nicky shook his head, his face growing bitter.

"I have been discussing this situation with Uncle Pavel for months as I foresaw the mess he was making for himself. He will not divorce her. He has found his one true love, apparently, so how can I let him have the children, darling? His little boy Dmitri is a grand duke after all, and in the line of succession, so I cannot see any other possibility."

It was my turn to sigh. Here was another little boy who wasn't mine who was in line for the throne and who, through a series of misalliances, would now be given to my barren sister as her boy, to raise as a possible future Tsar.

I thought then, 'Should I tell him now?' but no, it was too soon. I did believe that I was carrying a new baby, but after everything that had happened the previous summer, I could not quite announce the news yet, so I merely pressed back against Nicky and felt his body soften into mine.

He smiled.

"It is sad, isn't it, darling? My family is so irresponsible when it comes to following the line of duty. Love is all. Look at Cousin Cyril and Ducky."

I laughed sourly.

"Oh, I would rather not. At least those two will never be permitted to marry and this love you speak of isn't real. If it were, Paul and Cyril would have found true brides and –"

"Like, I did, darling, with you, my one true bride, my angel, my forever love?"

I was not in the mood for romance, as I seldom was when I was nesting, so, to put him off, I asked with feigned curiosity, "Whose ball was it where all of this nonsense occurred?"

Nicky looked crestfallen but he was never one to bother me with his affections if I seemed less than receptive, so he lit another cigarette and answered my question.

"It was at Anichkov."

"And we were not invited to this?" I asked sarcastically.

Nicky laughed.

"Of course we were. I refused the invitation as I refuse every invitation that comes our way, although I don't know how much longer I can continue to do so now that you are well again, darling."

I smiled secretly to myself – for at least another year, if my suspicions were correct. In fact, if I told him my good news right now, he would have to cancel our upcoming season in Petersburg.

Again I let the moment pass, saying only with a yawn, "Yes, I suppose you are right, hubby. We shall have to see more people now that I am well. Well, it has been a long day, dearest, and wify is a sleepy one, so goodnight, my wee one."

He kissed my forehead and thus another tense day came to an end.

Chapter 20

The night of our last great imperial ball seemed to go on forever. Of course, at the time I did not know it would be our last ball for at least fifteen years and probably much longer than that, given our current circumstances – I only wished it would be. Funny, remembering that now.

My gown, or better I should say robe – for that is what was worn back then – was an exact copy of Empress Maria Miloslavskaya's coronation costume. She must have been a woman of great fortitude because the towering headdress alone weighed nearly ten pounds and almost crushed the top of my skull. Indeed, I was already in such misery from wearing it, I hardly noticed the hairdresser clucking about my earrings, two fifty-carat diamond drops which he feared would tear my earlobes off. To prevent such a gruesome happening, he wound gold wires over the tops of my ears, a thing which would cause me such increasing agony over the course of the night that it distracted me from the pain of my skull being flattened by my headdress.

Oh that night, that endless, ghastly night …

Outside, the poor lined the Nevsky Prospekt and other streets as far as the eye could see. They at least were enjoying themselves watching this strange tableau inside the ballrooms. A thousand guests had received invitations and all had accepted, not, I think, because they had finally come to accept me, but because we were at last entertaining them, which was a decided rarity.

It only took me minutes to realize, upon our entrance, that Nicky and I had got our costumes horribly wrong:

279

Tsar Alexei must have been much taller than Nicky who looked even shorter than usual in his costume, like a sort of antique chess piece, while I was the sole woman to wear either a towering headdress or a heavy robe. Everyone else, my sister and Minnie included, were sporting the most charming paste hair toppers and slim, silhouetted dresses.

I couldn't bend my head to eat at the banquet or move from my chair, and I noticed that while Minnie predictably led the titterers at my stiff immobility, she was far from alone. Nor could I dance the opening measure with Nicky as I was concentrating very hard on not fainting from the pain in my head and ears. Furthermore, I had chosen to wear the ancient curved slippers of Tsaritsa Maria, the toes of which caught on everything. The other ladies, of course, were in regular dancing slippers.

I had got it wrong again … always wrong, always, but inside me I carried a baby, maybe a boy this time, although I tried not to think about that. Still, what if it were a boy? He would reign over all these people. He would be tall, like me, and strong, like previous Romanov tsars. His word would be absolute and the person he would revere above all others would be his mama. That is how I got through that cursed night, by imagining their discomfiture when I had a boy.

We were not permitted to leave until nearly 2am, and after Maria had removed my terrible headdress and cumbersome robes, and rubbed salve on my poor, bleeding ears, and I was clad only in my pretty linen and lace nightgown and Nicky in his, I turned from my place at the dressing table and held out my hands to Nicky.

He was smoking by the bed and looked at me with a puzzled expression.

"Darling, why are you still up? It has been a long night for you, I know, and you must be –"

I yawned and stretched elaborately.

"… Tired. Yes, I am, dearest, but then your son is weighing rather heavily on me tonight, so I suppose it is only to be expected."

He went still. I couldn't read his thoughts at all.

"Sunny …?"

I nodded.

He crushed out his cigarette and stumbled towards me. Falling to his knees, he laid his head in my lap and sobbed like a little child. My maternal instincts, so aroused already by my condition, suffused me with warmth for him so that I gathered his head to my breast and laid my cheek against his hair.

"Yes, precious one, my agoo wee one, it is true and it is our boy, I know it is, I feel it with certainty."

I felt him shake against me. He raised his head. I was so taken aback. He didn't look overjoyed at all; he looked … well, frightened.

"Nicky, what is it, dearest? Don't be worried on my account, I feel perfectly well, at least I do now that Maria has removed that house, that palace, from my head."

I laughed a bit to encourage him to smile back at me. He didn't.

"But don't you see, Alicky. Oh darling, you say you are perfectly well, but what if …"

He hung his head. I raised his chin and met his sad eyes.

"What if … what, Nicky?"

He shook his head and stood up to cross to the bed and light another cigarette.

"You know what."

"What if it is not a boy? Is that what you mean?"

"How clever you are, darling. Yes, exactly. What if it is not a boy? What will happen then?"

He seemed strangely angry at me all of a sudden. I was confused and hurt. Had I not just given him the news every man, particularly a man who wears a crown, wishes to hear?

I stared at him stonily, feeling all of a sudden very, very tired after all.

He shook his head, attempted to smile, failed to do so, and sat down on the bed with a groan, holding out his hand.

"Come here, my sweet one. Come and let us try to sleep. I am delighted, of course I am, I have simply been caught unawares, and if it is a boy, I will be over the moon, naturally. And if you give me another beautiful daughter, I shall count myself, as I do each day, the luckiest of men. Come to bed, darling."

I remained where I was and said mutinously, "But it *is* a boy. Say it, Nicky. I want to hear you say it and then I will come to bed. Say yes, Alix, it is a boy."

He crushed out his cigarette and slid into bed.

"Yes, Alix, yes, darling, yes, my life, it is a boy, a boy as beautiful and proud as his perfect mother. And speaking of his mother, would you ask our son if he would mind coming to bed as his father has to get up in oh-too-few-hours-to-count to attend to the ghastly job of

282

being Tsar, a job to which I am sure he will be much better suited."

I giggled and ran over and leapt upon him, tickling him until he was gasping with laughter.

"Oh no, he won't. No one will ever be a finer tsar than his father. Oh dearest, I have just had the most wonderful thought …"

Nicky yawned heartily and mumbled, "I hope it is about how fast the three of us can get to sleep."

I giggled and swatted at him.

"Of course, Rip Van Winkle. No, but seriously, darling, shall we name him Alexis after your favorite ancestor and to mark tonight?"

He did not answer me; I suppose he was already asleep.

Chapter 21

"Your Majesty, the new *freilinas* have arrived. Where would you like to receive them?"

"Oh no, really, Maria? I don't know why we cannot put a stop to these silly creatures coming here, do you?"

She shook her head and grinned at me.

"No, Your Majesty, I don't. I only wish you could. I never know what to do with them and they tend to be a bit high-handed."

I nodded in full agreement.

The *'freilinas,'* as they were called here, or 'ladies in waiting' as they were referred to in England, were one of the stupidest and most annoying aspects of my position. They had existed in royal courts apparently since the beginning of time. They were the daughters of noblemen, or *'boyars'* here in Russia, and it was considered a great honor for them to "serve" the ruling empress.

'Serve' was rather a strong word for their function, or lack thereof, as they would arrive at Tsarskoe Selo or Peterhof, or wherever we happened to be in residence, occupy a large bedchamber, wear white satin court dresses with my picture on a ribbon, simper at the soldiers, and then go home after two months and tell breathless stories of the life at my court.

Minnie had them, as did Xenia, as did all the grand duchesses, and they seemed to find them as much a part of our disconnected lives as they did the furniture. The Dowager-Empress, in fact, seemed positively to glory in being followed about by her gowned ladies who fell over themselves to be the first to agree with her every utterance. I, being of a more serious mien, and not being one to attend tea after tea or to entertain callers, found them irksome.

They, I think felt the same about me, for my court was not so much a court as a private home, and so there I was, stuck with them and they with me, as they sat about in my boudoir for hours at a time.

I would sternly instruct them to do some sort of useful work, such as sewing shirts for the poor or at least embroidering so that their creations could later be sold to raise money for peasants, but they were so lazy and untalented that it was usually a waste of everyone's time. They all liked to chat, chat, chatter endlessly, of course, usually about such lofty matters as their dresses or their next ball, and overall I found them so empty-headed and purposeless that I often ended up with the most terrible headaches, at which point I would take to my bed and order Maria to tell them to be quiet, which they resented. In the end, I would say goodbye to them with barely disguised relief on my part and with the bare minimum of courtesy on theirs. So it was only to be expected that I was less than delighted by Maria's news.

Sighing heavily, I rose.

"Send them to the Maple Room, Maria. I shall be there presently. I suppose they will want tea too."

She laughed.

"Well, I know one of them will. Wait until you see the Taneyeva girl, Your Majesty. She looks like a puff pastry on feet and will probably eat you and His Majesty out of house and home while she's here."

Maria was terribly impertinent and I mostly loved her for it, so I laughed and shook my finger at her.

"You are a bad servant, Maria. How awful of you to poke fun at a daughter of one of the great families. I am sure she is a most gifted and pleasant young lady."

We both laughed at that.

I tried to think, *Taneyeva* – the name sounded familiar. Oh yes ... *Taneyeva* ... her father was Nicky's Court Chancellor and a musician of some note. She had been presented to me over the winter season. Well, maybe the pastry could play the piano at least. We could all hope for something.

When I entered the Maple Room, the five young women were all standing waiting for me. I noted, amused, that the fat one hovered apart, as though her peers thought her unattractive appearance was diminishing to them all.

They all curtsied with great depth as their mothers had taught them to do in my presence, but when the others rose, the fat one only succeeded in sprawling face down on the floor, before rolling over to try to untangle herself from her skirts in order to be able to rise to her feet again, and in so doing managing to spin herself into the tea table, which crashed down upon her, spilling hot tea and biscuits all over her ungainly form.

She writhed in pain and shrieked, "Ach, ach!" at the top of her lungs.

I began to laugh so hard that I nearly fell over myself and I heard Maria giggle beside me until I elbowed her in the side.

I gestured to the young ladies that they should assist their fellow freilina and they did so with a show of great reluctance.

Miss Taneyeva, once upon her feet, looked even more ridiculous than she had on the floor. Her headdress was askew, she was stained by tea and coated in cake crumbs, and her face resembled nothing so much as a round, red, sobbing moon.

I found her rather repugnant and was horrified to see that she was going to renew her attempt to curtsy to me.

This was most annoying. I didn't even want these silly creatures and not one of them spoke English, only French or Russian, and with neither of these languages was I particularly conversant. In fact, the threat of being obliged to speak them in public was one of my greatest anxieties, the fear of making mistakes that would bring yet more ridicule down upon my head.

"Welcome to our court, *mesdemoiselles*. Maria here will be your chaperone and will instruct you as to your duties. I do not have a great deal of time, so if you have any questions, please address them to Maria."

On that I turned to go.

There was a loud thump as I exited the room. I guessed that it had come from the Taneyeva girl, but I knew that if I turned to see what had happened, I would lose all my dignity and composure.

That night in bed I told Nicky about my new ladies and he collapsed against me in giggles.

"Oh, I know who you mean, darling. Poor Taneyev. He brought his girls to meet me one day and I thought even then that the poor fellow would surely need to use his entire fortune to dowry off one of them."

Nicky cut our season short to predictable protests from his mother and led our little family back home to Tsarskoe Selo so that I could rest in comfort, not that I managed to rest at all because for some reason Japan decided to declare war upon us.

This came as a distinct shock to me as I had never thought about the existence of Japan or its people at all. On the other hand, I had liked the funny robe that their ambassador had sent to me. It was called a *'kimono'* and it was very comfortable.

So one can only imagine my horror and distress when Nicky sprung this news upon me one afternoon at tea with no warning. While I didn't know anything about Japan, I knew that war meant great evil to people of all standings, so I was not pleased by his explanation.

"You see, Alicky, those filthy yellow monkeys have declared war upon us without notice or reason, and against all the laws of God and man, the savages."

"How, Nicky?"

I was in shock at this sudden announcement and wanted to order him to stop it all, but he looked a hundred years old, so I thought I had best find out the facts, eleventh hour though it was.

His hands were shaking so badly that it took him several tries before he could put a match to his cigarette and speak. After inhaling and exhaling nervously for some moments, he straightened himself and said in almost a whisper, "Alicky, last night they … they … those beasts … Oh, it is too terrible."

I nodded as I tried to keep my own fears in check.

"Yes, darling, but you must tell me. It cannot be as fearful as you are making out. Tell me, Nicky."

He nodded.

"Yes, of course. Yes, well, you see, I have just received word from Fredericks that the Japanese government has formally declared war on us."

"Yes, I know, Nicky, and it is terrible, and you must tell them it is not acceptable. You need not look so frightened, dear. You are the Tsar and you will notify them that we shall not engage ourselves in their shenanigans and that, moreover, we hardly recognize the existence of their country at all. I suppose that penalties for their arrogance will have to be –" He was goggling at me as though it was I, and not the Japanese, who had run mad. "What is it? Why are you looking at me like that?"

"Alix, you don't understand. Prepare yourself." His voice broke and he began to sob.

I wanted to go to him, to comfort him, but I was frozen in sudden terror.

"Nicky, what –?"

"They attacked us last night. They attacked our ships at Port Arthur, Alicky. They murdered our sailors. I have called for Admiral Makarov, you see, and our fleet … So many dead … Oh God save and help Russia, Sunny."

I couldn't take it in: what he was saying; what it meant; only that I understood he was frightened, but …

"What ships, Nicky? What is Port Arthur? Where is it?"

He looked at me with such surprise that his tears stopped abruptly.

I felt calmer on seeing this. He merely needed to be subjected to firm questioning to pull him together, and then all would be well.

"Darling, Port Arthur is in Manchuria and is Russia's sole warm water port."

I nodded as if this made any sense. "Oh yes, and so the Japanese have attacked us in Manchuria ... Is that part of Russia, too, Nicky?"

He laughed bitterly.

"That depends on who is asking and who is answering. As you might have gathered, we see the answer quite differently from those yellow monkeys."

I nodded, still trying to make sense of any of this.

"All right, so Russia says it's ours because –?"

"Because it is ours. We have been colonizing it for years and we must have a warm water port for trade and defense purposes. Vladivostok is ice-bound all winter, so we looked and found Port Arthur."

"Did we acquire it?"

He shook his head in irritation.

"None of this is important. What is important, Alix, is that the yellow peril has attacked our fleet, killed our valiant Russian soldiers, and declared war on us, and we are forced to fight for the dignity of Russia and for justice, and that is all that matters. Now I will have to go into Petersburg immediately and meet with my ministers and Mama. When a formal response of a declaration of war from our side is decided upon, I would like you with me."

"I still understand nothing Nicky. A formal declaration of war ...? You just said we were already at war. Don't people already know?"

He scowled and sighed and fidgeted, and then finally shrugged and stood up ready to leave.

"Yes, well obviously, but it is how things are done. We must answer them formally and then prepare for –"

"*Prepare?* Haven't they already attacked us? How long will it take us to prepare us for war and why do you say you will need me at your side? When and for what? Does it mean that I have to go to Petersburg too? We have just got back from there and you know I need rest in my condition."

In as cold a tone as I had ever heard him use towards me, he said. "There will be a *Te Deum* at the cathedral to pray for our soldiers' safety, Alix. I would like Russia's Empress to be by my side at that moment, but, if not, I am sure Mama will be there anyway. I will then proceed to Moscow. I will not ask that you accompany me there while you are pregnant, but I thought merely travelling to Petersburg should not be too taxing for you."

I inclined my head. "No, I do not suppose that it shall, and of course I shall be there, trailing down the aisle of the church behind you and your mama. Maybe Sergei can escort me –"

"No, Sergei is the Governor-General of Moscow and will be busy preparing our regiments to engage the Japanese –"

"I was being facetious Nicky. Your sense of humor seems to have deserted you along with our fleet in Port Arthur, more is the pity. Anyone in a uniform will do as my escort, I am sure."

He shook his head.

"Russia is at war, Alix. Are you really thinking about court protocols orders of precedence at a time like this?"

I laughed.

"I suppose I am, yes. Why wouldn't I be? Until ten minutes ago I had never even heard of Port Arthur, let alone Japan, and now we are at war, something that doesn't seem to be as much of a shock to you as it does to me. So why should I not concentrate on the pecking order between your mother and me? I do not know what else to think about. I do not understand any of this."

"We are at war, Alix. No one needs to know more than that. What we will all need to understand will be revealed to us over the coming days. All nations are tested by war, even great ones such as ours. I must go now. Will you be all right? Shall I send for Botkin on my way out?"

I shook my head.

He left without another word.

When I heard the door close, I rose from my chaise and wandered over to my tall windows. Outside snow was falling. It was only February and many months of winter remained.

I wondered whether it was winter in Japan too or only here. I wondered if the poor men in Port Arthur were homesick and how all the boys in their little huts all over Russia, boys sitting by their cozy peat fires – for in Russia winter was a time of rest for the peasants – would feel about participating in a war in a faraway country, a country they probably didn't even know existed, as I had not, not really. It was a name, and maybe not even that to them. How would they feel when they were gathered up to go there and fight? Boys, sons, other women's sons, yes, but I felt sure they were just as precious to their families as the little one sleeping under my breasts was to me.

I rang for Maria. I did not know or understand this sudden war. I don't think women can ever understand a war, but I was the Empress and I would do what I could to alleviate a suffering that I had never seen coming.

Maria entered.

"Your Majesty? "

"Maria, it seems we are at war with Japan."

She nodded.

"Yes, I know, Your Majesty. The news is all over the palace. Everyone is talking about it, I mean."

I had to smile then, if only sadly. It seemed that everyone knew important things before me, who was supposed to be the most important of them all.

"Well, no matter. What I want you to do now, Maria, is to let Count Fredericks know that I wish him to organize a workshop area in the big palace next door. Also, find this crop of useless ladies-in-waiting some garments suitable for working in. I expect that our small crew will soon be joined by the ladies here at Tsarskoe Selo, if only so they can gawp at me. But I cannot concern myself with that. Every hand will be useful, no matter how pampered those hands, don't you think, Maria?"

"I ... well, I suppose so. I mean, of course, Your Majesty, but may I ask what the ladies will be working on? I mean, they aren't going to like hearing that word anyway, and they will ask me what is involved, and so it would be better if I knew what to tell them, if you don't mind, that is."

I sighed. There were always questions.

"Yes, Maria, I suppose they will. Well, we are all going to make things for the poor soldiers and then put them into packages and tie them up nicely, and dispatch them off to them to cheer them up."

She gaped.

"To Port Arthur, Your Majesty? However will they get there?"

Really, servants were like dull-witted children, even the best of them.

"Obviously, Maria, our little presents will be delivered the same way that the soldiers get supplied, by train and ship. Now, no more questions. Go and do what I have told you. Oh, and send me Tuttles. I need to think about what to wear when I join His Majesty in Petersburg."

She looked thunderstruck. "Should you be doing all this, Your Majesty? Can I call Dr. Botkin?"

"No, you may not call Dr. Botkin, Maria. What you may do is what I have already explicitly asked you to do. And I am quite well, thank you."

Finally, she left me in peace, although I felt bad for having snapped at her. It was not wrong of her to have been concerned for my health.

Oddly, though, what I had said was true: I felt very well indeed and I pondered how closely my own nature matched that of my sweet departed mama. Her health, too, had been quite fragile and yet she was always able to draw on some invisible well of fortitude when she needed it. I suppose it is a gift given to ruling women, for our duties are myriad and heavy and we must also always lead by example

I heard Tuttles knock and called her in, giving her orders to bring out several different outfits for my inspection. While she was thus occupied, I wandered through my tall windows and stood upon my balcony, not really feeling the icy air. My boy kept me warm, and besides cold air was my element, as it had been Grandmamma's.

I stared across the long, snow-covered lawn at the darkened windows of the big palace, Empress Catherine's great pride and joy. Soon it would be humming with life again as my ladies and I prepared our little treats for the poor soldiers. I thought that if the worst happened, it could even be turned into a hospital for officers, but no, that would not occur. This would not be a real war. The silly little Japanese people would probably be soundly punished by our enormous army before my packages could even reach our soldiers.

Monkeys, Nicky had called them.

"Fancy us fighting monkeys, darling. Well, it won't come to much and one day Mama will tell you all about it, and how your papa defeated them and how glad the nice Russian people were about it all. You'll be just like him, a hero, but maybe more sure of yourself. I'll see to that and —"

"Your Majesty?"

I turned. Poor Tuttles, shivering mightily, had crept up behind me. I giggled.

"Ah, you have caught me, Tuttles. I was just talking to the Tsarevich here." I patted my stomach." She stared at me, confused, and I shook my head. "Never mind. Let us go and see what sort of fine feathers you have picked out for me to parade in, shall we?"

So that is how it all began, the terrible war with Japan, the "war of minutes," the "small, useful war," as one idiot minister called it with hubris and an optimism which sickens me even now to recall.

Count Fredericks, in a display of unanticipated efficiency, got my workshop up and running within a week, and each day I would join my ladies for an hour or so to check up on their progress and mutter encouragement. The ladies, who quite obviously despised these tasks, greeted me with only the shallowest of curtseys, their knees hardly bent at all, save for the fat one who seemed to be in her element. Poor Anya, she alone gazed at me with such obvious admiration and joy at my mere presence that I began to grow rather fond of her. Also her stiches in the shirts were most competent and I did not have to order her to redo each one as I did the other ladies.

The *Te Deum* in Petersburg had been surprisingly lovely and moving as well, and I was quite overcome by seeing so many thousands of people bowing and even kissing the shadows cast by our carriage on the way to the cathedral.

I thought that maybe this was a war of justice and would be for the best for all of us, a sort of clearing of the air. All the silly, bad-humored people who had always complained about nothing would be brought together in unity for our glorious Motherland. That is what Nicky said, as did his ministers, with the exception of Sergei Witte who remained implacably opposed to the war, but he was old and stupid, and as Nicky said, a man greatly lacking in vision and, worse, patriotism.

Yes, things were looking fine for us and then Nicky received a telegram from my brother-in-law, Prince Henry of Prussia. My sister Irene had three fine boys, Waldemar, Sigmund and her baby, little Heinrich, a perfect blond angel. Their pictures were all about my boudoir. Waldemar had been born with the terrible English bleeding disease, Sigmund had not. Waldemar, like Grandmamma's poor boy Leopold and my lost little brother Frittie, was watched quite carefully and was now as old as my Olga. No one had said that her little one Heinrich was ill, but then no one liked to talk about the English disease at all. So when Nicky told me that tiny Heinrich, aged four, was dead at the same age as my own brother, it came as a thunderbolt from the blue.

Apparently he had climbed up on a chair, as little ones are wont to do – as my own wild Anastasia did at every opportunity – and he had fallen off the chair, as toddlers will also do, and hit his head, causing only a tiny bump that was barely noticeable, and died in agony within hours from a brain hemorrhage because he too, as it turned out, had the English disease, more formally known as hemophilia.

I grieved for my sister but I feared for myself even more. Nicky said I should not think about it that way. God was with us, and God's will and God's love were surrounding us and protecting us, and protecting our son. Russia would win the war handily and I would bring forth a great prince, a healthy, beautiful boy, for wasn't that the sole reason we had been waiting for him for so long?

I agreed that he was right, shook off my fears, and wrote to my sister. Then I donned black – black again for my nephew – and tried so hard, every second of the day, not to think about Heinrich's death at all, not about anything in fact.

Spring arrived, disguised as ever by mud, my baby grew and the war continued.

I had decided that each soldier would receive a pouch of tobacco and stamps, and a new shirt, and a pair of warm socks, so I soon found myself engaged in a much larger undertaking than I had originally foreseen, for the Japanese were not quite so easy to defeat and more and more of our soldiers were being sent away to fight them each day.

Nicky had originally called upon his adored Admiral Makarov to take charge of the fleet but that fleet had been destroyed and the admiral along with it. Scattered and increasingly nervous new naval officers were being sent out to replace the casualties, forced to sail nearly halfway around the world, from our Baltic coast to our Pacific one, to reach the war. On one of these trips they encountered and then mistakenly sank a small fleet of British fishing boats in a place called the Dogger Banks in the North Sea which stretches between Britain and Continental Europe. The world went nearly mad with anger, and England threatened to join the war on Japan's side against us, so each day we seemed to lose more ground.

As my baby continued to grow almost in defiance of the worsening news from elsewhere, Nicky suggested that it was time for me to retire from supervising the workshop. His mother had written to him and told him it was unseemly for me to continue to appear in public in my condition.

I did so despise Minnie but, in truth, I was glad of the excuse. My workshop was no longer the cheerful place of chatter and optimism and stories of flirts with young officers it had once been amongst at least a few of the young ladies. The young officers were dying in droves each day and the overall casualty lists published in the newspapers were now taking up four pages daily.

I was huge and hot and tired, and it was with the greatest of relief that I boarded the train to take up our summer residency at Peterhof.

Chapter 22

Nothing was the same as it had been during previous summers at Peterhof, except that once again I was heavily pregnant. *The war, the war, the war* ... It was all anyone spoke about and Nicky was never available to sit with me or to play with the girls as he had been during summers past.

Still, it was a very good summer in other ways, for I was feeling marvelous with very few pains anywhere, not even in my legs, although I was no longer walking and returned to my wheeling chair whenever I wished to leave my bedroom or boudoir.

Better yet, there was no Minnie that summer. She was the Head of the Russian Red Cross and was being kept busy in town overseeing her hospitals and committees. Xenia and her family, along with Olga, had remained behind as well, and although I did like them very much, I found the absence of Xenia's hooligan sons a relief, as did my girls, I think.

Nevertheless, all was not as it could have been, for Nicky's bilious old chairman of the committee of the ministers, Sergei Witte, seemed to have taken up permanent residence at Peterhof, and whenever I took it in mind to sit upon the beach for a while, I could hear his and Nicky's voices spiraling towards me from the windows. Moreover, when Nicky wasn't with Witte, he was with Sergei, who had arrived from Moscow with Ella and also Paul's children, Dmitry and Maria, uninvited. Nicky seemed pleased that Ella would be with me to "keep me company," and was oddly silent as to why Sergei had chosen to abandon Moscow. They spent hours discussing the war as well, but in their case their voices thundered much louder through the windows.

Ella, who caught me trying to listen into their conversation one day, shook her head and sat down beside me on the sand, sublimely careless as to the damage it was doing to her white linen and lace summer dress.

Oh Ella … we fought, we made up, we fought some more, and, despite it all, I was glad to have her there and I told her so.

She smiled but looked distracted.

I reached over and patted her hand.

"You needn't look worried on my account, Ella. I am an old hand at this business and, truly, I have never felt better."

She nodded.

"I know, Alicky. It is not that. It is … Oh, never mind."

"No, please, Ellie. Won't you tell me what is going on? Nicky simply shakes his head when I ask him and tells me just to rest and concentrate on the baby, as if I could do much else. Look at the size of me."

I patted my enormous stomach complacently and winked at her.

She pretended to look scandalized but laughed anyway and shook her head.

"I am not supposed to tell you anything. Sergei and Nicky have both said that I shouldn't and I would be in frightful trouble if anything I passed on to you upset you."

"You'll be in trouble with me if you don't tell me, and anyway, if I have to, I shall interrogate Maria. Servants know everything. It would be better, though, if I didn't have to stoop to that. I know ... let's talk about why you aren't in Moscow right now."

She shuddered despite the warmth of the sun. Then, pasting on a dreadful attempt at a grin, she tried to lie to me.

"I wanted to be with you for when the baby comes."

I shook my head.

"Thank you, Ella. Sergei too? Has he deserted his post to serve me as a midwife as well? Is he medically qualified suddenly? Should I dismiss Ostrovsky or even Botkin?"

Her shoulders slumped, which was uncharacteristic of her, and she clutched her fingers. Facing out to sea and not at me, she mumbled something that sounded like 'Prince Mirsky.' This made no sense to me: what could Minnie's old friend the historian Mirsky have done that could possibly have upset Ella. As far as I knew, she didn't even read.

I poked her to make her sit up.

"Ella, what on earth does Prince Mirsky have to do with your acting so strangely now?"

"It is all his fault."

She was once again managing to both irritate and frustrate me beyond belief, and I felt my head begin to pound and told her that she was making me ill with her nonsense.

She glared at me.

"Well, isn't that typical of you, Alix? *What's going on? What's happening? Oh tell me everything, Ella.* And then, when I try, you get angry with me and pretend to be sick, as you always do. I told you I do not want to talk about it."

I inhaled as deeply as a woman in my condition could and tried to curb my natural impulse to swat her over the ear.

As calmly as possible, I tried again.

"Yes, well, you see, Ella, you have not in fact told me anything. You have only made an allusion to there being some trouble and mentioned the name Prince Mirsky, and so I am as at sea over whatever it is that is concerning you as I should be if we were seated on The Standart."

Ella hesitated to speak once again and then did so.

"You know that Prince Mirsky was made Minister of the Interior two years ago when Sipyagin was assassinated, don't you?"

I nodded, not because I did know, but because I didn't want smug Ella to know something that I had no clue about. I dimly recalled that one or the other of Nicky's ministers had been shot dead by some filthy anarchist a few years before. Apparently his name had been Sipyagin. Now Prince Mirsky had his job.

I felt rather clever at having pieced this all together from Ella's incoherent speech and my headache began to recede.

I nodded grandly. "Obviously I am aware of this, Ella. Nicky shares everything with me."

She nodded in her turn.

"Good, then I imagine he has already spoken to you about the strikes and the riots all over the country, strikes and riots which I think can be laid directly at the feet of that idiot Mirsky."

"What strikes and riots?" I blurted out before I could stop myself.

Ella colored and looked away.

"So no one has told you anything about them, then?"

I reached out for her hand. She gave it to me.

"No, no one has said anything, and Elly, I am sorry, I really don't know anything about the ministers at all. I was just ..."

She leaned her shoulder into mine with a gentle bump.

"It's all right, Alicky. If Sergei had his way, I would scarcely know what time of day it was, but living as we do in the very center of things, I cannot help but hear about them." She took a deep breath. "So, last winter, after the war started, well it was all supposed to make all those ugly people, the ones who throw bombs and who say bad things about us all the time ... it was thought ... that is, well even Sergei ... he said it would make them all rally around the country and everyone would stop demanding more freedoms and land and, oh, whatever it is that they want. They always want something, don't they?"

I was on firmer ground here and able to nod with great conviction. Yes, the people always wanted something and there was always some rabid agitator wheedling himself into their midst to whip them up into a fury, for they were none of them clever enough to know what was in their best interests or wise enough to leave all of that to Nicky and God to decide for them.

"So, you see, when the war began, those awful zemstvos began –"

"Oh they are horrid! Do you remember when Nicky ascended the throne and those monsters came to him to ask for more of a voice in government?" I interrupted, excited to be able to contribute to the conversation.

She nodded.

"Yes, his 'senseless dreams' speech, I remember it well. Well, it seems they never really put aside their senseless dreams, you see, so when the war began, they once again started agitating for a voice, and Mirsky somehow, and completely against Sergei's advice, talked Nicky into giving them one."

I waved my hands dismissively. "Nicky would never do that."

"But he did, Alicky, that is what I am telling you. Mirsky persuaded Nicky that letting them assemble and talk would syphon off some of their anger, like with a pus boil, but you see it didn't work and now there are strikes and demonstrations against the war all over Russia, against the war and –"

She hung her head.

"And?"

"… And against you and Nicky and the government. And it is growing rather serious, you see –"

"*Against me? Why me?* What have I ever done to anyone? It surely cannot be true that they dislike me for anything I have actually done, nor Nicky for that matter, not the real people. They love us –"

"Alix, they don't *know* you. To them, to all those people out there," she gestured out to sea as if wishing to include all the fish therein and all the birds of the air, "you and Nicky are just ideas, distant figures. It has always been that way in Russia. There is that old saying the peasants have, "God doesn't hear us and the Tsar is too far away." But now they want you to hear them. Now they no longer endure what they consider to be their privations with resignation but with anger. This war has not damped down some scattered glowing embers, as it was supposed to do, but instead it has stoked a raging fire that no one seems to know how to put out."

I wanted to refute every word she had said, and yet Minister Witte's worried presence and Nicky's continual hangdog air of preoccupation seemed to go some way towards confirming that it might be the truth.

The baby turned over in my stomach. I gasped a little and pulled Ella's hand over to me to feel him. Her eyes widened.

"He is so active."

I smiled, my fears of a moment ago evaporating.

"Isn't he? And he is strong too, Ella. You will see. All of this ..." it was my turn to gesture pointlessly at the waves, "... all of it, this little war, these absurd demonstrations, it will all come right when he is born, and then people will love me and know that I labor for them, love me and Nicky too. An heir. That is all that is needed to settle them down. You'll see."

Ella didn't look as convinced as she might have been but she attempted a smile anyway and said, "Yes, of course, Alicky, that is all anyone is waiting for ... Speaking of waiting for things, I am for tea, are you? I'm getting hot. Let's go inside, dear, and ring some up. Maybe Sergei and Nicky will join us. That will be nice, won't it?"

I felt somehow that my attention was being diverted from something but I could not quite identify from what. Anyway, I did want my tea, so I let Ella help me rise and we both laughed when, after settling me in my wheeling chair, she got me stuck in the sand and had to return to the house to summon two burly servants to carry me in.

That night, as Maria was brushing out my hair, a large silver looking glass on the wall crashed to the ground, and despite landing on soft carpet, shattered into dozens of pieces.

Maria dropped the brush and crossed herself, and I cried out in fear.

"Maria, did you brush against it?"

She shook her head, her eyes round.

"No, Your Majesty. And it shouldn't have broken. The carpet, it's –"

"I know. Oh God, it is an ill omen, isn't it? My baby…"

I leaned over, clutching my stomach protectively.

Nicky rushed into the room and stared, startled, at Maria and me and the wreckage on the floor.

He scowled at Maria.

"What is this? Have this cleaned up immediately. Her Majesty and I will cut our feet. What is wrong with you? Get on with it, Maria."

She goggled at him before running out into the corridor, for she was nearly as unused to a show of intemperance from Nicky as I was.

He looked at me concerned.

"Darling, what is it? Were you hit by flying glass? Are you all right?"

He approached me gingerly while at the same time trying to avoid stepping on any shards. Nevertheless I heard some of them crunching under the soles of his shoes and each tiny sound seemed to become magnified in my room like bones snapping.

I flinched and he pulled me to him.

"Let me look at you. Have you been cut? What happened in here anyway?"

I began to cry and gasped out about how it seemed as though the mirror had been hurled from the wall by a mighty force, because how else could it have broken? What did it all mean?"

He shushed me with the age-old words of the nursery.

"Hush, darling. Nothing is there. You are fine. Everything is fine. I am here."

When I had calmed down a bit and he had manfully lifted me and carried me into the adjoining room to allow the servants to clean up the glass, he sat me gently upon my chaise, lit a cigarette, and said in a conversational tone, "You know, darling, we are right on the sea here at Peterhof and that makes for damp plaster. As to why it shattered, I imagine the mirror was as ancient as this building – it has probably always been here – and old glass is so brittle that it breaks if you breathe on it too hard."

I nodded because I wanted him to be right and because I didn't much want to talk about it anymore. Dr. Botkin had brought me some soothing drops, so what was the point of belaboring the issue? Yet I knew, for example, that the mirror was one I had ordered just two summers ago and Peterhof had never struck me as being damp at all, not like the ugly houses in Livadia and

Poland, but what could he have said if I had said those things back to him?

Nicky might be the Tsar of all the Russias but there was another world beyond this one. I knew about it, Philippe had known about it, as did my friends Mitsia and Stana. Even my dearest departed mama had understood that the unseen coexisted side-by-side with this tangible world and that at times, to those who were sufficiently sensitive, the veil between them could become very thin. However it would not help, I sensed, to attempt yet again to enlighten Nicky on this subject, for despite all his supposed submission to the will of God and his endless allusions to having been born on the Day of Job, he did not truly believe that we were all at the mercy of unseen forces. No, he preferred to think that he was the master of his own ship and the commander of all his domains, his manner of conducting this war with Japan being but one example of this. He did understand the concept of destiny, or at least as he perceived it to be, but to him all that it meant was that if one were given power, one was thereby predestined for success and for God's especial guidance and protection.

Maybe that was for the best, for if he understood, as I did, how easily evil can enter into our lives, he might not have been able to shoulder his duties as Emperor. No, Nicky was too easily prone to despair and to throwing up his hands in the face of living human opposition. If he thought that there were other forces that might be ranged against him, he might well have wilted even further and not done his duty.

I marveled inwardly that I, who understood it all so clearly, who knew these things and who constantly looked to others to teach and advise me, who did not look away, was more resolute than my beloved one and was more capable of confronting any adversity with determination and courage.

I said none of this, of course, merely letting him cosset me, and feed me tea and biscuits, and rub my swollen feet, and eventually lead me back to bed. However, once there, only one of us fell asleep, for despite my sleeping draught I was acute to the night and lay awake staring at the slightly lighter patch on the wall where the mirror had been. I knew its breaking had been a message, a portent of loss and terror. What form that terror would take is what I did not know. I shudder to remember it now, but at the time I hoped it meant only that we would lose the war and not that it referred to the baby inside of me, such as that it would prove to be yet another girl after all.

My foolish fears were laid to rest at noon the next day. I had no sooner sat down to luncheon with Nicky, Ella and Sergei, when I felt a familiar tugging in my abdomen. I signaled to a servant that I wanted to be replaced in my rolling chair and, in response to the enquiring looks of the others, I merely smiled serenely.

"I think it is time. No, Nicky, you stay with Sergei. Ella will bring you the news when there is any news to tell. Elly, let us go, shall we?"

She jumped up hastily and shooed aside the footman in order to push me in my wheeling chair herself.

Once inside my bedroom, she rang for Botkin and Ostrovsky and Maria, and the room filled rapidly with people, but even before the chloroform was administered

I was beginning to drift away to that place where every laboring woman goes, a protected area of determination and fear and hope all at once.

I came to in a silent room. Nicky was there, his face bathed in tears, and at first I thought my baby had failed to survive, but then I heard a cry and I knew.

"A son? Oh God, please tell me it is true. Have I really had a boy?"

Nicky knelt beside me.

"Sunny, my angel, my one-and-all, you have given Russia her Tsarevich. Ella, bring him to his mama."

Ella crept over and deposited him into my shaking arms. *My boy, my life.*

Nicky, who had rushed off with my enthusiastic permission to send telegrams and to receive congratulations, was not with me when the guns began to salute the arrival of our newborn, so only Ella, Maria, Baby and I were there to listen together to one hundred and one, one hundred and two and one hundred and three volleys to honor Baby, and my little one and I were long asleep before the sound of the three hundredth gun fired to announce my victory to the world.